Bonnie and Clyde: Dam Nation

Saving the working class from a river of greed.

Book 2

Clark Hays

Kathleen McFall

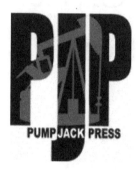

PUMPJACK PRESS

First Printing 2018
First Edition
ISBN: 978-0-9974113-6-2
Library of Congress Control Number: 2017964761

Cover design by *the*BookDesigners

Pumpjack Press
Portland, Oregon
www.pumpjackpress.com

Also by Clark Hays and Kathleen McFall

Bonnie and Clyde: Resurrection Road (Book 1)

The Cowboy and the Vampire Collection (four books)
A Very Unusual Romance
Blood and Whiskey
Rough Trails and Shallow Graves
The Last Sunset

Also by Clark Hays

Just West of Hell

"The strongest bond of human sympathy outside the family relation should be one uniting working people of all nations and tongues and kindreds."

Abraham Lincoln

"This morning I came, I saw and I was conquered, as everyone would be who sees for the first time this great feat of mankind."

Franklin Roosevelt
In remarks dedicating Boulder (Hoover) Dam

CHAPTER 1

Rearview cowboys

The first time he saw the car, Royce was late for work.

It was just after nine in the morning. The small parking lot behind the newspaper office was already full and so he squeezed his battered Chrysler LeBaron into a barely-big-enough spot between a dumpster and a delivery truck in the back alley. He elbowed the rusting door open, and grimaced when a rat ran out from behind an overturned trash can.

Walking quickly, Royce took one last drag and flicked his cigarette to the curb outside the building, and it rolled under the black sedan. The parked car stood out next to the collection of rusting pickup trucks and dented Buicks lining the dusty street in Lubbock, Texas.

What a beauty, he thought. A brand spanking new 1984 Fleetwood caddie. He wondered, with more than a little envy, if a fellow reporter inherited some oil money. Stopping long enough to admire the gleaming finish, he scowled at his own reflection in the tinted windows, rubbing the ragged three-day stubble on his cheeks. Comparing the car to his junker, Royce sighed and headed into the morning editorial meeting that was likely already half over.

The second time he saw the car, Royce was grabbing lunch.

It was five minutes past noon. He was on his way to take photos at a pie-eating contest. He carried a bag with two cheeseburgers, an order of fries and a chocolate shake. The black sedan was parked three spots down to the left of his rust bucket.

Odd coincidence, he thought, tossing the food onto the passenger seat and grinding the ignition to life.

As he pulled out, he got a good look at the two men in the front seat. The passenger was a pale man with a mustache; a darker-skinned man sat behind the wheel. He couldn't make out their features, but both wore black suits—out of place in Texas in June, or ever, really—and dark sunglasses, Ray-Bans, like his. One man's cowboy hat nearly touched the roof of the car, the other man's hat was a good six inches lower. He tipped two fingers from the wheel in their direction, but neither acknowledged him, just kept staring straight ahead. Maybe getting stoned, Royce thought.

The third time he saw the car, it was four hours later and he was driving down the county road leading to Bonnie Parker's house.

He spied the sedan in the rearview a hundred yards or so back and mirroring his speed, the topography of the cowboy hats easy to spot. A flood of adrenaline dropped an ice ball into the pit of his stomach.

Impossible, he thought, I am not being followed. That only happens in the movies, not on a rural road outside of Lubbock, and never to a talented but underappreciated reporter.

He looked at the rearview reflection of the car again. Shit. Bonnie warned him, but he hadn't given her concern any credence.

He turned up the radio volume and lit a cigarette, blowing smoke out of the open window, aiming to steady his nerves as he thought this through. He took a deep drag and unconsciously mouthed the lyrics some country crooner was singing about digging up bones.

Nope, Royce thought, stubbing the cigarette into the overflowing ashtray. Three times in one day is one too many.

He tromped on the gas pedal and the old LeBaron labored to pick up speed. The black sedan held back, either trying not to be obvious or maybe not following him at all. Royce felt a sudden sense of hopefulness that this was his overly-active imagination talking, but just to be sure, he drove past the turn-off to Bonnie's house, speeding along for several miles until he came to a junction at the top of a rise. He pulled onto the gravel shoulder and waited.

He watched as clouds billowed far across the dusty terrain—likely rain, probably not a tornado. Could be an afternoon summer squall building. A trio of crows circled above the nearby cotton field doing barrel rolls and playing tag. In the distance, Royce saw the straw hat of a field worker blow off a man's head. His companions pointed and laughed as he jumped off his tractor to chase after it.

The black sedan crested the hill and drove toward Royce's idling car.

Royce pulled a map from under the seat, unfolded it and pretended to study it. As the car passed, Royce glanced sideways, careful to look like he was still staring down at the map. It was definitely the same two men from earlier at the restaurant parking lot.

A little way up, a traffic light dangled from a wire across the road, swinging and creaking in the Texas wind. Just as the sedan approached, the light turned yellow and the car stopped.

No one from these parts stopped at a yellow light.

Royce wiped away the sweat dripping into his eyes and opened the glove compartment to be sure the .38 Special revolver was still there. He tried to remember the last time he fired it, tried to remember if it was even loaded.

The light turned green. The sedan hesitated for a long second, then turned right and drove slowly down a side road toward what Royce knew to be field after field of cotton. He waited and watched, the wide-open flatlands making it easy to track the car. About a quarter-mile down, a farmworker lumbered his tractor onto the road, trapping the sedan on the other side.

Royce knew any Texas farmer worth his salt would make a city car wait until he was good and done, so he threw the LeBaron in reverse, spun it around and with only the barest of looks for oncoming traffic, bounced and rattled back onto the county road and raced off in the opposite direction, praying to the saint of old cars that the drivetrain wouldn't fall away under the strain.

He chanced a look back in the rearview and could see the black car struggling to pass the tractor. He lost sight of it as he rolled down the decline of the little hill. With the engine groaning and tires squealing, Royce made it back to his exit, and rattled down the dirt road leading to the old yellow clapboard house.

Bonnie was at the screen door and knew he was driving uncharacteristically fast. She hauled out a double-barreled shotgun as he slid to a stop.

"I think someone's following me," he said through his rolled-down window.

She pressed a button inside the door and the garage opened. "Pull in out of sight."

In the garage, Royce parked next to Bonnie's red Cadillac. Still holding the shotgun, she opened the door into the house. A bedraggled black cat with one good eye, Moonie, crouched by her feet.

Inside the house, Royce sat down in the now familiar but still uncomfortable floral chair, heart racing.

He watched as Bonnie, a tiny woman pushing eighty with the posture and grace of someone half her age, carried out a cut-glass decanter and poured Royce a glass of whiskey over three ice cubes, then poured one for herself. "This'll steady your nerves. Now tell me what happened."

Royce took a good long drink. "I saw the same black car three times, and the drivers were suspicious looking, in dark suits. Nobody wears suits. And then they followed me on the way out here."

She got up to peek out through the blinds. "No sign of them of them now."

"I gave them the slip."

"Well, good for you," she said. "That kind of driving reminds me a little of Clyde."

She sat across from him now in what had become customary positions for their interviews and pulled a crochet throw blanket over her knees. She was always cold. "But I wonder…" Bonnie said, her sugary accent sweetening the question. "Did you consider introducing yourself?"

"Introduce myself? What the hell for?" Royce asked. "It was because of you that I outdrove them. You warned me this could get dangerous."

She smiled and tugged the blanket. "Oh, there's no doubt about the danger. But next time, make sure there are plenty of people around and then give it a try. Clyde and I always found riling things up tended to bring out a wealth of unexpected information."

Royce gulped down the whiskey and rattled the cubes in the glass out of habit. "Like figuring out if the threat is real? Is that what you're getting at?"

She topped off his glass, but didn't respond. Royce took a deep breath. "I am a little on edge." He rubbed his tired eyes. All of his vacation time, and then some, was gone along with far too many late nights spent checking out this old woman's wild story that she was the real Bonnie Parker, that Bonnie and Clyde didn't die in the 1934 ambush in Sailes, Louisiana—that it wasn't them in the car.

Royce stiffened, as the waning adrenaline gave way to irritation.

After weeks of investigating and interviewing, traveling to California, all on his own dime, he finally got the break he needed. Although, the ramblings of an ancient and probably demented Hollywood special effects man weren't necessarily evidence that would stand up in court, it was certainly enough to go public and exhume the bodies and get proof, one way or the other.

"You're still mad at me, aren't you?" Bonnie asked.

"I'm sitting on a career-making story and you won't let me publish it."

She sipped the whiskey. "The story will be even better when you figure out who really died in the car fifty years ago, and who we were working for all those years."

"The identity of Sal?"

"Exactly," she said.

"The same Sal who is long dead and buried, along with any evidence she ever existed?" Royce asked.

"You're feeling a little out of sorts today, it seems. Did that black car spook you?"

Royce raised an eyebrow. "What if it did?"

She leaned forward and patted his hand. "You're mad because it's not really me stopping you from publishing the article."

"Yes, it is you, and nobody else," he said, regretting the petulance in his voice.

"No, sir, I only reminded you that you gave your word. It's honor holding you back."

His shoulders slumped. He had come so tantalizingly close to, well, he could only imagine the many wonderful things that would happen once he, Royce Jenkins, small town newspaper reporter, became known worldwide as the investigative journalist who broke the story of the century. A Pulitzer. Book deal. Better parties.

Hell, any parties at all.

He sighed. Stupid integrity. She backed him into a corner, and why would he expect anything less from this fierce little woman, this survivor from some of the darkest days in modern America?

"Fine. I've found out how they faked your deaths. Now we will figure out who died in your place and who you were working for."

"Then we publish," she said, smiling, the motion causing her cheeks to pop out of her slight, wrinkled face like a baby chipmunk. "One down, two to go."

He pulled out his narrow spiral-bound notebook and put the micro-cassette recorder on the table between them. "Let's get to work before the black sedan shows up again."

She laughed. "I am sympathetic to your skittishness. I know how scary it is to feel like you're being followed," Bonnie said. "Like an animal being hunted down."

"Yeah?" Royce said, clicking on the recorder. "Guess that was your life when you were on the road."

"We always knew we were being followed when we were living as Bonnie and Clyde," she said. "But later, when we became Brenda and Clarence Prentiss, it was different. I felt like a cornered fox with that Texas Ranger tracking us during our second assignment."

"What was your second assignment?"

"We were trying to stop someone from blowing up Hoover Dam before they finished building it."

CHAPTER 2

Summoned

They sat close on a threadbare blanket spread out on the sand and watched as the sun set into the Pacific. He had his arm around her and she rested her head lightly against his shoulder.

"Merry Christmas, Bonnie Parker," Clyde said. "I got you a little something."

Clyde reached under the corner of the blanket and handed her what was clearly a bottle wrapped in an old newspaper with a shred of blue cloth around its neck tied into a sloppy bow.

"Oh, honey," Bonnie said. "You are the sweetest man." She ripped off the paper, looked at the corked bottle of local mescal and smiled. "It's perfect. Let's crack it open right now. But first, I got you a little something too." She pulled a book out from beneath the worn red sweater crumpled up beside her.

He whistled low under his breath. *"Tropic of Cancer* by Henry Miller. That sounds real special."

"Someone left it behind at the hotel last time we were up there, so I gave the desk clerk ten cents for it," she said. "It's supposed to be mighty racy. So racy they won't even publish it in the States."

Clyde thumbed through the worn pages.

"I want you to read it out loud for us," Bonnie said, standing and stretching.

"That is something I will look forward to," Clyde said, looking up at her smiling down at him, her face lit by a halo of golden orange shadows from the setting sun.

Bonnie tugged on the strap of the pink polka-dot two-piece bathing suit she had also found at the hotel.

The former owner was two sizes bigger and Bonnie had to tie it in knots to keep it on, and then only on dry land. The first—and last—time she swam in it, the top came off in a wave and Clyde took his sweet time helping her track it down in the surf.

"Be right back," she said, walking into a tiny shack—little more than a canvas roof over a table and sink, with two hammocks slung between trees outside—on the edge of the white sand beach. She sliced two limes onto a saucer, then poured them each a glass of liquor.

Walking back the few steps to where Clyde was reading the pieces of the newspaper that had recently wrapped up the bottle, she set down the saucer, handed him a glass and clinked hers against his.

"You ever wonder how things are going back in the good old U. S. of A?" he asked.

"Not really," she said, brushing the sand off her calves and staring at the thick and twisted burn scars snaking around her leg. "I think about my momma some and how I wish I could tell her the truth, that we're still alive, but I figure she's on the other side of grief by now. Telling her at this point would just throw everything into disarray again. How about you?"

"Sometimes I think back on how we saved the president," Clyde said. "And probably America in the process. I wonder how old FDR is doing these days."

"Hard to imagine things have gotten much better this soon," she said. "I can't remember the last time I saw a newspaper that wasn't a month old. And I'm okay with that."

He took a sip of mescal, bit into a slice of lime and sucked the juice out of it, then tossed the rind into the surf. "It's perfect being here with you, like paradise."

They were silent for a while, listening to the waves rolling in and the call of seabirds gliding past. She took a sip, then dumped the rest of her glass into his and stretched out with her head in his lap. He traced his fingertips along her temple, smoothing a strand of hair behind her ear and she closed her eyes.

"Think we'll ever hear from Sal again?" she whispered.

"Nope," he said. "I think we paid our dues when we brought them three barons down. It's been, what, six months and not a peep. She's got someone new to send on her crazy suicide missions."

"Don't know how she would even know where we are," Bonnie said.

"If she lost track of us, that's her fault," Clyde said. "She's supposed to be the big spy master. And if we get wind of anything nasty befalling our family, all we got to do is go to the press and let the fact that we're still alive sink her boat."

"You always know just what to say," Bonnie said. The cooler evening air mixed with the ocean breeze and she pulled the edge of the blanket over her feet.

"Want me to try and catch us a fish for supper or do you want to go into town and eat at the hotel?" Clyde asked.

"I'm a little tired of rice and beans."

"Fish it is then," Clyde said. "But I'd give twenty dollars for a hamburger."

"It would be our last twenty dollars," Bonnie said, resting her hand on his thigh. "We're running low on funds."

He drained the glass and leaned back onto his elbows. "Guess we may have to rob a bank soon."

She sat up and pulled on a sweater to cover her shoulders as the sun dropped below the horizon and the breeze picked up. "Darling, I don't think there's that kind of money in these parts."

"I heard Al Capone comes down here to get away. Got to be bootleg money stashed somewhere."

"You want to take on the Chicago mafia on account of us running out of money?"

"I ain't gonna work for a living," he said. "Besides, ain't nobody can touch Bonnie and Clyde. Haven't you heard, we can't be killed?"

"You mean Brenda and Clarence Prentiss," she said.

"Senor Prentiss," a small voice called from the shadows, as if on cue.

Bonnie reached for the knife on the plate of limes and Clyde rolled toward the .45 under his fedora on the edge of the blanket, but Bonnie saw their visitor and grabbed his arm. "Baby, it's just a kid," she whispered.

A young Mexican boy stood shyly by the shack, holding a letter with both hands. "Senor Prentiss, I have una carta, a letter, for you."

"Well, bring it here, son," Clyde said. He took the letter and gave the boy a nickel. "Gracias, now get on out of here. Shoo, sal de aqui. And stop sneaking up on people."

The boy scurried out of sight.

"I'm impressed," Bonnie said. "You're learning Spanish."

"Just 'get out of here' and 'more booze,'" he said with a smile. "Now, who do you suppose knows that Mr. and Mrs. Prentiss are hiding out in Puerto Penasco?"

"Her timing is unbelievable."

Clyde opened the envelope and pulled out a single sheet of paper. After scanning it, he handed it to Bonnie. She squinted to make it out in the dying light.

Be at the La Posada Hotel in Winslow, Arizona by December 27. Room is reserved for the Abercrombies. Don't make me come to Mexico. I hate sand. And Mexico. Sal.

CHAPTER 3

Marching orders

"Probably real nice here in the summer," Clyde said, looking out the window at the shallow fountain pools in the expansive hotel gardens.

"Or hot as hades," Bonnie said.

A small flock of turkey vultures gathered next to the central fountain and a man in a wide-brimmed hat shook a rake in their direction, yelling something in a language Clyde did not recognize. The birds mostly paid him no mind, hunching their shoulders and shuffling back out of reach, but the largest one—his scrawny old man's head gleaming red—spread his wings wide and pecked his beak toward the gardener, causing the man to drop the rake with a shriek and retreat. Clyde laughed at the sight.

Bonnie looked over his shoulder. "Odd time of year for those birds to be here. Hope it's not a sign."

La Posada Hotel was a stately red-clay oasis for the wealthy in the Arizona desert.

At this time of year, the hotel wasn't full but Sal wasn't taking any chances, booking their rooms in the private guest wing where they wouldn't see anyone—or be seen. The note at the hotel said to stay put, room service only.

They were more than happy to burn through Sal's money, which was why a small army of waiters rolled a parade of lunch carts to their room, loaded down with a pile of sandwiches and salads, along with a bottle of gin, three beers and four slices of cherry pie with fresh-churned ice cream.

The waiters left, overjoyed by the huge tips signed to the room.

The desert sun beat down from a cloudless and cobalt sky, warming the room and slowly melting the ice cream.

Bonnie poked at her salad—peas, cubes of ham and cheese, and chopped hard-boiled eggs tossed with mayonnaise and served in a lettuce leaf. "Feels like we're back in prison here."

"This is a far cry from the bloody 'Ham," Clyde said, thinking back on Eastham Farm prison and his missing toes. "Besides, you said you were tired of beans and rice." He reached for a second club sandwich. "I kind of like this hotel. Nice to have a little bit of fancy back in our lives. And you'd make a heck of a Harvey girl."

"Maybe you'd like me to get one of those cute little outfits and dress up all pretty for you later. Here's your coffee, sir, would you like me to bring you an extra blanket, sir?"

"I wouldn't stop you," he said. "I mean, assuming you'd be willing to get under it with me."

Bonnie laughed and leaned in to kiss him, running her hand up his thigh and pressing her lips against his.

"Give it a break, would you?" Sal asked, startling them both. She stood in the open doorway, a spare key in her hand.

"A knock would be the polite way to announce yourself," Bonnie said, feeling her blood start to boil at the sight of this wretched woman.

"Merry Christmas to you too, Sal," Clyde said, tipping his fedora back. "I hope you got everything you wanted from old Father Christmas." He waved at Sal's thick right-hand man, Carl, standing behind her. Carl looked over, and nodded, but only slightly.

More than I ever got from him before, Clyde thought.

"I didn't have to come down to Mexico to drag you back up here," Sal said. "So yes, the holiday was fine."

"Sweet as sugar you are," Bonnie said, coolly.

Sal wore a tweed suit with a light blue satin blouse and black heels, barely an inch high. Sensible, thought Bonnie, always sensible. Her hair had grown out since they last saw her, and it was shiny with a flip curl at the ends. She looked more fashionable, like someone was finally giving her lessons about how to dress like a woman. Or maybe she had a man now. Either way, it suited her.

Sal sat down at the room service table, crossed her slender legs and pulled a thick folder out of a leather attaché case. "I'd love to sit around and drink bad coffee and reminisce with my favorite murder-happy criminals, but I'm not particularly fond of you or Arizona for that matter. Let's go over your new assignment so I can get out of here."

"Hold on, darling," Bonnie said, resting her hand on the folder. "Why don't you tell us how our families are doing first?"

"They're not in jail, if that's what you're wondering," Sal said. "They're being watched, of course, and contact from you remains strictly off-limits. If they find out you're alive, the deal is off and you don't get to stay alive and they all get tossed in prison for life. But otherwise, you know, they're fine. Broke, but that ought not to come as a big surprise."

"Can we send them money?" Bonnie asked.

"Absolutely not."

"That don't seem real fair," Clyde said. "Whatever wild goose chase you got us on next, it won't help if we're worrying about our kin."

Sal tilted her head while she thought about it. "How about this? You get through this next assignment without messing anything up and I will figure out a way to get some money to your family. Not much, but almost anything would seem like a fortune to them. Does that seem fair?"

"Depends on how hard this new assignment is, I suppose," Bonnie said.

"Compared to driving around and randomly shooting at people to save President Roosevelt, it's going to be a lot harder," Sal said. "You're both going to have to get real jobs."

Bonnie poured two fingers of gin and tossed it back. "Real jobs? That's certainly not part of the skill set of a certain Bonnie and Clyde."

"But certainly to be expected for a couple of regular folks like Brenda and Clarence Prentiss," Sal said. She opened up the folder. "Have you heard of Boulder Dam?"

Clyde nodded. "Yeah, not too far from here. They're trying to block the old Colorado River to make electricity."

"And to move water downstream for crops," Sal said. "Mostly to California."

"It's a big old project, way I hear," Clyde said. "Hundreds of people, good, steady jobs."

"Try thousands of jobs," Sal said. She pulled out a pile of black and white photos of the dam and construction site along the Colorado River.

"Look at the size of that thing," Clyde said.

"Our very own version of the Egyptian pyramids running along the state line between Nevada and Arizona. And all thanks to taxpayer money, business know-how and the muscle and sweat of workers," Sal said.

"Why do I get the feeling things aren't going so well at the eighth wonder of the world?" Bonnie asked.

"There's all kinds of things going wrong," Sal said. "Missed deadlines, budget overruns, accidental deaths, but that's normal on any big job, and this is the biggest. There's something else though."

She pulled out several pages of reports and pushed them in their direction. "Read these later. But for now, suffice it to say someone is trying to sabotage Boulder Dam. Two people have been murdered, and there's evidence someone wants it to fail."

"Why on earth?" Clyde asked.

"That's what we need you two to figure out," Sal said. "But the one thing I know for sure is that the dam has to hold. There will be no bomb-throwing knuckle-heads giving our government a black eye on my watch. That would be disastrous, and not just for the site itself—it would put a halt to funding for other New Deal infrastructure projects necessary to get this country and our economy back to work."

"Who do you think is good for it?" Bonnie asked, looking more closely at Sal's face. At this close range, she saw new wrinkles around her eyes, and she looked tired. Still, Bonnie pegged her at no more than thirty years old.

"It could be the unions. There was a strike a few years back that didn't end well. It could be anarchists or even commies looking to keep America down. Might even be the mob—they've been circling around Las Vegas, ready to take over management of the gambling and houses of ill repute there."

"Figuring out that mess sounds like a mighty tall order," Bonnie said.

"About seven hundred and twenty feet tall, to be precise," Sal said, pointing to one of the photographs.

"That's like one-seventh of a mile," Clyde said.

"My, my, we are good with numbers, that's a surprise," Sal said.

Bonnie poured another drink to keep herself from reaching out and slapping the smug look off Sal's face.

"How long do we have to sort it out?" Bonnie asked.

"Not long," Sal said. "They start filling up the water behind the dam in February, and that massive chunk of concrete absolutely must hold, so a month at best. FDR himself is coming out later in the year to celebrate the opening."

Sal shut the folder. "I have jobs lined up for you. Clyde, you'll drive a water truck at the dam site. Bonnie, you're in the hiring office in Boulder City. When you get there, find my man Herman Daniels. He's a high scaler. Infiltrated the union. He's been poking around and the last time we talked, he had a solid lead, but needs help."

"So, you bring us in, the big guns," Clyde said, hooking his thumbs into his suspenders and puffing out his chest.

"Or maybe more accurately, the desperate ones, willing to do whatever needs to be done," Sal said. "There's a new car waiting outside for you. Fully loaded, if you get my drift."

Sal stood, and looked down at Bonnie and Clyde. "Be on the road by tomorrow morning. I'll stay in contact by phoning Bonnie, or Brenda, as needed during her shift at the administration offices."

She turned, and walked across the suite without a word, her footfalls soundless against the rich carpet. She stopped, annoyed, at the closed door.

"Carl, do I really need to ask that you open the door when I am so clearly making my exit?" she asked.

He smiled sheepishly, opened the door and watched as she disappeared down the hall.

"Good luck, you two," he whispered, then closed the door and hurried after her.

CHAPTER 4

Party line

Clyde slept soundly in the soft bed after a long evening of sex, champagne and more food. Restless, Bonnie sat on the sofa, smoking and thinking, listening to Clyde's rumbling snore.

She picked up the map off the coffee table and stared at the ink rings circled around Boulder City. After dinner, but before dessert, they planned their route. In just a few days, the unthinkable would happen—they would join the workforce. She shook her head and tossed the map back on the table next to Clyde's copy of *Tropic of Cancer*. Reading that out loud was what got them riled up earlier.

Idly, she paged through the list of services and amenities at the hotel, wondering if they should delay their departure in the morning long enough to get her hair done properly.

She flipped a page, then another, and found herself reading about the brand-new telephone service at the hotel. State of the art. The latest technology. Long distance. Affordable.

Bonnie hadn't been totally honest with Clyde about what she was feeling regarding her mother. She missed her fiercely, and guilt about the sadness and shame she brought to her momma's life ate at her nearly every day.

Pragmatic by nature, Bonnie knew there was nothing to be done other than live the consequences of her bad choices, and there certainly wasn't any value in going on about her feelings. It wouldn't do anyone any good.

But a phone call couldn't hurt, could it? Tonight, Bonnie longed for her momma's voice, to sustain her for whatever fresh hell waited on the Colorado River.

For better or worse, Bonnie had already decided in her heart to risk the call, but now her mind needed to justify it. They would be gone by daybreak, so even if someone was listening in, the risk would be minimal. In a few days, they'd be part of the faceless workforce at Boulder Dam. This was the best chance she was likely to come across for a while. Clyde would never have to know.

She stubbed out the cigarette in the ashtray, took one look at him sleeping—the sheets pulled away from his thin waist, one strong arm around a pillow that, in his dreams, was probably her—and then pulled on a shawl and tiptoed out of the room.

At this late hour, the hotel felt completely deserted, the silence tall and echoing. The reception desk was empty and she cleared her throat, surprising a young man who lurched out from the back office.

"I'm so sorry, ma'am," he said, taking in the sight of a pretty young woman and quickly straightening his tie unconsciously. "What may I help you with?"

"I am impressed by how modern everything is here," she said, lapsing into a soft and flirty lilt. "You must be so smart to work all that fancy equipment, like how you can place long distance phone calls."

"Yes, ma'am," he said, standing up a little taller. "We've all been trained special."

She let the shawl slip down, showing off her bare shoulders. "Are you telling me that you could help me call someone in Dallas, Texas, right now?"

"Yes, ma'am," he said. "And I'll prove it you. Is there someone you would like to call?"

"I wouldn't mind seeing if my sister was home," Bonnie said.

Years earlier, when they were on the run, Clyde insisted her momma put in a phone, as expensive as it was, and she hoped her momma still had it. Now, she wrote the number from memory on a scrap of paper and slid it across the counter, touching the back of his hand when he reached for it, lingering there an instant too long.

"I'll be happy to place that call," he said, his voice inching upward a notch. "I'll let you know when the connection is made, it may take a just a little while."

"How do I pay for the call?"

"We can charge it right to your room, or if you like, we also have the ability to reverse the charges," he said, as proud of the latest technology the hotel had secured as if he bought the equipment himself.

She pursed her lips and put her finger up to her mouth. "Shhh, it's a secret. The call is about a surprise birthday party for my husband, so I'd like to keep it private," she said. "Would it be possible for me to pay cash upfront?"

"Sure, that'll be fine," he said, sliding a card with rates across the counter. "You can pay for a three-minute segment, the minimum, is that enough time?"

Bonnie nodded. "And you just became my second favorite man."

A toothy grin flashed across his face.

Bonnie paced the lobby perimeter while the attendant provided the information to the local county operator, watching for Clyde, her eyes tracing the floor's elaborate red stonework as she nervously walked back and forth.

Finally, the young man motioned toward the wooden phone booth at the far edge of the lobby. She slid into the seat, lifted the receiver, and heard the sound of the phone connecting.

"Hello?"

Her mother's voice—calm, tired and comfortable—took Bonnie's breath away, and she gripped the handset tighter.

"Hello? I think this was our ring. Hello, who is there?"

Without even knowing it was about to come out, Bonnie let out a quiet moan, a choking sound mixed with hurt, into the receiver, and then, horrified at the lapse, she quickly went dead silent.

"Hello?" This time her mother's voice was lower, with a curious, cautious tone. "Hello?" she repeated. Bonnie didn't answer, couldn't answer, and the silence between Arizona and Texas was heavy.

"Is this who I think it is?" her mother whispered, a flood of relief and love in her voice, and Bonnie nearly lost her resolve. Her heart was hammering in her chest. "I've been having one of my feelings lately," her mother said.

Bonnie wanted to say something, anything, to let her momma know she finally had cause to be proud of Bonnie, to lift the burden of grief and disappointment. But she said nothing.

"I know it's you," her mother whispered hurriedly, and then something else seeped into her voice. "I'm warning you, stop making trouble. Darn kids." Something scraped against wood, and she heard a door shut.

"Who is it Mrs. Parker?" A man's voice. "Is it your daughter Bonnie?"

"Of course not," Bonnie's mother said. "My Bonnie is dead and buried, thanks to you. Why are you badgering an old woman?"

Bonnie slammed down the phone as if it was on fire. After a minute or so passed, she stood shakily and pushed open the door. Walking past the reception desk, the attendant called out, asking her how the call went.

"Just fine," she said weakly. "It'll be a big surprise all right. Thanks for your help."

After she went back upstairs, the attendant scribbled their room number on the slip of paper and used a tack to stick it on the wall next to other recently called numbers. The switchboard buzzed and the boy pushed the cable into the appropriate hole. Odd, he thought, for a call to come in so late.

"Hotel Posada, how may I help you?" He paused, listening. "Why yes, a call was just placed to Texas."

Bonnie softly opened the suite door and let out a breath she hadn't realized she was holding, relieved when she heard Clyde's steady snore. She kicked off her shoes, dropped her clothing onto the floor and slid into bed. Even as he slept, sensing her presence, Clyde pulled her into his arms. She felt safe in his embrace but as Bonnie tried to fall asleep, the man's voice in her mother's house echoed in her ears.

CHAPTER 5

On the road again

Clyde whistled appreciatively at the brand new green Ford V8 in the hotel parking lot, keys in the ignition. "Think this is for us?"

Bonnie opened the back door to find two BARs, a duffel bag of guns and explosives, and an envelope of cash. "Absolutely," she said.

"Guess we best be getting on the road," Clyde said, holding the door open for Bonnie, then slipping behind the wheel. He turned the key and the engine roared to life. "Kind of hoped Sal would see us off, maybe threaten our families one more time, just for old times' sake."

Bonnie laughed, and pulled on large round sunglasses that covered nearly half her face. "You have a peculiar sense of humor, Clarence Prentiss."

He tipped his fedora a little lower. "Which way, darling?"

"Straight shot, head for Flagstaff and hook right at Kingman. Ought to be there by late afternoon if we hurry," Bonnie said.

"I don't know about you, but I ain't in a hurry to start my job."

She settled back into the seat and smiled. "Well then, let's take our own sweet time."

The winter sun shone hard and bright across the dusty flats, wisps of clouds floated through the blue sky like bolls of fresh picked cotton, and tumbleweeds rolled across the nearly deserted road. As they drove, they passed through soaring rusty sandstone cliffs and deep narrow canyons, layered with orange, purple and red-colored rock.

"Ain't it amazing how big and beautiful this country is?" Clyde asked.

"Yes, and so different from Texas. And from Pennsylvania. Or New York."

He put his hand on her thigh. "It might be prettier here, but that week we spent in a hotel bed off of Times Square, after taking on them three barons, was about the happiest I think I've ever been."

"Me too, baby," she said, wishing she could turn back time as an anxious feeling settled over her like a wet muslin shroud.

As they drove on, Bonnie tried to shake off the sense of dread by reading through some of the material Sal gave them about the dam. "Says here, the amount of concrete in that dam could pave a road from California to New York City."

"Damn," he said, grinning.

"That's a terrible pun," she said, punching his arm. "Don't say it any more until after this is all over." She shuffled through more of the papers. "Right now, there's more than five thousand men working to build that structure, and so far, nineteen have died."

"Job that big? More than likely the bosses ain't telling the truth about that," he said. "I wonder if any of 'em are buried in the concrete."

Bonnie held up a photo of a half-dozen deeply tanned shirtless men harnessed into cables scaling the cliffs adjacent to the concrete dam face. "This is what Sal meant when she said her inside man, Herman Daniels, is a high scaler. Boy, one slip and that's a bad banged-up death at the bottom."

"That looks fun," Clyde said. "I might have to try that instead of driving a water truck."

"Over my dead body," she said.

"I'm built solid and I'm pretty good with heights."

"Darling, you almost fainted on the top of the Empire State Building."

"That was just something I ate," he said. "I bet I'd take naturally to high scaling."

"Kind of like how you take naturally to being a yeggman," she said.

He scowled, thinking back to the botched safe cracking in the New York mansion of the three barons.

She pulled out a second photo and cocked her head a little to the left as she looked at an image of another shirtless man, this one standing alone amid rock rubble, beams and discarded pipes. He was drinking greedily from a canteen, the muscles in his stomach ribbed like a washboard and his pants slung low around his hips.

Clyde glanced over at the photo and Bonnie's intrigued expression. "All right, that's enough staring."

She laughed. "That hunk has nothing on you."

Bonnie read more, occasionally reciting facts about the dam out loud. Clyde kept one hand casually on the steering wheel and the other on her. After a while, she put the papers down, pulled a cigarette from the glove compartment and lit it. She partly rolled down the window and blew out a stream of smoke, letting the dry desert air flow into the car.

They stopped for lunch at a roadside diner in a small, dusty town that wasn't more than three buildings and a gas station. After a meal of egg salad sandwiches and black coffee, they got back on the road. It wasn't long until the motion and the sun made Bonnie drowsy and she began to nod off, finally giving in and snuggling against his shoulder. Clyde let the familiar peaceful glow triggered by the sight of her, alive and happy, radiate through him.

When they reached Kingman, Clyde forgot which way to turn. "Bon," he whispered. "Right or left?"

"Look at the map," she said, sleepily.

"Can't find it," he said. "Never mind, just go back to sleep, baby." He pulled a coin from his pocket, and tossed it, then checked the outcome. Tails. "Right it is," he said.

When Bonnie woke more than an hour later, they were closing in on Boulder City and traffic was picking up. Cars, trucks, heavy equipment, even bicycles and people crowded the road into the company town. Men spilled out of low-rise wooden buildings along the highway, and women wearing not much more than lingerie sat lazily in chairs in front of two of the shacks.

"Guess that's where the men blow their paychecks," Bonnie said.

"Not much in the form of competing entertainment in this desert," Clyde said.

He honked at a man pulling a hand wagon blocking his way, and steered clear of a group of children.

They queued up behind a line of cars waiting to enter Boulder City. They passed by a sign outlining a lengthy list of regulations on the federal reservation. Property of Bureau of Reclamation. All residents must be employees of Six Companies or the Bureau. Guests must obtain passes. No exceptions. No alcohol. And so on.

At the security gate, Clyde showed the guard the paperwork documenting their jobs. Always suspicious, the guard looked inside the car but saw no obvious reason to detain them.

The late afternoon sun cast a rich, deep orange light across the sandy streets of Boulder City. The first thing they noticed—what anyone would notice—was the large water tower looming over the center of the town.

After Clyde passed through its shadow, like a Texas rain cloud, they passed a hotel, a movie theater, a diner and a five and dime. Ladies walked the sidewalks, chatting and carrying bags.

Not far from there, they drove by the mess hall where a crowd of people milled around, and past the company store.

On Wyoming Street, they counted two clapboard churches, and a third at the intersection of Utah and Arizona around the corner from the American Legion Hall, where a lonely Christmas tree, decorated with colored balls, leaned precariously. A few blocks past was a plain schoolhouse, and in the distance, a building with an ambulance parked out front.

They kept driving. Away from the center, the brand-new town was laid out at precise angles, with row after row of nearly identical cottages lined up like a battalion of weary desert soldiers, each standing at shabby attention over a tiny front yard of gravel and a few cactus plants. Washing hung between the homes, flapping in the afternoon breeze blowing in from the desert. Children played stickball in the street.

"How many people live here, you figure?" Bonnie asked.

"Not sure, but with close to five thousand workers, some with families, plus all the bosses, it adds up quick."

"The shopping looks fine enough," Bonnie said, "but one stiff wind seems like it might blow the houses away. Definitely not the kind of place I want to settle down in. I hope we don't have to stay here too long."

"Compared to the lot of millions of unemployed men in the rest of the country, maybe it ain't so bad," he said. "Steady wages. A roof over their head. Food. Schooling for the kids."

He turned the car around at the end of the street where new cottages were still under construction. From that vantage, they could see nicer buildings on the surrounding sandstone bluffs, green lawns, shade trees and trimmed hedges standing out against the dusty brown and orange cliffs.

At the highest point stood a large hacienda-style house with white stucco walls and a red tiled roof. Dozens of smaller but still grand homes—at least compared to the workers' housing—lined the opposite hillside.

"Guess we know where the bosses live," Bonnie said.

"Sure, get the nice cool breezes up there," Clyde said.

Driving back through the center of town and to the other side, they came to the end of the road where the town stopped and the desert was trying to reclaim it.

Clyde pulled the car next to a makeshift baseball diamond. Folks cheered as two boys chased around the bases, dust billowing as one of them slid in to home only to be tagged out.

"Seems like a good spot to get some information," Bonnie said, nodding at the bleachers behind first base where the wives and mothers of Boulder City congregated. "Can you track down their husbands?"

Clyde pulled his fedora down a little tighter and buttoned his jacket closed over his .45s. "Now, how would I know where working men congregate?" he asked, slipping a bottle of gin into his pocket. "But I'll figure it out fast enough."

He kissed her, and went off on foot looking for the missing men.

CHAPTER 6

Every jot and tittle

"Try journalism," Royce said to himself, tapping on the keyboard and banging out copy about a high school spelling bee for the afternoon deadline. "Never a dull moment, unlimited opportunity," he muttered. "Bullshit. B-u-l-l-s-h-i-t. Bullshit."

He hit "save" on the WordPerfect program, said a silent prayer to the computer gods and watched as the screen flickered in response. For the hundredth time that week, he cast a longing glance at the electric typewriter gathering dust on the shelf.

He pulled out the disk, tossed it to a startled Terrence—looking eager and well-put together, hair combed down carefully and his white, crisp short-sleeved shirt recently ironed—and told him to run it to production.

After the pale young man left, cradling the disk like a rare treasure, Royce pulled up the article he was working on for the weekend edition about a boy wonder on the high school baseball team with a rocket for an arm and a long list of colleges and even a few professional suitors hoping to curry favor.

Unlike many of the mind-numbingly boring topics he was assigned to write these days, this one turned out okay. The young man was humble and grounded, his mom—raising him on her own—was kind and laughed easily. He interviewed them in the kitchen of their small apartment last week, and hoped a little publicity might speed up the process for the red-headed kid.

He read through the copy, made a few edits and then a few more. When Terrence walked back in, Royce saved the story and ejected the disk and tossed it to the boy. "Here's another one for production, Terrence. You're a smart kid, but you need to learn to make one trip instead of two."

"Sure thing, Mr. Jenkins," Terrence said, used to the ribbing. "Thanks for sharing your wisdom so freely."

"You bet, kid," Royce said, pushing his chair back from the desk.

Larry, his editor, poked his head in the office door. "Terrence doing your job for you again?"

"Dammit, you're on to me," Royce said. He looked down at his wristwatch. "And you can save the lecture, I'm ahead of deadline on both stories. Photos should be coming out of the darkroom any minute now. Got a great shot of the kid with his mom."

"Good," Larry said. "I'm gonna give that one front page just below the fold."

"Sports section?"

"No, true front."

"Wow, that's great," Royce said. "You must really like Terrence's writing."

Terrence grinned and blushed.

"Get that on down to production, son," Larry said. "Royce, let's talk in my office."

Royce had a lot of respect for Larry, a man who cut his teeth reporting on the oil boom and bust for a Houston daily before getting called up to the big leagues with an offer from *The New York Times*, on the energy beat. After a decade in the Big Apple, Larry shocked the journalism world by giving it up to run a small-town newspaper in Lubbock. Royce didn't understand his rationale, but was glad to have him as a boss.

Larry closed the door to his office and motioned for Royce to sit. Larry took his seat and, without saying a word, opened the bottom drawer and pulled out a bottle of whiskey. He silently poured a shot for Royce and one for himself in a pair of paper cups.

Uh, oh, Royce thought. Never once had he seen Larry drink in the office before the sun had set. Larry knocked back his shot and motioned to Royce. "Go ahead."

Royce mentally counted the number of vacation days he had used up and the unexplained charges on his expense account, the days late to work and the missed editorial meetings, and made a quick calculus. He was about to get fired. He drank the whiskey in one gulp and steadied himself for the axe.

Larry filled the cups again and then stabbed the intercom button on his phone with his middle finger, knobby and missing to the first knuckle from a long-ago printing press accident. "Belinda," he said to his secretary. "Hold my calls."

"You got it, boss," Belinda said, her voice crackling through the wires.

He looked at Royce. "You said you're working on something big."

Royce thought about Bonnie, the pledge he made to her, and a story that, if he managed to get it over the goal line, would re-write American history. And also make *The Dispatch* the best-known paper in the country. "Yeah, real big," Royce said. "Real, real, real big." His voice got a little louder each time he repeated the words.

"You have yet to tell me what this real big story is about," Larry said flatly.

"If word gets out, I'm afraid the whole thing will crack," Royce said.

"You sure it's not because the story has already cracked?"

"To be honest, Larry, it could still go either way." Royce felt unexpected relief at letting out that pent-up thought.

Larry swiveled and looked out of the venetian blinds at the heat shimmering off the parking lot macadam, and then past that to the distant low-rise buildings of downtown. He was silent for nearly a full minute, and Royce felt his career teetering in the balance.

"Royce, do you think I'm a good editor?"

"As far as editors go," Royce said, the highest praise he could muster.

Larry grinned, and ran his hand over his bald head, a reflexive motion established from years long past when he had a full head of hair.

"I'm moving you full time to obituaries," Larry said, turning back around.

"What the—" Royce said. "Why not just fire me?"

Larry held up his hand, the missing knuckle tip giving it an unsettling skyline. "I want to tell you about two phone calls and one in-person visit I've received, all having to do with you."

Royce barely heard him, as his mind raced at the news of the demotion, trying to remember how much money he had in his savings, whether his sister would mind letting him crash with her and her loud-mouthed boyfriend, and what he was going to tell Bonnie. He slouched down into the chair.

"Both phone calls were from the U.S. Chamber of Commerce, a group which, as you know, has a lot of pull with the federal government."

"What did he want?" Royce asked.

"She, not a he," Larry said. "It's 1984. The world is changing, try to keep up. The first time she called, she played nice and asked about the paper, said she had heard about the fine work we were doing down here in Lubbock."

"Someone in D.C. recognized our journalism?"

"That was the tip-off that she was putting me on," Larry said.

"What did you say?"

"I suggested she buy a subscription to the paper, maybe take out some ads," Larry said. "Like any good editor would do."

"That's it?"

"On the second call, she got more focused. Asked questions about you, how long you've been here, what kinds of stories you're working on, that sort of stuff."

"That's odd," Royce said.

"This morning, a man from the local office of The National Grange stopped by," Larry said. "He's retired, but still kind of a big shot around here."

Royce sat up straighter in the chair.

"Seemed to know something about a story you're working on," Larry said. "He hemmed and hawed, but I got the distinct sense it was not something that pleased him. Seemed to imply it would hurt our reputation, maybe even our ad revenue."

"And?"

"And I don't much like being caught flat-footed like that," Larry said. Royce felt a stab of guilt. He wasn't only jeopardizing his own professional future with this story about Bonnie and Clyde. He swallowed, and tasted the whiskey on his breath.

"So, you're demoting me to obituaries?"

"I'm also promoting Terrence, our young eager-beaver intern. He'll write the first drafts of the obits and you guide him to get them into final form."

Royce was confused. Why would he get a demotion to writing about dead people but then not have to write about them?

"I don't get it," Royce said. "Why sideline me?"

Larry shook his head. "Why are reporters so goddamn dense to their own lives?" he muttered. "I'm trying to free up your time."

Royce leaned back, finally understanding.

"My instinct tells me you may have something big by the tail here," Larry said. "You've stirred up some folks and that's generally a good sign. I'm willing to give you latitude on this, and I'll increase your expense account, for now. Whatever this is, you treat it right. Dot your I's and cross your T's, and source—"

"Every jot and tittle," Royce said, finishing one of Larry's favorite sayings.

"That's right. I'm taking a big risk, so don't let me down."

"Thanks, boss," Royce said. He stood and shook his hand.

Larry pulled his hand close, causing Royce to lean in. "One more thing, Royce," Larry said. "Watch your back."

CHAPTER 7

Social lubricants

Clyde knew Boulder City was dry. Bosses liked their workers sober, Clyde thought, but he also knew that didn't mean much of anything in a town where likely every third person had access to homemade hooch. And that made his store-bought gin a rare commodity.

After wandering around for a while, he finally found what he was looking for behind a row of supply buildings not far from the railroad tracks, at the end of a rocky, cactus-strewn, barely-there path. Dozens of men stood around passing glass canning jars filled with a murky liquid, throwing dice, smoking and laughing. Clyde walked up and the talking fell away.

"Howdy, fellas."

"Howdy yourself, stranger," a man said from the shadows. He sat on an overturned milk crate like it was a makeshift throne, chewing on a toothpick. Wiry muscles lined his white arms, now tanned dark by the relentless sun, disappearing under the frayed cuffs of a short-sleeved denim work shirt.

"Name's Clarence Prentiss," Clyde said.

"That supposed to mean something to us?" the man asked, slowly taking in Clyde's appearance, the rumpled suit and soft, unblistered hands.

"Not a goddamn thing," Clyde said "But I just landed in town with my gal. We both start work tomorrow and I was hoping to get some information."

"What kind of information?" the man asked.

"The kind that'll get you a swallow of store-bought gin," he said, pulling the bottle out of his pocket. "Just want to get the lay of the land."

The sight of the full bottle was like dropping a stone in a pond, as a ripple of tanned faces turned simultaneously and rough hands reached out. Clyde pulled the top off the bottle. "Been out of work a long while and saving this bottle for the special occasion of ending that dry spell." He took a long swig, then handed it to the man on the crate.

"Much obliged," the man said, taking a swallow, eyes closed to savor the taste. "Name's Dino." He passed the bottle to a man behind him. In less than two minutes, it was empty and the men largely forgot about Clyde and returned to their dice games, drinking their rotgut and bragging about sexual exploits.

"What do you do here, Dino?" Clyde asked.

"Pouring concrete now," Dino said. "Before that, I was on the crew blasting the diversion tunnels. You ever worked on a dam before?"

"Nope, and don't plan to now. I'm a driver. I'll be driving water trucks."

"Not a bad job," Dino said. "Hot in the cab, especially in the summer, but at least you ain't busting your back or dangling over the canyon on a wore-out rope. Just mind the edge, it's a hell of a drop."

"Thanks for the tip," Clyde said. "Say, a pal in Dallas told me to look up Herman Daniels when I got here. You know where I can find him?"

A shadow of suspicion clouded Dino's eyes. "Them fancy clothes of yours, and soft hands, you don't strike me as a union man."

"Herman's a friend of my sister. She used to be sweet on him. I need to have a few words."

"Fair enough," Dino said. "I was afraid you was with management, maybe snooping around. They don't take too kindly to union talk. You can sure expect to get the pitch once you start drawing wages, from Jimmy Hall. He's the head organizer for the union here, for what that's worth. As for Herman, he's likely just getting off shift right about now."

Dino used a little stick to draw a map in the dust. "Herman ain't married, so he lives in the dormitories down there with the other single boys. Believe he's in room twenty-four."

"This company gives you housing?" Clyde said.

"Gives?" Dino said with a laugh. "They wouldn't give their own mothers a Christian burial without charging their fathers for it. We pay rent to the company to live in them dingbats."

Clyde left them to their recreational drinking and gambling and walked to a row of two-story dormitories. He banged on the east corner door where Dino said Herman bunked, but no one answered.

A few men lingered outside on the porch smoking. After taking the stairs two at a time, Clyde walked down the second-floor corridor. Craning his neck to get a look inside an open door, he was surprised at the small rooms, with barely enough space for a bed and little else.

At the end of the hallway, he knocked on the door with 24 scrawled on it. Inside, he heard noise, but no one answered. He shoved the door open and saw a young man with tousled blond hair in tattered overalls, looking at Clyde with panicked eyes.

A man lay on the floor next to him, blood pooling around his neck. Dead, thought Clyde, quickly taking in the situation. Throat slashed. A bloody knife was next to the body. Clyde pulled out his .45.

"Wait, don't shoot," the man said. "I just walked in and here he was, dead on the floor."

"Says the man crouching over a corpse," Clyde said.

"He was my friend, I live next door," the man said. "I wouldn't kill him. They're trying to frame me, and with my own knife."

"They've done a hell of a convincing job," Clyde said. "Who are you?"

"Name's Jimmy Hall," he said.

"Who's this?"

"Herman Daniels," Jimmy said.

"Just the man I was looking for."

"I didn't kill him, I swear. He was dead when I got here."

"Hold your hands out," Clyde said, looking for traces of blood. The man's hands were clean, shirt too. A wound like that tends to spray, Clyde thought. And the blood was already starting to congeal.

"I guess I believe you," Clyde said, holstering his pistol.

"Why do you have a gun, and who are you?" Jimmy asked.

"Both good questions," Clyde said. "But maybe we should save the gossiping for later and get you out of here before anyone sees us."

"Shouldn't we ought to call the cops?" Jimmy asked.

"Won't make him any less dead, but I can't say the same for you," Clyde said, and then, at the sound of a car pulling up outside, peeked out the window and swore. "It's the laws, and they're packing heat and got their sirens off. That means they ain't planning on doing too much arresting."

Clyde acted fast, picking up the bloody bone-handled hunting knife, wiping the blade off on the bottom of the dead man's pant leg, and then slipping it into the leather sheath and dropping it in his own pocket. "Come on," he said.

With the men in the dormitory focused on the lawmen on the front porch, Jimmy and Clyde ran down the back stairs until they reached the showers. Inside, Clyde pried a window open, looking around for any bystanders. "Coast is clear," he said. "Get ready."

When footsteps thundered up the stairs toward number 24, they scrambled out the window and then tried to act nonchalant, hands in pockets, as they walked in the direction of the baseball field.

Bonnie sat with a group of women watching the children play a half-hearted game that was winding down with no scores on either side. She held a cigarette in one hand and with the other laughingly traced red lipstick on to the lips of the woman next to her. She saw Clyde approaching and started to wave, but he tipped his head ever so slightly.

She looked over his shoulder and saw two policemen hurrying toward them, guns drawn.

CHAPTER 8

Making new friends

Bonnie excused herself from her new friends at the baseball diamond and joined Clyde and the handsome stranger just as the police caught up to them.

"Where you been, Jimmy?" one of the cops asked, catching Jimmy by the arm.

"Hey, easy buddy," Clyde said. "What's your beef with Jimmy? He's been with me and my gal, catching up on old times. Ain't that right, Jimmy?"

The confident edge in Clyde's voice took the cops by surprise.

"That's right, officer," Bonnie added. "What seems to be the problem?"

"You two mind your business," the second cop said.

"It is my business," Clyde said. "We finally get a chance to catch up with the man who left my sister at the altar, and you want to roust him?"

"Look, I keep telling you, your sister's the one who told me to leave," Jimmy said, catching on quickly. "I wanted to marry her. Honest."

"Are you calling my sister-in-law a liar?" Bonnie asked.

"Shut up all of you about your hillbilly family laundry," the first cop said. "We found a body in the dormitory.

Room next to yours. Throat cut. And with your—" he caught himself. "With a knife."

"Oh, my saints," Bonnie said, clapping the back of her hand to her forehead "A murder?" She pretended to faint into Clyde's arms.

"What's the big idea, copper?" Clyde shouted, carefully lowering her to the ground. "Look what you done to my girl. Watch it with the rough talk."

He knelt beside her and held her wrist, carefully tapping her cheek. "Baby, it's okay." Her eyes fluttered open and she looked up at the two cops, now both holding their hats in their hands.

"Now listen, you two need to beat it," Clyde said. "I wish Jimmy was responsible, but we've been jawing about what he done to my sister for the better part of an hour. Ever since we pulled in from Texas."

The two cops looked at each other. "We'd better talk to the chief."

But then the second one glared at Clyde. "What's your name, boy?"

Bonnie felt Clyde's fist ball up at being called boy, and she wrapped her hand around his, out of sight of the cops' stare. Ever since his prison experience, the accumulated rage Clyde felt toward the laws was always just a thin scratch below the surface.

"Clarence Prentiss," he said, jaw clenched.

"You keep your nose clean, Clarence Prentiss," the cop said.

"You let me worry about my nose," Clyde said. "Don't you got a murder to solve?"

They watched as the cops headed back toward the dormitory.

"That was close," Clyde said. "Jimmy Hall, meet my wife Brenda Prentiss. Brenda, this here is Jimmy. He's either a murderer or else someone tried to set him up but good. And it was our pal Herman that paid the price either way."

Clyde pulled the knife from his pocket and handed it to Jimmy. "Here's your knife back," he said. "You might want to either keep better track of it, or get rid of it all together."

Brenda stuck out her hand. "Pleased to meet you, long as you're not a cold-blooded killer."

"I'm a lot of things, but killer ain't one of them," Jimmy said, shaking Bonnie's hand. He had a strong grip, rough with callouses.

"Head of the local union though, at least according to my new pal Dino," Clyde said.

"That's right," Jimmy said, nodding. "You must've snuck in some hooch. And it ain't much of a union so far. It got busted up years ago, but we're rebuilding."

Behind them, the baseball game fizzled out and the mothers shooed their children out of the field and toward home. Bonnie waved at a few, and thanked them for their advice. Jimmy lowered his voice. "It ain't hard to see why someone would try to frame me, but I can't figure why someone wanted to kill Daniels. I'm not real sure why you helped me back there, but I sure do owe you."

"I can think of one way you can wipe that slate clean," Clyde said.

"Yeah?" Jimmy asked.

"Me and Brenda start work tomorrow and since we got a little bit of daylight left, how about you give us a quick tour of the dam site so we can get the lay of the land up there?"

"How can I say no to the couple who just saved my bacon?" Jimmy asked. "Especially since I know Clarence here has a gun."

"Oh, we both do," Bonnie said, patting Jimmy's arm.

Clyde tipped his hat at the guard as they drove through the Boulder City security gate and noticed him peering closely at Jimmy in the backseat, then scribbling notes in his logbook.

"That guard seems mighty interested in you," Clyde said as they drove toward the dam.

"Six Companies ain't exactly on cordial terms with the union," Jimmy said. "Thanks to old FDR, we got new rights, but they can still find ways to make life hard."

"Old habits are tough to break," Clyde said.

Bonnie turned around and offered Jimmy a cigarette. He declined but took the lighter casually from her hand and lit hers. Clyde tapped the brakes hard enough to jolt Bonnie into turning forward on the front seat, and she made a face at him.

"What do they have against unions anyway?" Bonnie asked, blowing a stream of smoke in Clyde's direction.

"That's easy. Money," Jimmy said. "If you got money, you got power. You can decide who works and who's idle, who lives and who dies, even. The collective voice of the working man is the only power that can stand up to money."

"And working women, too," Bonnie said, turning back to face Jimmy. "But I'm sure you were getting there."

"Absolutely," Jimmy said. "Unions want a world where every member of the working class gets respect, a fair shake and a shot at a decent life. Well, most unions want that. We got some things to work through still, like making sure we're welcoming of all folks and not just white folks, and not just men, and not too overly focused on the skilled trades. These things take time to build right, but we're making inroads."

"I'd like to make some inroads past all these cars," Clyde said, speeding up to pass a family of four in a sturdy new car. "Who are all these folks? Sure as hell ain't workers."

"The dam is close to being done, and with all the reporters out here now writing articles, there's a jam of tourists," Jimmy said. "Six Companies put in an overlook, that's where I'm taking you now. We call it the Byrd's Nest on account of how pissed off it made the site boss."

"That'd be Henry Byrd?" Clyde asked. "What's he like?"

"He's good at his job," Jimmy said. "And his job is getting thousands of men and machines to work together to shove a giant concrete wall into the middle of a canyon where, not long ago, an unruly river ran through. That's not an easy task."

"I hear a 'but' in there," Bonnie said.

"He treats the workers pretty rough. We call him Hurry Up Byrd, because he rides us so hard. Thinks of us as expendable, which is no different than most bosses, because we kind of are to them. Expendable, I mean."

"Good wages, food, housing. I seen lots of men would kill for that," Clyde said.

"Just because there's men lining up to do your job, even for cheaper, doesn't mean the company should get to twist you by the balls—ah, sorry, Brenda, didn't mean to talk rough."

"I've heard worse," she said.

Clyde thought back to Eastham prison when he worked in the cotton fields from sunup to sundown for no pay at all, all the prisoners giving free labor to the cotton bosses for petty crimes and sometimes no crimes at all. It was so bad, he chopped off two of his own toes to escape. These workers here had it way better, he thought, but the anger coming from having no choice in the matter was something he understood.

"You gonna strike? No wonder they don't like you much."

"I didn't say nothing about a strike," Jimmy said. His voice was defensive. "Last time they tried, Hurry Up, with the backing of the Bureau thugs, broke it but good. Fired the lot of 'em. But FDR is on our side, and I've got ideas about how to even things up. Turn left here."

Clyde pushed the car into low gear as they made their way up a narrow winding canyon road. Bonnie held her breath, fearful at each hairpin turn. Finally, they topped out at a ragged parking lot blasted out of the canyon walls, full with cars and people taking photographs.

"Sunset is a favorite time for the tourists," Jimmy said as they got out.

They heard a distant rumbling noise, like a slow moving thunderous earthquake.

"What is that?" Bonnie asked.

"You'll see," Jimmy said.

Clyde came around from the driver's side, she hooked her arm into his, and they followed Jimmy to the edge of the canyon by a waist-high curved stone retaining wall. Jimmy waved them over to an open spot. Once there, Bonnie and Clyde turned at the same instant to look down the canyon.

"Holy shit," Clyde said.

Bonnie, at a loss for words, just gasped.

A massive white concrete wall stretched across the canyon, from edge to edge, the blazing smooth brightness of it a shock against the dark lava rock of the steep and shadowy canyon walls. In the dried up, diverted riverbed far down at the bottom, an army of men worked, a steady procession of trucks rattled back and forth, and drilling equipment reverberated in clattering echoes that bounced against the canyon. On the opposite side of the gorge, the Nevada side, a locomotive belched steam and chugged out of sight around a bend, nestling into a groove blown out from the side of the canyon back toward Boulder City, while another train car pulled in.

Men walked across a lurching catwalk that spanned the canyon close to the dam, and a maze of cables with cages dangling hundreds of feet in the air crisscrossed the canyon, ferrying people, concrete and large metal cylinders up, down and across.

"Watch over there," Jimmy said. "That cableway is about to drop its load."

In the distance, they could make out the work crew on the eastern corner of the dam—which was still being filled in—as the four men pushed the swaying metal container hanging from a cable, tipping its load of wet concrete into a wooden mold. The empty container then zipped back to the loading platform on the cliff while the men standing on the adjacent, already-hardened dam blocks used shovels and rakes to smooth the new material inside the mold.

"Think of it like a giant brick wall," Jimmy said. "Each of them boxes is one brick in the dam, only we're making the bricks as we go."

"Why not just pour the whole thing at once?" Clyde asked.

"They calculated it would take a century or something like that for all that concrete to dry," Jimmy said.

"The smaller boxes dry faster," Bonnie said.

"Yeah, and there's piping inside each block too, where they pump in cooling water," Jimmy said.

"Say, what's that behind the dam?" Clyde asked, pointing at two concrete cylinders that looked like looming watchtowers.

"That's the intake for the electric power generation," Jimmy said. "They're connected to tunnels that will push the water into seventeen turbines inside the generator house at the base of the dam."

Bonnie looked downstream in the direction they drove up a few minutes earlier. "All that desert down there will get water and electricity?" she asked, imagining a future where the yellow-red valley would be transformed into rich agricultural land.

"Yep, and farther than you can see from here, all the way down into California," Jimmy said. "See that little mountain over there?" He pointed to an area just south of the dam site where a peak crested against the backlight of the sun.

"Yeah, what about it?" Clyde asked.

"That wasn't there three years ago," Jimmy said. "All the rock piled up into that little mountain was blasted out and moved from this canyon."

"Damn," Clyde said. "That is the second most incredible sight I've ever seen."

"I know you are going to say something sweet about me right now, Clarence," Bonnie said, "but if you say 'damn' one more time for a joke, I swear I'm going to murderize you."

Jimmy laughed. "I like you two, even if you do pack heat."

"Can't be too careful these days," Clyde said.

Bonnie looked up. The sun was out of sight behind the horizon now, and the sky was turning an indigo blue color she loved so much. A single star flickered above, and she watched as a series of floodlights came to life across the dam and in the canyon below, illuminating the site for the night shift, like a thousand spotlights on a theater stage.

"Takes some mighty smart people to pull this off, got to be real organized," Bonnie said. In the few minutes they had been there, she counted six containers of wet concrete being delivered to the face of the dam.

"It does," Jimmy said. "But mostly it depends on the muscle and sweat of those thousands of men working down there every minute of every day. They're breaking their backs while a bunch of fat cats get rich off them and the government."

The crowd was starting to thin and Clyde nodded toward the car. "I can't believe I'm saying this, but we better get back to town. We have to go to work tomorrow. Jimmy, I got some questions for you about where to go in the morning."

"You got to catch a ride on Big Bertha," Jimmy said.

CHAPTER 9

Last night of freedom

By the time they got back to Boulder City, it was dark and the night had turned chilly.

After asking for directions twice, Clyde finally parked in front of their assigned cottage, indistinguishable from all the other cottages save for the number on the door, and the fact that it was dark on the inside.

As they walked up to the front door, a neighbor ducked out from beneath the line of laundry connecting their two houses. She wore an apron frilled with clothespins, and her pale, weary face was proof of a long day doing chores. She looked Bonnie and Clyde up and down, tucked a flyaway strand of hair behind her ear and forced a smile.

"You must be the new neighbors. I'm Clara. Y'all need any help getting settled in?"

"Thanks, honey. I'm Brenda and this here is Clarence. I think we got it covered, but maybe later you can clue me on where to shop and all."

Clara seemed relieved they didn't actually need any help. "We can catch up tomorrow morning after the men go to work."

"I got a job too," Bonnie said. "Maybe tomorrow evening?"

"That's unusual," Clara said. "They don't usually let married women work, got a rule, only one breadwinner."

"That's news to me, hope I don't get there and not even have a job on my first day," Bonnie said, hoping her faked surprise would satisfy her new neighbor's curiosity.

"Well, you lucked out another way too. The family you would have been bunking with just moved on to the Bonneville site two days ago. You got it to yourselves, at least for a little while."

Clyde pulled Bonnie tight, and gave her a kiss on the cheek. "That's probably just as well."

"Oh, Clarence," she said, swatting his arm, "You're such a devil."

Clara smiled, and Bonnie saw the exhaustion in her eyes. "You must be newlyweds," she said. "The dam has a way of sucking the life out of you. Or maybe it's the desert. Either way, best be on guard against it. And the lizards. And the sand getting everywhere. Nice to meet you both." She turned back to gathering the laundry.

The door to their new house wasn't locked. They walked into the small common room. There was a kitchenette on the far side with a two-burner propane stove. On either side were doors to small bedrooms, each with a rack for clothes and a metal double bed frame covered with a thin mattress.

"It's not exactly the Taj Mahal," Clyde said.

Bonnie looked crestfallen. "I always dreamed of what our first house together would be like, and it was a hell of a lot better than this."

He caught her up in his arms, temporarily dislodging the sour look on her face.

"Don't be that way, Mrs. Prentiss. This ain't a real house, and I bet you can fix this dump up nice. We'll go down to the company store and spend some of Sal's cash on over-priced curtains, a few pots and pans and maybe a Turkish rug or two. Next thing you know, we'll be inviting the neighbors over for fancy cocktail parties."

"Clara doesn't seem like the cocktail type," Bonnie said.

"We can find out. I got another bottle of hooch in the car and it looks like her husband is still awake."

"I don't know, Clarence," she said, the name still sounding foreign when they were alone. "We both have to work tomorrow and it's been a long time since either of us turned in a full day of honest labor."

"Stop reminding me," he said, dropping her back to the floor. "I'm not sure I'm cut out for it."

"Then we'd better get to the bottom of all this nonsense fast, otherwise you're going to get all thin and wiry and sunburnt like Jimmy."

"Are you a little sweet on him?"

She pushed him out the door. "Go get our things."

"That's not an answer," he said.

He returned a few minutes later with her suitcase and two BARs, wrapped in a quilt, and slid them out of sight under the bed.

She hung her clothes on the metal rack as Clyde retrieved the duffel bag and a trunk stuffed with more clothes and a few books over a false bottom where they had pistols and knives and other tools of their new trade.

"You ready for this?" she asked.

"I'm driving a water truck," he said. "How hard could that be? I'm way more concerned about you pulling off a gal-Friday in an office. Short of a stint waitressing, which—as I recall—you were terrible at, you ain't worked a lick in your life."

"I bet I'll do a better job pretending to be a secretary than you pretending to be a roustabout."

"You're on," he said, shaking her hand, and then pulling her in close for a kiss before guiding her toward the bed. "And right now, we've got to ante up a little."

"But we don't have any curtains," she said, already unbuttoning her blouse.

"Then Clara and her old man are in for a real treat," he said, kicking his shoes off and reaching for *Tropic of Cancer* book on top of his suitcase. "Because I left off on a section juicy enough to make old Scratch himself blush."

CHAPTER 10

Clyde's first day on the job

The honking of Big Bertha, the transport truck, rumbling down the street woke Clyde abruptly and he swore, then groaned and disentangled himself from Bonnie's sleepy embrace.

"Don't go," she murmured, throwing her arm over him.

He looked longingly at her velvety smooth back revealed as the sheet slipped off. "Leaving you is the hardest thing I ever have to do," he said, crawling out of bed and pulling on a stiff new pair of denim overalls, a white tee shirt and a pair of work boots—Sal thought of everything. "Missing breakfast is the second hardest."

"I'll get some food today," she said sleepily.

"And maybe an alarm clock," Clyde said, kissing her on the neck and bolting out the door, still buttoning his overalls as he ran toward the truck trundling around the corner out of sight.

The men hooted and hollered as he caught up and then leapt onto the back fender, holding on for dear life—along with two other late risers—as the truck cleared the edge of town and sped up.

Strapping young laborers, their muscles sinewy from hard work and skin tanned by the desert sun, filled the truck. They each carried a tin box strapped over their shoulder and Clyde realized he not only missed breakfast, he didn't have lunch either. It's not the first time I've gone hungry and probably won't be the last, he thought.

"Hey, first day," someone shouted over the engine noise, and Clyde recognized Dino. "You ready for this?"

"I think so," Clyde said.

"Be careful, sun gets fierce in the hole. Be glad it ain't summer."

The truck made a wide turn and accelerated, and the momentum swept Clyde off balance, his feet sweeping out in an arc. The men in the truck erupted in good-natured laughter as Dino reached out, grabbing Clyde by the belt loops and pulling him back to safety.

When they finally got to the top of the canyon, the men filed out of the truck and stood in line to punch time cards, and then purposefully moved toward their respective jobs. A crowd of dirty, tired workers—finishing up the night shift—stood nearby, yawning and impatient, waiting to catch a return ride to Boulder City.

He followed the men to the punch-clock booth, then looked blankly at the time-keeping contraption. A heavyset man in overalls with hair combed around the edges of his otherwise bald head and an Errol Flynn mustache, sensing a slowdown in the line, looked up from his clipboard and snarled. "What's the hold up?"

"Uh, lack of familiarity," Clyde said. "It's my first day."

"Gonna be your last if you don't punch in."

Once Clarence Prentiss officially reported for duty, Clyde walked to the edge and looked down at the canyon worksite. It was just as daunting as the night before, somehow even more impressive in the flat, clear morning light. The black basalt canyon, carved by millions of years of wind and water, seemed ancient and otherworldly, freshly sculpted by tons of dynamite and jackhammers—the scars were almost an affront to the grandeur.

But the dam itself, he whistled under his breath, it was a thing of beauty, an engineering marvel.

"Prentiss, Clarence Prentiss," yelled the foreman, disrupting his reveries.

"Here, sir," Clyde said, raising his arm and moving away from the cliff's edge.

"Quit your daydreaming and get your ass down to the bottom," the foreman yelled. "You're driving on the canyon floor. Truck is at the base. Take a monkey-slide down."

He pointed to the large open cage on tracks sliding up the steep face of the canyon carrying a few dozen men.

"Monkey-slide?"

"The cableway," he grunted, and then laughed. "Also called the widow-maker."

Clyde watched the gondola-like cab arrive with a bump, and when the gates opened, men spilled out of it like minnows from a tipped over bait bucket. Clyde stood stock-still as people swept by him, emptying and then refilling the car.

"Did you want a gold-plated invitation, your majesty?" the operator asked, motioning him on.

"No, it's just...so damn high." Some of the other workers already onboard laughed.

"Don't worry," Dino said, pulling him on. "These things hardly ever fail. And this one ain't the widow-maker. The foreman was joshing you. She's way over there." He pointed to a cage straddling the middle of the canyon.

"Hell of a way to go," Clyde muttered, then said a little prayer to Bonnie and got on the creaking cable car. He ground his teeth together and gripped the side so tight his knuckles ached when the metal box lifted off and—the bottom scraping against the vertical rock face—slipped into open space. As the cage slowly labored down to the bottom of the canyon, Clyde fought the cold, sick ball of dread in his stomach.

By the time he stepped off, breathing a sigh of relief to be on firm ground, his knees ached and his back burned from standing frozen for the few minutes it took to get to the bottom. Dino pointed him to the truck depot and the crew boss handed him a map.

"Here's your route. Six stops. Then you'll come back, fill up the water tank and do it all over again. Each circuit will take about two hours. Then you keep doing that until your shift is up. Think you can do that?"

"Yes, sir," Clyde said.

"You ever driven a truck like this before?"

"If it's got wheels and an engine, I've driven it." He eyed the steep canyon walls. "Not especially good with heights though."

"Lucky for you we're working on the dry side. Two months ago, you would have been hugging the cliff walls. There's only one steep stretch now, from the bottom up to the east diversion tunnel. If you get spooked, shut your eyes. These trucks damn near know the way."

Clyde pulled open the door to the cab and jumped in. The keys were in the ignition and the water tank was full. He turned the engine over, shoved the truck into gear, gave it a little gas and it lunged forward. Clyde smiled, impressed with the strength of this battered beauty.

He tossed the map on the seat beside him and squinted at the sun. The temperature was climbing and the cab warmed up quick. Even though it was winter, the desert heat collected inside the canyon, and Clyde felt sweat breaking out across his chest, dripping down to his stomach.

At the first stop, Clyde pulled out the hose and filled up the small standing water tank. It was bone dry. A few men came by and he held the hose out as they splashed their faces, wetted their shirts and filled up canvas canteens. At the next stop, he repeated the same steps, and this time a few of the men asked to be soaked down to escape the building heat.

At the last stop, he drove out of the construction site for the powerhouses at the base of the dam and aimed the truck toward a steep, switch-backed road leading up to the high-mix concrete plant. He shifted into low gear and pushed ahead, white-knuckling the stretch and ignoring the drop off. At the crest of the road, he stopped and filled the water tank, bringing relief to the grateful workers.

With the truck's tank finally empty, he rumbled back to the depot and filled it up again from the water tower. The foreman told him he needed to speed things up. Clyde started out again, remembering why he hated so-called honest labor. If it was really honest, someone would get a busted jaw for talking down to him. After just one morning, he could see how the monotony and repetition of this work would kill a man, if a loose boulder, equipment malfunction or heat prostration didn't get him first.

During lunch, Dino shared his sandwich, but it did little to dampen Clyde's now fierce hunger. Still, he made a note to give Dino some hooch later.

As the sun arced across the clear blue sky, Clyde started on his last run. His shirt was soaked through with sweat, several mishaps with the water hose had muddied his new overalls, and blisters were coming up under his new, stiff boots.

Finally, his stomach grumbling like a metal plow through gravel, he made his last stop of the day at the sixth water tank. As he waited for the water to fill, he heard the clang of metal against metal under the parked truck. Curious, he walked back over and peeked under the chassis and saw two pairs of legs in clean pants and unscuffed loafers standing at the front of the truck.

He picked up a rock the size of a baseball and walked around to the other side of his truck.

A man smoking a cigarette stood looking down at another man, now flat on his back and under the truck. He could tell they didn't belong—no dirt on their clothes.

"Hurry," the standing man said. "The mook'll be done any minute."

"The mook's already done," Clyde said. The man spun, pulling out a switchblade. Clyde clobbered him on the side of the head with the rock, knocking him to his knees.

He picked up the knife and dragged the other man out by the feet, smiling when he heard his head clang against the axle. "What the hell you doing to my truck?" Clyde asked.

"Don't blow your wig, fella," the man said, standing slowly and looking at his friend who was addled from the blow and slowly touching the wound, studying his bloody fingers, confused. "Just slow down, take it easy."

"You're tampering with my brakes and you want me to take it easy?" Clyde said. He punctuated the question with jabs of the switchblade directed at the man's gut. "Tell me why I shouldn't let the air out of you?"

"Look, fella, it's nothing personal," the man said with a surprising calmness. "I got no beef with you. My employer is of the opinion that the owners of this operation have not been paying appropriate tribute for protection against unforeseen accidents."

"Like failing brakes?" Clyde asked.

"Exactly," the man said. "We wanted to send them a reminder. Unfortunately, that reminder would have been in the form of you."

He reached into his jacket and Clyde lunged forward with the knife ready.

"Hold on," the man said, extracting his wallet carefully between two fingers. "I'm just trying to compensate you for the misunderstanding." He pulled out a twenty and handed it to Clyde.

Clyde realized this might be a lucky break. If the sabotage of the dam was by mobsters running a simple protection racket, he and Bonnie could tie it up fast, report in to Sal, and get the hell out of Boulder City after just a single day of pretending to work.

"Keep your money," Clyde said. "Let's think of this misunderstanding as an opportunity for me to move into a different line of work. It's my first day, and I can already tell I ain't cut out for this business."

The man smiled, but let it fade quickly. "You seem smart enough and able to handle yourself." He let his eyes drop to the other man, now on his knees, slowly opening and closing his mouth like a stranded fish.

"Sorry about your friend," Clyde said. "How about we call it even and you put in a good word for me with your boss?" He hopped into the cab. "I did some work for someone you may know, Joe Mignolia in New York."

"Maybe I'll give him a call," the man said.

Clyde knew he was being tested. "That'll be hard. He's dead. That's why I'm here. On the run."

"Naturally, I'll have to confirm. But if it turns out clean and you're ever in Las Vegas, come by the casino. Ask for Lefty."

"Which casino?" Clyde asked.

"The only game in town," Lefty said. "Let's just say that if our paths cross again, it was meant to be."

"Fair enough," Clyde said. "Say, you didn't finish cutting the brakes, did you?"

Lefty smiled and shook his head. "Not quite."

Another test, Clyde thought. He roared away and watched in the rearview mirror as Lefty helped his friend to his feet.

CHAPTER 11

Bonnie's first day on the job

After Clyde left, Bonnie tried to sleep longer, but the bed felt lonely without him so she got up and made a cup of coffee. She moved to the stoop to drink it and smoke a cigarette, watching the company town come to life.

Kids traipsed to school, heads down and lunches tucked under their arms. Wives and mothers hung washed-out overalls and diapers to dry in the pale sunlight. Husbands off the night shift trudged inside to sleep. A few cars rolled by, a few new moms pushed trams, a few people nodded at her politely, others looked at her curiously.

I am not cut out for civilized society, she thought.

At ten to eight, she walked to the Six Companies administration office, a sleek, white-washed building in the center of town next to the water tower.

An American flag was planted out front on the only patch of green lawn she had seen so far in the whole town, other than in front of the cliffside boss houses. She pushed open the door, not sure what to expect.

A group of women filing, typing, talking and smoking stopped what they were doing to look Bonnie over, admiring the matching violet skirt and jacket she picked up months ago in Nashville.

Standing inside the doorway of a smaller office, a woman with ivory skin, jet-black hair swept up into a swirling bun and emerald green cat eye glasses gave her the once-over. She chewed gum with mechanical precision. "Can I help you, honey?" she asked between short, wet, enthusiastic smacks.

"I'm Brenda, Brenda Prentiss. Today's my first day." She straightened her beret.

"Oh right, good, I'm Claudette." She motioned Bonnie to come join her. "Say hello, ladies."

The six women in the room waved and said hello in unison, then quickly returned to their work and conversations.

Claudette led her into the smaller office and pointed at a tiny desk covered with papers. "That's your desk. Let me know if you have any questions."

"Well, I have one straight off," Bonnie said. "What am I supposed to be doing?"

Claudette looked at her over the rim of her glasses. "You don't know what you were hired to do?"

"Not really? Am I supposed to type or something?"

"Oh, heavens no," Claudette said. "The typing pool is that crowd of gals you just passed through."

Bonnie heard typewriters clacking and the clipped, soulless sound of voices droning through dictaphones.

"You're a backup to the main secretary, me. Your job is, in this order, to make sure there's always plenty of coffee for Mr. Fitzsimmons." She gestured at the closed door behind her desk. "He really likes his coffee, always black, real hot and preferably delivered from someone young and pretty. You've also got to answer the phone when I'm at lunch or taking a break or having a smoke, which is fairly often, and take care of the filing."

She pointed at the mound of papers piled on Bonnie's desk. "I've been saving it up for you. There's a big stack of employment contracts for you to file today. The tan ones go in the big drawers, alphabetical by last name. And that part's important. The last gal couldn't get it right. And the little stack of red folders get locked inside the brown metal cabinet there." Claudette pointed, her perfectly manicured pink nails adding emphasis.

"What's the difference?"

"The red ones are the troublemakers the company is keeping an eye on." She paused. "This is serious stuff, confidential information. You can't go telling nobody about what kind of files they have on the men."

Bonnie nodded. "Of course not."

Claudette lowered her voice and leaned in, motioning Bonnie closer. "But it's pretty entertaining reading, especially if you like the bad boys like me."

Bonnie winked and smiled. "Only choir boys for me."

Claudette giggled. "You don't know what you're missing, sister. Now keep an eye on things while I go have a smoke."

Bonnie watched her leave, admiring her shapely figure—she looked like Fay Wray. Bonnie wasn't much for making friends—what was the point in this life of theirs—but if she was tempted, Claudette would likely fit the bill. Easy going and fun, by the looks of it. Wouldn't ask a lot of questions.

Turning back to the work, Bonnie began flipping through some of the red files, humming a little tune softly. Jimmy Hall was at the top. She scanned through a laundry list of union agitating and other official misconduct. His file ended with a cryptic scrawl related to suspicion of murder, but with no evidence. Yet. There was a note to check Clarence Prentiss more closely.

"Not even a full day on the job and you're already pegged as a troublemaker," she said, shaking her head. "It's your lucky day, Clarence Prentiss." She erased the notation.

The next five files were more union agitators, each with notes related to their job performance. After that was a file for a new hire, a Dante Iescco. An Italian immigrant and potential anarchist. He was suspected of stealing dynamite, and they were keeping an eye on him until some Boston lawmen got here to take him back to stand trial for some kind of bombing. Bonnie checked to make sure Claudette wasn't coming back, then copied the details down onto a scrap of paper and tucked it away in her bra just as the phone rang.

The sudden noise startled her and she snatched it up. "Hello," she said.

There was a long pause, and then a woman's voice said, "Who is this?"

"Uh, this is Bonnie," Bonnie said, then felt a sick feeling wash through her stomach.

"I must have misheard you," the woman said, her voice icy. "I was trying to reach Brenda. Brenda Prentiss. And I know for a fact, there's no Bonnie in your office."

It was Sal. "Are you trying to fail, trying to get your family sent to prison?" Sal asked.

"Shit," she said, shaking her head, just as the main interior office door opened and Mr. Fitzsimmons, her new boss, stepped out. He was tall and thin, emaciated even, a scarce head of hair combed over so far it reached his pink ears, and a nose that reminded Bonnie of a pirate. Or a pirate's parrot.

"No, ma'am, my name is Brenda Prentiss," she said. "It's my first day."

"I assume someone just walked in," Sal said.

"Yes, ma'am."

"I prefer this subservient side of you," Sal said. "The strain must be immense, so I'll get to the point. We've got trouble. Hank Black thinks you're still alive."

"Oh, yes ma'am, that's a familiar name, but could you remind me why it's important?" She flipped through some of the folders on the table and smiled up at Fitzsimmons as he rattled his empty coffee cup in her direction.

"He's a Texas Ranger who was at your, uh, at the ambush."

"Thank you, I don't recall seeing that in the file," Bonnie said, as Fitzsimmons put the cup down in front of her, practically on top of the telephone, and walked back into his office.

"That's because he wasn't in the papers. He kept his name out of everything. Didn't want to make it seem like he was after the glory. He's a law and order man who wanted to see the job through. He was spotted at your mother's house two days ago. You haven't done anything stupid like talk to her, have you?"

"No, ma'am," Bonnie said.

"Black is like a dog with a bone," Sal said. "If he shows up there, we're all sunk. The whole thing comes apart."

"I'll make sure to add that to my agenda, and by the way, your connection is, well, your connection has expired."

There was a long pause. "Daniels is dead?"

"Yes, that is correct," Bonnie said.

"Fuck," Sal said. Bonnie was surprised by the genuine remorse packed into that single word. "His last report came in just after I left you at La Posada. Said he was really worried about the dam."

"We will fulfill your order just as soon as possible," Bonnie said. "Did he happen to mention who was sending the, uh, package?"

"In an unsecured phone call?" Sal asked. "Of course not. You'll have to start from scratch. Just keep your heads down and don't blow this for me."

She hung up and Bonnie cradled the receiver.

"Mrs. Prentiss," Fitzsimmons called, just as Claudette walked back in. "In this office, we like to convey a certain disposition. Please end your calls with 'have a pleasant day' or something similar."

"Of course, Mr. Fitzsimmons," Bonnie said. "Yes, sir."

"And if I ever hear you curse again, on the phone or elsewhere, you'll be gone."

"Yes, Mr. Fitzsimmons."

"And, one more thing, Mrs. Prentiss."

"Yes, Mr. Fitzsimmons?"

"Did you think my coffee will magically fill itself up and walk back in here?"

CHAPTER 12

Going once

A potted fern withered on the sill of the only window in the basement. Nestled in the corner of a worn red couch, the armrests stained dark from years of use, Bonnie pushed cardboard puzzle pieces around on a card table, looking for color matches. The box top on the couch beside her showed a lighthouse on an ocean coast.

"These things are so aggravating," she said. "Whoever thought old people would like these is either a sadist, or doesn't know how old eyes work." She tried to wedge a piece together with several others then shook her head and threw the piece into the middle of the table, leaning back on the couch pillows. "Did you ever see those two fellows in the fancy car again?"

Royce thumbed through his notebook, finding his place, and then queued up the micro-cassette recorder. "Nope. I was likely overreacting. But hanging out with America's most famous outlaw queen, long presumed dead, tends to induce a little paranoia."

"Only a little?" Bonnie said, standing. "How about some hot chocolate?"

"Sure, but are you out of whiskey?"

"I'm feeling a little out of sorts today, but I am happy to get some for you. It adds a nice kick to the hot chocolate. But I'll stick to cocoa." She plugged in an electric tea kettle and fussed around in the cupboard. "With marshmallows or without?"

"Without."

Bonnie ripped open two packets of instant mix, dumped it into mugs and waited for the water to heat up.

This was only the second time she'd invited him downstairs. Unlike the upstairs, which was barely furnished, dusty and lonely, the basement was full of photos, memorabilia, crochet quilts and throw pillows. A big television sat in the corner next to a record player with two large speakers.

Earlier, as they walked down the stairs—Royce ducking his head beneath the exposed beams—she explained that even as the decades passed, Clyde still felt the need for tight security. They rigged up this two-room basement with alarms and trip wires, and before he died, Clyde was looking into one of those new-fangled video surveillance systems.

He watched Bonnie's eyes drift to the now empty space not so long ago occupied by Clyde's hospital bed. Royce felt a tragic, helpless sadness seeing her smile droop and her relentlessly bright eyes dim, wondering what it must be like to love someone for half a century, and then suddenly have to live without him.

He let his mind drift, imagining Bonnie and Clyde sitting together and drinking hot chocolate, watching television—maybe Laugh-In or Dallas—and doing jigsaw puzzles. Even outlaws get old, he thought.

She filled the cups and placed them on the end table beside the puzzle, then settled back into the couch. "Have you ever been to Hoover Dam?"

Royce nodded. "A family vacation when I was a kid, on our way to the Grand Canyon."

"I still remember how I felt when I first laid eyes on that dam," she said. "Back then it was called Boulder Dam, you know?"

He clicked on the recorder. "How did you feel seeing Boulder Dam, now called Hoover Dam, for the first time?"

"Small," she said, eyes clouding over with memories.

"Small? How so?"

"Part of it was just the sheer size of it all, like it literally made me feel small. But then there was another part, how each of us—me, Clyde, Jimmy, Claudette, the workers—each one of us had this tiny part to play in this big, important thing. We were all tiny cogs in a giant machine, and each one on their own, none of us mattered a whit, but working together made us all part of something grand and exciting and useful."

She paused, searching for exactly the right words. "That sense of being small, but somehow still connected to something bigger, it really stuck with me after that. And I know Clyde felt it too. I think being there, seeing people working on something with so much potential to change lives, knowing their efforts all added together would shape the future—well, it finally forced us to see the world a little more generously."

"What do you mean?" he asked gently.

Bonnie shook her head silently, as if regretting the intimacy, but continued. "We did some terrible things, me and Clyde. What we did in New York, saving the president, that all seemed like a lark, and Sal was forcing us. But Hoover Dam, seeing so many people brought together, working toward a common goal, I think that was when we started to feel different, like maybe no matter how small the actions, we could do something to help others, help the country. And maybe that would allow us to atone for the past."

She threw her hands up, ashamed of the monologue.

"Forgive an old woman's rambling." She took a sip of cocoa, leaving behind a chocolate mustache she dabbed with a lace handkerchief trimmed with embroidered violets. "You made a mistake passing on the marshmallows. Let's get back to the story."

"Tell me more about this Jimmy fellow," he said, flipping through his notes. "The head of the union. You said he was real handsome. Did you have a little crush on him?"

"Don't be ridiculous," she said, a little too quickly. "He had real charisma, though," she said with a smile. "And he was smart, had some good ways of explaining things that made it easy to understand. That comes in handy when you're trying to get folks organized around an idea."

"Like what?"

"He talked about circles," she said. "He would draw these pictures. One circle was industry. One was government. One was labor, you know, the working man. He said the goal was to always have the three circles in tension with each other, but mostly equal-sized. And then he would put a big X over the labor circle and explode it into dozens of small dots, and say how without organizing, it was just a bunch of little bugs, like mosquitos, stinging and occasionally drawing blood but always at the mercy of being swatted by the other two."

"That's not bad," Royce said.

"He always said when the worker circle was equal, it had the power to share in profits and to vote as a bloc to be sure government policies were favorable to the working man. Said the balance was better for the country overall."

"I can see why bosses might find someone with such a simple but strong way of explaining things a threat back then," Royce said.

"Back then?" she said, shaking her head. "I don't think much has changed."

"Unions are strong today," Royce said, confused.

"If you believe that, you aren't paying attention," Bonnie said. "To my mind, the mistake was they always thought too small, much smaller than the vision Jimmy and others like him had. Turned back into a bunch of bugs buzzing around, fooling themselves into thinking they're influential because they've grown to the size of horseflies but still easy enough to swat down, with the help of money and laws from the other two circles."

"I've been hearing about this new workers' union in Poland that's challenging the Soviet Union," Royce said.

"Solidarity. That's a good example of what Jimmy was talking about," Bonnie said, sipping the hot chocolate. "Takes workers organizing from the ground up across all jobs to accomplish something revolutionary, to change the status quo," she continued. "There, in Poland, it's to disrupt communism. Here, we need something to challenge capitalism, to keep it from devouring itself and everything in its path. But that's the opposite of what the unions are doing. More like appeasement. And mark my words, it's going to bite us all on the ass someday."

"I don't know," Royce said. "I don't think unions are going away any time soon."

"I hope you're right," Bonnie said. "Otherwise, corporations will be calling the shots and the only thing they'll have to guide them is profits and shareholder demands. And when that happens, without unions, when the government starts dancing to the tune of greed, the working man and woman will always come in last."

"Was that your experience with Six Companies at Hoover Dam?"

"Don't get ahead of the story," she said, reaching out to pat his hand.

Royce smiled. "All right. We ended last time with that Texas Ranger on your trail."

"The devil who gunned down two innocent people he thought was us," she said. "Oh, that reminds me." She handed him a brown envelope. "I have something that might be of interest to our mutual investigation."

He pulled a glossy magazine-style brochure from the envelope. It was from Sotheby's New York announcing upcoming auctions of art and historical artifacts. He looked at her curiously.

"Open it to page twelve," she said.

A two-page layout advertised a sale from the shootout of Bonnie and Clyde with the headline: *Own a piece of outlaw history!*

The text explained that a private—and anonymous— dealer was selling an entire collection of rare artifacts from the Sailes, Louisiana ambush site along with other paraphernalia purchased from family members over the years. Photos of a bloody glove, a fedora covered with bullet holes like Swiss cheese, and a piece of the blasted car were in the catalogue.

"That must be weird for you."

"You have no idea," Bonnie said. "But look at item fourteen."

"A gold wedding band inset with rare blue stones worn by Bonnie Parker when she was gunned down," Royce read. "The inscription and jeweler's mark render this a one-of-a-kind possession." Royce handed the brochure back to her. "Sounds like a lovely ring."

"Likely is," Bonnie said. "But it's not mine."

She watched Royce's expression change as the implications sank in. "Looks like I'll be making a trip to New York," he said.

CHAPTER 13

Welcome wagon

After a nerve-wracking return ride to the top of the canyon in the monkey-slide at the end of his first shift, Clyde caught the transport truck back to Boulder City.

Blistered and tired and hungry, he limped toward their cottage. The sun was already sinking and Bonnie was on the front step smoking. She brightened at the sight of him and ran down the path, colliding into his arms.

"How was your first day, baby?" she asked, kissing him.

He shrugged. "Long."

"Come on now, I haven't seen you in near on ten hours. Can you give me a little something more?"

"It was a normal work day, Bon."

She arched her left eyebrow and he looked around at the houses nestled up against theirs, but saw no sign of nosy neighbors. "Brenda, I mean Brenda. Nothing happened and now I just want to have something to eat and stretch out on the bed and get some shuteye before I have to get up and do it all over again tomorrow."

She stepped back, looking him over, up and down. "You are a filthy mess. My guess is them overalls could stand up without you even being in them."

"Maybe you could help me out of them?" he asked.

"So, you're not too tired for fooling around?" She took his hand and led him to the small stoop. "Have a sip of coffee. That's just what you need."

He looked in the cup, saw it was rye whiskey, and drained it.

"That hits the spot," he said, sitting on the front step, and sighing with deep fatigue. "How was your first day?"

"I filed some papers, fetched a lot of coffee for an asshole who watched my ass and was talked down to at least fifteen times. I think there's a bright future for me here."

She refilled the cup, took a sip of whiskey and then lowered her voice. "I also found out we've got a Texas Ranger by the name of Hank Black on our trail." She left out the part about how it was likely her fault. "He was at the ambush."

"He was one of them fellows who thinks they gunned us down?"

She nodded. "Yep. So it would be awkward if he ran into us here. Oh, and I may have found out who's behind the sabotage."

"The mob," Clyde said. "I ran into them today, too."

"No, it's the anarchists," she said. "When did you run into the mob? You said nothing happened."

"Well one thing happened, I guess," he said. "They tried to cut the brakes on my truck so's my fiery death would send a message to the bosses."

"What happened?" she asked.

"I wrecked and died," he said with a straight face. "I'm a ghost."

"Then you ought not to feel this," she said, pinching his arm.

He laughed and slapped her hand away. "What exactly is an anarchist?"

"People who don't think we need government to tell us how to live," she said.

"Like, no government at all?"

"I think so. They believe any kind of government is a fancier, trussed up way to trick people into their own oppression, or something like that. Things would be better if people learned to get along and took care of each other."

"Seems overly hopeful of an idea about people, if you ask me," Clyde said.

"They certainly have a favorable view of human nature," Bonnie said. "It's something I need to think through a little more, because, you know, based on what we've seen, I suspect without the government, it would be a dog eat dog world, and the big dogs—the ones with the most teeth—would end up being in charge anyway."

Clyde nodded. "So, why'd you peg the sabotage on them anarchists?"

"Six Companies has files. I took a look at some Italian fellow, a new hire. Him and his brother, the bosses think they're bad news."

"So, we've got a ranger on our tail, and the mafia, anarchists and union boys all coming in as possible saboteurs," Clyde said.

"Saboteurs?" Bonnie asked.

"Yeah. It's French I think, for someone who sabotages."

"I know what it means. You just surprised me."

Grinning, Clyde walked into the tiny house and looked sadly at the empty table and bare cupboards. "I wish I knew French for 'I'm so hungry I could eat my own shadow.' I was kind of hoping you'd have supper ready."

"I worked a full day too, Clarence," she said.

"Yeah, but—"

"Don't you dare say, 'yeah, but you're a woman,'" she said, standing in the doorway, hands on hips.

"I was gonna say you were sitting in a chair all day."

"And you were sitting in a truck all day."

His shoulders slumped. "I ain't gonna win this, am I?"

"Let's go spend some of Sal's money and have a nice meal at the diner," she said. "I hear there's a fella there who makes the best pies in the whole state."

"Think I should bring my heaters?" he asked, looking at the shoulder holster draped over the chair, holding the matching .45s.

"It's just a bite to eat," she said, checking her make up. "What could go wrong?"

After Clyde cleaned up, they walked arm in arm across town to the diner.

"Maybe we'll see some famous movie stars here in town," Bonnie said, her eyes shining eagerly. "Claudette told me that Bette Davis stayed here last year. Wouldn't it be something to see her, or Jimmy Stewart?"

"I don't understand why everybody is so damn anxious to see Hollywood types," he said. "They ain't no different than the rest of us."

"Yes, they are baby," she said. "They're famous."

"We were famous once too, and it didn't amount to a hill of beans," he said. "I just wonder if they ain't got something better to do than come out here and gawk at people working and sweating and toiling."

She squeezed his hand. "One day of hard work and you're already a communist."

"If being a communist means wanting to make sure I get a square deal for my work, rather than everything finding its way into some fat cat's bank account, call me a communist."

"Better not let the company men hear you say that," she said. "You'll end up with a nice new red folder."

After a meal of steak, potatoes and apple pie, they strolled back toward their house.

"Hey look, it's Jimmy," Bonnie said, waving as he walked toward them. She felt Clyde tense at the familiarity.

"Hey, Brenda," he said. "Clarence, how are you?"

"Full all the way," Clyde said. "That diner can put down a spread."

Jimmy cocked his head. "How'd you afford a meal like that on a truck driver's wages?"

"You ought not to ask too deep about another man's finances," Clyde said.

"Sorry, don't get your feathers all ruffled. Hey listen, we've got an organizing meeting tonight. Why don't you come with me?"

"That sounds like a good idea," Bonnie said, giving Clyde a breather to catch his temper before it turned violent. "We can learn what all the union fuss is about."

"Sorry, Brenda, this one's just for men," Jimmy said.

Bonnie frowned. "Because only men work? Or because women can't think through these big old complicated topics like organizing for a common goal?"

Clyde nodded. "Probably both," he said, happy to see her crush on Jimmy evaporating before his eyes. "But most definitely a man thing. Why don't you wait for me at home? And maybe see if you can rustle me up something for lunch tomorrow."

She glared at him, but brightened when she saw Claudette waving at her from across the street. Claudette ran up, breathless, and introduced herself to Clyde and Jimmy, her eyes lingering a second too long on Jimmy, who fidgeted uncomfortably as he tried to keep from staring at her.

Claudette was dolled up in a tight red dress, with a fashionable bra underneath that made her chest stick out like traffic cones, and she had pin-curled her dark hair.

"Brenda, come with me to the dance," Claudette said. "I need a gal to pal around with."

"That sounds perfect," Bonnie said, sticking her tongue out at Clyde.

He watched her walk away, then fell into step with Jimmy. "I don't know much about unions," Clyde said.

"Your last job didn't have one?"

"My last job was what you might call a freelance position."

They turned a corner and stopped in front of the Methodist church. A group of men loitered on the wooden front porch waiting for the meeting to begin.

"I've been hearing rumors about sabotage," Clyde said. "Think it could be some of the union folks?"

Before Jimmy could answer, a flatbed truck barreled around the corner and half a dozen men in cloth masks leapt out, brandishing baseball bats and wrenches.

"I don't suppose that's the welcome wagon," Clyde said.

CHAPTER 14

Dancing with anarchy

Bonnie hooked her arm through Claudette's as they walked toward the recreation hall.

"Don't get your hopes up," Claudette said. "There won't be many men there and even if there was, the older ladies watch us like hawks, and nobody dances too close. Plus, the music is terrible and there's no hooch, of course."

"Sounds like a prison dance," Bonnie said, laughing.

"It's mostly a chance to catch up on the gossip," Claudette said. "You'll have fun enough. I'll introduce you to some of the other married ladies. Their husbands are all at that union meeting. They'll look after you."

Bonnie slowed. "You aren't staying?"

Claudette smiled slyly. "I'll stay a little while, but I've got a date with my new man."

Bonnie nodded. "I see. So, you'll be off having fun and pitching woo while us old married gals drink fruit punch and gossip."

"Well, it's not like that exactly," Claudette said. They drew close to the recreation hall. Tinny music drifted through the crisp evening air, the melody mixing with a light scent of juniper. "I mean, the dance is exactly like you described it, but Dante isn't really the pitching woo type. He's got big ideas."

"You little tramp," Bonnie said. "Dante Iescco? The anarchist? You *do* have a thing for bad boys."

Claudette squeezed Bonnie by the arm. "I can't help it," she said. "He's so cute and so serious. When he gets all spooked up about injustices and fighting the government, it makes me weak in the knees. Too bad you're married. His brother Mateo is almost as cute and twice as earnest."

"Will they have booze?" Bonnie asked.

Claudette nodded, her eyes sparkling.

"Let's both skip the dance," Bonnie said.

"Say, how did you know he was an anarchist?" Claudette asked.

She led them down a gravel pathway littered with lumber, hacked off pipes and twists of barbed wire, passing behind the most recent row of still unfinished houses and along the tracks behind the railroad depot.

"I saw his red folder today," Bonnie said. "Don't worry, his secret is safe with me."

"They have to be really careful," Claudette said. "Since I told them Fitzsimmons is on to them, they meet outside."

They walked a quarter mile past the depot to a little gully where a fire flickered. Two men crouched beside a campfire—both dark-skinned with thick black hair—talking animatedly, until they saw the women.

At the sight of a stranger, they both stood, and one fumbled under his jacket. Bonnie saw a flash of a splintered wooden handle and rusted metal, and cursed herself for leaving her little automatic back on the nightstand.

"What is this?" the older of the two asked.

"Calm down, Dante," Claudette said. "This is Brenda. She's sympathetic to the cause." She elbowed Bonnie in the ribs lightly to make sure she played along.

"Very sympathetic," Bonnie said.

Neither man spoke for a few long seconds.

"Relax, fellas," Bonnie said, letting her sweetest southern drawl do the work of flirting. "I don't really have a head for politics, so how about you handsome men share some of the booze and tell me what's got you all riled up?"

Claudette, still holding her arm, sat them both down on an overturned box next to the fire and took two mugs filled with red wine, handing one to Bonnie.

"Come on, Dante," Claudette said. "Brenda here is just a hard-working gal like me who probably has been blinded to, you know, the reality of things by the newspapers and politicians, like you always say."

Dante and Mateo spoke quickly in Italian, and after the exchange, Dante relaxed and let his hand move away from the butt of the old pistol, then sat down beside Claudette, draping his arm around her shoulders. He introduced the other man—Mateo—and laughed, running his hand through his thick hair.

"You both seem innocent enough," Mateo said, his words thick with an Italian accent that sounded sultry and romantic to Bonnie.

"Like a preacher's daughter," Bonnie said, batting her eyes. "Why don't you boys explain it all to me, but real simple so I can comprehend it."

"We are anarchists," Mateo said. "We want to end the tyranny of governments and allow men to live the lives of freedom they deserve, with no rules, only the freedom to associate as they wish. Men are able to govern themselves, they do not need kings and tyrants."

"You're not into free love, are you?" Bonnie asked, draining the wine and rattling the cup for more. "Because that always struck me as something that only worked out well for men. Like, I'd be all for it if women could have as many husbands as they want."

"That would be ridiculous," Dante said. "It goes against the laws of nature for women to have more than one mate."

"Oh, so there are laws then," Bonnie said, maintaining the lilt to her voice so her words sounded less threatening. "The laws of nature?"

"Yes, there are certain natural laws that must be taken into account," Mateo said, refilling her cup. When he sat back down, his pants rode up and she could see the handle of a knife stuck into his boot. "The wolf will never embrace the lamb, nor the lamb the wolf. That is natural law."

Bonnie scooted closer to the fire and pulled her sweater tighter. "Well, certainly not if the wolf has dynamite and is trying to blow the lamb up."

"You have been fooled by your so-called journalists," Dante said. "Anarchists aren't trying to blow up the lambs, we are the lambs. We believe that with education, men—and women—can learn to govern themselves without being oppressed by a government made up of wolves."

Bonnie nodded, like she was thinking on their words, and paused before responding.

"Was a time I might have agreed with you boys," she said. "But these days, I have to come at it from another angle. This Depression was caused by men, and a few women, who have so much money, they don't have to follow any laws, natural or otherwise. I think all your words sound real pretty, but at the end of the day, we need the government to save us from people who have all the wealth and power, and no compunction about using their riches to work against the greater good."

Claudette shifted uncomfortably on the crate. "Take it easy, Brenda. You're gumming things up here."

"Your government is dangerous, and so are the robber barons it spawns," Dante said. "This dam is a symbol of American ingenuity and progress, and also a symbol of capitalism engineered for the few on the backs of the workers. If completed, it would signal to the world that American democracy mixed with capitalism is the only way."

"Well, theoretically, it's not a bad combo, all things considered," Bonnie said. "Does that mean you all are trying to sabotage the dam so it doesn't get finished?"

Claudette gasped.

"You ask questions like the police," Mateo said, inching his hand closer to his boot. He turned to Dante and spoke again in Italian.

Bonnie snorted. "Me? A copper? That's rich. I just want to make sure my man is safe if you try to blow anything up."

Claudette looked at Dante who was slowly pulling out an antique revolver. "I am very sorry Claudette, but this evening will not turn out well."

"What are you talking about, Dante?" Claudette asked. "You know you've got my heart. Put that gun away." She took a slug of wine, certain he was playing a game.

"We do not kill women," Mateo said. "Dante, put the gun away."

Dante yelled something at Mateo, and Mateo responded, his voice also rising, in their native language. Bonnie and Claudette wondered what they were saying, turning their heads back and forth as the conversation escalated. She couldn't make sense of language, but the one thing Bonnie knew for sure was that Claudette's boyfriend was both stupid and drunk on red wine. A dangerous combination.

Finally, Dante stood and pointed the gun at Claudette, and then Bonnie.

"Honey, what are you doing?" Claudette said. Disbelief slipped into her voice, with the sudden recognition that her boy may not just be bad, but crazy too. She held on to Bonnie's arm tightly.

Mateo cursed, but made no move to stop Dante.

"This doesn't seem like a very enlightened way to solve problems," Bonnie said. "Not very anarchist at all, really. Put the gun away."

Dante cocked the hammer, and Bonnie was transfixed, hardly believing that this was how it was going to end for her, sitting next to a fire in the desert with a drunk anarchist pointing an antique gun at her. Time seemed to slow down but then she heard a soft thud. The chamber fell out of the pistol, landing on the sand by Dante's feet.

They all looked down at it, then Bonnie laughed. "You are the worst anarchist ever."

"Dante, you are a fool, but you have started something that now has to be finished," Mateo said.

He pulled his boot knife out with a flourish, but Bonnie was faster. She yanked a burning piece of wood from the fire and shoved the glowing tip into his face. Mateo yelled in pain and dropped the knife. Dante bent down to retrieve the chamber from the pistol and Bonnie clubbed him hard across the back of the head, singeing his hair and knocking him sprawling.

She caught Claudette by the arm and pulled her up to her feet. "Time to scram," she said, half dragging her into the darkness. "I hope you are reconsidering your fondness for bad boys."

Behind them, Dante found the missing gun part. He blew sand out of the chamber, wobbled unsteadily, then wedged it back into the frame of the pistol and fired at their shadowy, retreating forms.

Claudette screamed and covered her ears, but the bullets whistled past ineffectively. Drunk men rarely shoot straight, Bonnie thought, if they can shoot at all.

With a curse, Dante reloaded, and the anarchists took off after Bonnie and Claudette as the women raced toward the lights of town.

CHAPTER 15

Busting the union busters

A knot of men wearing black hoods spilled out of the back of the truck and advanced toward the church where the union meeting was about to get started, waving baseball bats and pipe wrenches.

Clyde whistled low. "No wonder no one comes to your meetings, Jimmy. You're supposed to give folks coffee and donuts, not beatings from armed assholes."

"We've had enough of your collective organizing bullshit," one of the hooded men yelled. "We know the union is behind all the sabotage at the dam. You're gonna cost us our jobs and we're putting an end to it right now."

"Fellows, the union ain't got nothing to do with that nonsense," Jimmy said, his voice loud but calm and authoritative. "We fight for all of us, to make sure they treat us square, and we're more than happy to work hard for a fair wage."

The workers who had been waiting inside the church came out onto the porch, saw what was brewing and milled nervously, knowing that trouble of any kind could get them tossed from Boulder City.

Working up the courage to help out Jimmy, a few of them started down the stairs, but the driver of the truck cracked opened the door and stepped one leg on the ground, aiming a shotgun through the open window toward the porch. "You boys stay up there. Our beef is with Jimmy. But we'll take on anyone who's feeling brave."

"Why don't you fellows take them masks off so we can have a civil conversation?" Clyde said. "Don't hardly seem fair we don't know who's bent on giving us a whupping."

"Mind your business, Prentiss," one of the men said, brandishing a length of pipe.

"Aw, shucks," Clyde said. "You already know my name. Something tells me either you're kind of sweet on me, or else you've had a looksee at my files."

"Which means you're a company man," Jimmy said, pointing at the masked agitator. "Why do you come at the union just for wanting the same deal you get?"

"We're working men, same as you," the driver said. "But we've had it with you trying to mess things up and get us all fired."

"That's not what's going on here," Jimmy said. "And you know it."

Clyde took off his jacket and draped it over the porch railing, tossed his fedora on top of it and then loosened his collar.

"I don't think they're interested in the truth," he said, rolling up his sleeves. "In fact, I think they're trying to muddy the water. Not sure why yet. But I wonder just how deep they're willing to wade in to get their point across."

"You ought not to stick your nose where it don't belong," the man with the pipe said, moving closer.

"Never been good at taking orders from nobody except my main gal," Clyde said.

"This ain't your fight," Jimmy said quietly.

"More than you know," Clyde said. "Plus, Brenda has taken a shine to you. She'd never forgive me if that handsome mug of yours got all busted up."

"Y'all would run if you had any sense," the man closest to them said. He raised his bat up nervously, threatening to take a swing.

"And y'all ought to know better than to poke at a rattlesnake," Clyde said, smiling easily.

He lunged in close to the man and caught him by the elbow, keeping the arm with the bat high over his head. With the bat out of commission, he jabbed the attacker in the gut three times hard and fast. The punches knocked the wind out of him and he sank to his knees with a groan.

Clyde pulled the bat from his hand and tested the heft.

"A genuine Louisville slugger," he said. "I've been hit by these before, and they leave a hell of a mark. The kind of mark that's easy enough to see in daylight when you ain't wearing a mask." Clyde took a savage swing at the next man in line, the one holding the pipe who had recognized him, catching the man flatfooted and smashing his nose with a sickening crunch.

"Jebub Chribe," the man moaned, dropping his pipe and staggering down to one knee.

The thugs still standing seemed uncertain, and one spun to address the driver. "Shoot him," he yelled.

"But that's cold-blooded murder," the driver said. "And everybody is watching."

"Shoot the sons of bitches!"

Before the driver could come to a decision, a shot rang out from behind them at the far end of the street. Clyde looked past the demoralized attackers, puzzled to see Bonnie running full tilt in his direction, dragging Claudette behind her.

Farther back, two men—cloaked in the shadows—stopped and one raised a pistol and fired another round toward the women.

"Son of a bitch," Clyde snarled.

Using the distraction, he sprinted toward the truck, lowered his shoulder and slammed his full body weight into the door. The driver, still with one leg on the ground and the gun out the window, had craned his head around to find the source of the shooting, and didn't see Clyde coming. The door, powered by all the force Clyde could muster, slammed into his leg so hard the metal warped and his shin bone shattered.

With an agonizing shriek, the driver fell out of the truck and onto the sandy drive, moaning and clutching the jagged shards of bone pushing against his pant leg. Clyde picked up the fallen shotgun, blew the dust out of the trigger and aimed it straight at Bonnie. She saw his play and dragged Claudette to the ground by the arm.

The second she was out of the line of sight, Clyde blasted a round at the anarchists, then another. They were too far away to do much damage, but the birdshot peppered them and Clyde smiled when he heard them howl, drop the gun and flee back into the shadows.

Bonnie helped Claudette up, swiping some of the dust off her new red dress, and looked at the scene before her: she counted three wounded men, and four more still able-bodied but looking nervously with their hands up as Clyde covered them with the shotgun. A gaggle of workers stood frozen on the front porch.

She tilted her head to his left, warning him silently as three uniformed men ran up from behind. He nodded and turned around.

"What the hell is going on here?" one of the cops asked, stopping in front of Clyde while the other two held back, guns drawn. "Hand over that shotgun, real slow like," he said to Clyde.

Clyde handed the gun over, nice and easy, the barrel pointed to the ground.

"Who the hell are you? And why shouldn't I cart you off to jail right this second?" the officer said, passing the shotgun to a deputy.

"It was self-defense," Jimmy interjected. "We were attacked in the middle of our lawful union meeting by these hooded jackasses."

The men on the porch shouted a chorus of agreement.

"Pretty sure I wasn't talking to you, Hall," the man said without breaking eye contact with Clyde. "Your time is coming, but not tonight. Let's try this again. I'm Chief Inspector Hoskins, head of security for Boulder City, authorized by Six Companies and the federal Bureau of Reclamation. Now, who the hell are you?"

He was a tall man with ruddy white skin, and a protruding belly that seemed out of place on an otherwise thin frame, like a bull snake that had just swallowed a rat, Clyde thought. Untamed red sideburns spun out from under a low-brimmed cowboy hat. Both hands rested familiarly on the butts of two revolvers at his waist.

"Clarence Prentiss," Clyde said, trying to rein in the adrenaline and anger.

Bonnie walked up, with Claudette in tow. "You're pointing the guns at the wrong people, Chief Hoskins. Clarence here just saved us from a couple fellows who were trying to murder us. I think they were anarchists," she said with a conspiratorial whisper. "We're lucky their old pistol misfired."

"Hooded vigilantes trying to intimidate working men, anarchists trying to murder young women. What the hell kind of a town you got here, Chief?" Clyde asked.

The rest of the union men spilled out onto the street, pressing in close to the chief and his two nervous deputies, talking excitedly about how they had all been ambushed by the masked men.

"Take their hoods off," someone yelled. "Let's see who these scabs really are."

"Nobody's doing nothing out here in the middle of the street," the chief said. "We'll take them back to the stationhouse and sort things out. Come on boys," he said, conceding to the mood of the street. "Help your pals up. You're all going to jail."

Two of the men helped the driver up, moaning as the motion jangled his broken leg.

"Ain't you gonna take their hoods off?" Clyde asked.

"That's none of your damn business," Hoskins said. "Just thank the lord I'm not taking you and Hall in too. Now get on out of here."

"Maybe I'll just take a peek, before I get on my way," Clyde said, stepping toward one of the assailants.

"I'll shoot you down like a rabid dog in the street if you do," Hoskins said, his right hand suddenly filled by a revolver.

"You can see how this might make it seem to regular folks that you are covering for whoever's really trying to bust up the union meeting," Clyde said.

"You let the law worry about sorting out right from wrong," the chief said.

"Seems right and wrong ought to be clear to anyone, regardless of if they're wearing a badge," Bonnie said.

The chief spit a stream of tobacco juice near Bonnie's feet and returned his attention to Clyde. "You best keep your woman under control, or I'll run you both out of town."

"I'm not 'his' woman," Bonnie said. "And if you can't keep the anarchists and the hoodlums and the criminals from running amok, we won't be staying here for too very much longer."

"That would be just a damn shame," the chief said.

Clyde bent down and picked up the baseball bat. "I'm keeping this behind my door now. Any of you hood-wearing crumbs come creeping around, I'll split your skulls open."

"Thanks for an interesting night," Bonnie said turning to Claudette, who was standing on the sidewalk, eyes wide, still trying to make sense of what all had transpired.

"Jimmy, would you see Claudette home?" Clyde asked. "A pretty little thing like her ought not to be walking alone after all this excitement."

Bonnie and Clyde walked off, arm in arm. As they got near the corner where the old revolver was lying in the dust, he checked behind him long enough to make sure they were unobserved and nudged Bonnie. She bent down and grabbed the pistol the anarchists dropped and tucked it into the waist of her skirt.

CHAPTER 16

Waking the neighbors

Bonnie looked up into the sky, crowded with blazing constellations and a river of light from the Milky Way, and caught a glimpse of a falling star trailing across the edge of the horizon. She made a wish before it blinkered out and disappeared into the darkness.

Clyde came to the door toweling off his face. He had on clean pants and an undershirt, suspenders hanging at his sides.

"You okay, baby?" she asked, turning back from her star-gazing seat on the cottage stoop to look at him. "Anything broken?"

"They never even laid a finger on me," he said. "Shoulder's a little sore from where I blocked into that old truck door, but I'll be all right."

"That poor fellow is going to walk with a limp for the rest of his life."

"That poor fellow ought to have made better choices," Clyde said. "He'll always remember the night he pointed a gun at Clarence Prentiss."

"Who do you think they were?" she asked.

He sat down on the stoop beside her and toweled his hair. A spray of water sprinkled her thigh. "Hard to say. Could be the mob in Las Vegas. Could be Jimmy is playing a long con and it was union men. Could be friends of your anarchists."

She shook her head. "Lots of fancy words and righteous anger, but I doubt those Italians have the smarts or the vinegar, much less the money, to wrangle a truck full of muscle and buy off the chief."

"So, not enough to mules to pull the wagon," Clyde said. "That moves them to the bottom of our list of suspects, but they ain't out of the woods yet. Maybe things will clear up if we can find someone with a banged-up mug."

"That was a good plan, leaving that as a clue," she said.

"Yeah, that's what it was," Clyde said. "A plan."

He drummed his fingers against the doorframe, cracked his knuckles, and then stood, whistling as he went back into the little house. She heard him rummaging through the empty cupboards.

"I worked up an appetite," he said. "We got anything to eat in here?"

"I brought back half a ham sandwich from the mess hall today. It's in the brown paper on the table."

She heard him tear off the wrapper and wolf down the sandwich, and turned back to watching the night sky.

Clyde liked to fight, a little too much for her comfort—it brought all the rage he kept mostly hidden right up to the surface. In the heat of it, she could catch a glimpse of the man he was trying hard not to be, and worried each time he let it out that he'd never be able to put a chain back on the beast.

But there was a silver lining. Fighting got him so worked up, he took it out on her—in the best possible way. The familiar ball of electricity started growing, spreading up into her lungs and her heart, and south between her legs, and she shivered a little. "Wouldn't want to be our neighbors tonight," she said quietly.

"What's that, Bon?"

"Oh, nothing," she said, stubbing out her cigarette and joining him in the kitchen. The single light bulb dangling from the ceiling cast looming shadows against the walls. He filled a glass with whiskey and smiled at her. "You're looking mighty fine tonight, Mrs. Prentiss."

"Seeing you in a scrape gets me all hot and bothered," she said, egging him on as she sat down next to him.

Clyde leaned over and cupped her cheek in his palm, then he traced the outline of her jaw with the backs of his fingers, trailing them up to her forehead. She looked at him curiously, surprised at the uncharacteristic quiet affection. "What are you thinking about, baby?"

"That you look near as beautiful as an angel," he said. She smiled and took his hand in hers. His knuckles were red, and the bruises were already coming forward. She rubbed the edge of his pinky finger where the three barons had cut off the tip.

"I appreciate the words, but I wish you'd share what you're really thinking."

He smiled and let his hand drop back by his side. "I was thinking you deserve more than what I can give you. More than this crazy life."

"I wouldn't want any other life," Bonnie said, puzzled by his mood.

He tipped the bottle to refill the glass, then scooted it toward her. "I spent all day in that truck thinking back to when we first met, and how I went away to take that job, a real job, but couldn't stand being so far from you. I never had a real job again after that, and that's how things fell apart."

She took a sip and forced a smile. "I'm not the innocent victim in this. I never told you that I was so lovesick for you, I led you to believe I was stepping out just to make you jealous."

"You made that up?" he asked, incredulous. "You twisted me up like a pretzel just so I would quit my job?"

She couldn't read the look on his face and waited, wondering what would come next.

He laughed, and slapped his knee. "Kitten, sometimes you're too smart for your own good."

Bonnie pushed the glass back toward him, but he took a swig from the bottle instead.

"I always felt guilty for giving up on the straight life on account of I was too weak without you," he said.

She took his hand in hers. "I'm the weak one. I couldn't live without you."

"We both made some bad decisions," he said. "Stupid decisions. Things snowballed, but we never should have let nobody get hurt, other than the screws at that hellhole prison."

"I know," she said.

"That Hillsdale heist's been on my mind, of late," Clyde said.

Bonnie always knew—or at least hoped—Clyde felt remorse, the same as she felt, for the deaths they'd caused, but she had never heard him say it out loud before. "You didn't pull the trigger." At least not on that one, she thought, but kept it to herself.

"The widow don't know that, and it don't really matter. We were there to steal from them. They should have told strangers looking to buy socks in the dark of night to go to hell."

He took another swig. "I'm getting good and drunk, and I have to get up soon and go to work, and I can't help but wonder what our lives would have been like, what all the people who died on account of us, what their lives would be like, if we'd just held on a little longer and found square jobs."

She took the bottle from his hand. "I think the fact that we can both feel so tore up means we didn't lose all of the good in us. Almost, but not all of it. And things worked out. If we hadn't become bandits, if we hadn't got so good at robbing banks and getting out of scrapes, the president of the United States would be dead and a lot more people would be suffering. The hard part is that nobody will never know that," she said. "Not momma, or your family, or the newspapers. The world will always think we were a couple of no account killers."

"We are a couple of no account killers, that's just the truth. But I don't care what the world thinks," he said. "As long as you know the truth, as long as you can see even one speck of good in me, that's all the matters."

"Oh, Clyde," she whispered. "I see a whole bushel of good in you. We can't go back in time, never, to undo those things we done. It's only forward."

"It's just that now I can't help but think of how that could have been you, left all alone, a widow," he said. He pulled her closer, guiding her to sit on his lap, facing him, legs astride his hips. "Don't you worry, no one is ever going to harm you, not while there's a breath in my body, I'll kill anyone that tries," he said. "Too late now to go straight."

She ran her fingers through his hair and darted her tongue into his mouth. He pulled her blouse up over her head and then unhooked her dainty lace bra, groaning at the sight of her uncovered breasts, rosy nipples stiffening in the cool desert air.

With a growl, he stood up, holding her with one arm around her waist and sweeping the table top clear with the other—sending the whiskey bottle, the glasses and books crashing to the floor—then laying her across it and tugging at his belt.

She raked her nails across his back and spread her legs, pulling him close as he entered her, and moaning his names. "Oh Clyde, oh Clarence, oh god."

He pressed his lips over hers, trying to prevent her from screaming the wrong name.

Across the tiny side yard, the neighbors pulled their shades down, and Clara clapped her hands over the ears of their oldest boy while glaring at her husband with a mixture of irritation and resentment.

CHAPTER 17

The Algonquin, revisited

"Very good sir," the bartender said. "A double shot of Dalmore. One of our most expensive. Excellent choice."

Royce grinned at the man's kind attempt to warn him of the cost without offending. His rumpled department store suit was a dead giveaway, he supposed.

"Make it two, and charge it to my room."

Before he left Lubbock, Bonnie insisted Royce stay at the Algonquin Hotel off Times Square, and that she would foot the bill for everything including—and she was very clear—the best whiskey at the bar.

Royce was hesitant to accept her largesse—taking money from a source was unethical to the point of career suicide—but with his credit cards overloaded and the certainty no matter how much latitude his editor was willing to give, high-priced whiskey would always be out of the question, his resolve wavered. She retrieved a bundle of hundreds from the safe.

"It won't do me any good when I'm dead and gone," she said, dropping the money in his lap. It was the most money he'd ever held in his life.

"Have fun, and bring back the ring that poor woman, the one they thought was me, was wearing so we can figure out where the hell it came from."

And this was research. Bonnie and Clyde—then registered as Mr. and Mrs. Clarence Prentiss—stayed in this very hotel on their way to saving FDR fifty years ago.

As he nursed the whiskey, rich and sweet and smoky, he tried to imagine them back then, two scared kids with ice-cold brutal streaks given an unexpected second chance, trying to bluff their way through averting a presidential assassination.

"I would have loved to seen them then," he said softly.

"The Vicious Circle?" the bartender asked, overhearing but misunderstanding.

"Yeah, sure. Dorothy Parker seemed like a real pistol."

"You can have a seat at the table," he said, gesturing. "Everybody does."

Royce took his drink into the lobby and sat at the infamous table of The Vicious Circle, thinking about Dorothy Parker and what she would have made of Bonnie and Clyde. Given the timing, it was entirely possible they crossed paths right here in this lobby, he thought, without even realizing the fame of the other.

"Cheers to infamy, of many kinds," he said quietly, raising a toast to all three, and then draining the whiskey.

He had an hour before the pre-sale reception at Sotheby's where registered buyers could view the collection. Bonnie had been collecting for years and had an eye for good art. Years ago, she bought an early Pollock and two sketches by Braque, among others—now in the basement vault—and so she was well known to Sotheby's. Her notoriety secured him easy access to the advance viewing.

He went to his room to freshen up, then pushed aside the thick drapes and looked down onto 44th Street. Trucks, cabs and cars growled and strained to make it through the narrow street, and even up on the fifth floor he could hear the frustrated honking as drivers leaned into their horns, blasting their anxiety at pedestrians, doormen and dogs.

What a city, he thought.

Bonnie couldn't remember the room number where they holed up so long ago, but she remembered the floor. He looked around the luxurious room, trying to imagine her as a lost, young girl sitting at the small table, sipping gin and sparring with Sal as Clyde's severed fingertip bled all over the bed.

He imagined she held her own in that situation, and pretty much any situation she was thrown into. Precisely what Sal needed out of them, Royce thought.

He checked his watch, swore and then hurried downstairs to hail a cab.

After a knuckle-whitening, ear-shredding, horn-honking and tire-squealing drive in and around and in between congested traffic, he arrived at the Sotheby's galleries on New York Avenue, the Upper East Side. He paid the driver, who stared at him, expectantly, waiting until Royce peeled off another buck.

Royce walked into the Sotheby's building and up to the reception area. The young woman behind the desk—a severe Nordic beauty with razor sharp cheekbones and frosty blue eyes—took one look at his ill-fitting suit and sun-tanned farmer's complexion and dismissed him silently but completely.

That changed when he gave his name and she saw the notation for Brenda Prentiss.

The receptionist immediately thawed and unloosened a beautiful smile, stood and came out from behind the desk to take him by the arm and escort him into the main gallery.

She had model good looks and that special, haute couture style that made short hemlines and deep cleavage seem not only sexy, but somehow necessary. It had been a very long time since he'd been in the company of such a woman. Oh, who am I kidding, he thought, I've never been close to a woman like this.

"You simply must enjoy yourself tonight," she said. "I will take it as a personal insult if word gets back to Mrs. Prentiss that her friend was bored for even one second."

She pecked him on the cheek and as she leaned in, he inhaled deeply to remember the smell—peaches and brown sugar and vanilla—and chanced a quick look down her shirt to the soft tops of her braless breasts. She caught him, but overlooked his transgression with a knowing smile.

He snatched a glass of champagne from a tray carried by a passing waiter and then examined a mannequin meant to be Clyde—with a blank face and a modern fedora. It was the shirt Clyde—or whoever was in the car—had on when the bullets began to fly. The fabric was coarse and fraying, but the bullet holes, dozens of them, were easy to make out. A brown stain covered the chest of the shirt.

Royce stepped closer, and the armed security guard next to the mannequin cleared his throat. "Sorry," Royce said. "Clyde would be happy. He was real short, but this mannequin is nearly six feet."

"If you say so."

Royce moved on to a glass case with items that had been found in the car. He saw the notebook Bonnie kept while they were outlaws on the run. The pages had been carefully reproduced so buyers could see what was contained inside the book. He recognized the handwriting from their time together.

Next to it was another case with a letter on yellowed stationery, allegedly from Clyde to Henry Ford:

Dear Sir,

While I still have got breath in my lungs I will tell you what a dandy car you make. I have drove Fords exclusively when I could get away with one...

Even fifty years later, he could see how Clyde Barrow was a charmer. Bonnie didn't stand a chance.

Royce turned to a tall display case behind him. Inside was a stand-in mannequin for Bonnie herself, full on with the rifle, cigar and red beret. He downed the champagne and thought of the photos he had taken of Bonnie, or Brenda, recreating the pose just a few weeks back.

"We tried to make it a good likeness, do you think we succeeded?" a man asked. He wore a suit that actually fit, silk probably, and stood next to Royce.

"How would I know?" Royce stuttered, before he realized the man was just making polite conversation.

The man put out his hand. "Good evening, and welcome to Sotheby's. I am Mr. Percy, assistant vice president of sales and marketing. I understand you are the representative of Mrs. Prentiss?"

"Yes, that's right."

"We were unaware Mrs. Prentiss collected historic curios," Percy said. "Her eye for art is so, well, rather exceptional. Please let her know we remain eager to evaluate the pieces she has indicated she may be willing to sell."

"I'll tell her that. Say, are all those clothes on the dummy really hers? I mean, did they all belong to Bonnie Parker?"

"No," Percy said. "There were many souvenir hunters and in the first days after the ambush of Bonnie and Clyde, the site was far from secure. Rather ghoulish, actually. Our team authenticated the hat, shoes, stockings and—" He paused. "The undergarments. Which have bullet holes. We have a sketch of the locations of the holes. Would you like to see it?"

Royce smiled politely. "That's all right, but would be it okay to take a photo? I think Mrs. Prentiss would be tickled by this."

"Of course," Percy said.

Royce pulled out the camera he borrowed from one of the photographers at his newspaper, and fiddled with the settings. The gallery was filling up—Bonnie and Clyde could still pack a room, he thought—and he had to dodge elbows and dirty looks as he took a few shots.

He turned back to Mr. Percy who apparently was not going to leave his side.

"Let's get down to business," Royce said. "Mrs. Prentiss wants to buy the ring she spoke to you about. I'm prepared to offer ten percent more than the highest bid, in cash, and the opportunity to auction her Pollock," he said, trying to make a deal too good to pass on.

Percy's eyebrows shot up and he looked physically sick. "I dearly wish we could oblige. The Pollock, that would bring in, well, a great deal of interest, but the collector withdrew the ring earlier today. Not more than an hour ago."

"Mrs. Prentiss will not be happy to hear that. Can you put me in contact with the owner?"

Percy's lips twitched, and Royce imagined he was considering the loss of the Pollock painting. "We are not at liberty to disclose that information."

"She will be unhappy she couldn't see the ring."

The man brightened. "We took photographs of the artifact for cataloging purposes. I have them in my office. We would be delighted to give them to you to pass along to her, with our good wishes."

"Well now, that's mighty kind of you."

Percy, relieved, guided Royce toward the back of the room.

As they walked through the crowded gallery, Royce saw two men in dark suits. Almost everyone in the gallery wore black, but these were the only two in cowboy hats, and they were looking at the people, not the artifacts—moving against the flow of gawkers. In his mind, Royce put sunglasses on them and sat them in a luxury black sedan. His heart revved up into a higher gear. They were the fellows who trailed him to Bonnie's.

He followed Percy into the office, closing the door behind them before the two men looked in their direction. Percy handed him a tan envelope and Royce pulled out the pictures.

"You can even see the inscription," Percy said. "I didn't realize Bonnie and Clyde were actually married."

"They weren't," Royce said. "Not to each other, at least."

"Then why was she wearing a ring?" Percy asked.

Royce folded the envelope and tucked it into his jacket pocket. "That is a very good question. Would you mind terribly if I wait here until the auction starts before I leave?"

"Of course not," Percy said, used to eccentric requests. "Shall I ask Annika to bring us some chamomile tea while we wait?"

"That would be just fine," Royce said.

CHAPTER 18

Alarm bells

When the new alarm clanged at the crack of dawn on the second day of work, Clyde flopped his arm around until he found the clock on the bedside table and threw it against the far wall. It clunked, and one of the bells fell off, but the floored remains continued to feebly ring, like a small dying animal.

"Lord almighty, I hate working for a living," he said.

"Oh, baby, now I have to buy a new alarm clock," Bonnie said. "And it's only been one day."

"Maybe pick up a few groceries, too," he said. "My stomach thinks my throat's been cut."

"I'm not going to turn into some housewife."

Clyde pulled his clothes on. "Bon, stop harping on that. The company store is literally two blocks from your job. I'm near ten miles from it!"

"Well, don't blame me when the magic is gone and you come home and ask me what's for dinner and then sit to read the paper while I go play bingo with the gals."

He sat on the edge of the bed and pulled her into his arms. "Even if I live to be a hundred, I can't imagine the magic ever fading away."

"You're late for work," she said, heating at the intensity of his words. "Get on out of here and I'll have something special waiting for you tonight."

He winked, kissed her, then ran out the door, hooking up his overalls and stumbling after the convoy truck already pulling away. "Hold on, Big Bertha!" he yelled.

Bonnie got ready for work herself, then sat on the stoop to finish her coffee. She let her thoughts drift back to the night before and the warm glow of joy from the closeness she and Clyde shared. Twice.

Clara, her neighbor, walked out on the porch with a basket of washing under one arm, two quiet, big-eyed children at her feet. She looked across at Bonnie.

"Good morning," Bonnie said.

"Reckon it is for you," Clara said. "Although I imagine you're feeling a mite tired."

"Sorry for all the commotion last night," Bonnie said.

"Good thing I got a radio, and that my oldest is a heavy sleeper," Clara said, putting the basket down and pinning up a pair of dungarees to the clothes line. The children scampered down to the road and started throwing stones at nothing in particular.

"How's that job of yours going?" Clara asked.

"Okay, as far as jobs go, I guess," Bonnie said. "You wishing you had a job?"

"I got a job," Clara said, nodding down to the children.

"You should get paid for it," Bonnie said.

"Paid for woman's work? That's a kicker. Still, thinking it might be all right to have a different kind of job, the kind that does pay, like you got, one day," Clara said, hanging up a slew of bleached diapers. A wail came from inside the house and Clara wiped her hands on her apron. "That's the boss calling," she said, leaving the laundry and walking back inside to attend to the infant.

On her way to work, Bonnie gave the two boys a dime each and told them to get something special for their momma, and then walked to the office.

Claudette was sitting at the entrance smoking and when she saw Bonnie she turned away from her. Bonnie sat down on the bench, and talked to Claudette's back.

"Listen Claudette, I know you like bad boys," Bonnie said. "But they tried to kill us last night."

"Tried to kill you," Claudette said, turning to face Bonnie. "And they didn't really mean it."

"They shot at us, Claudette," Bonnie said, exasperated. She plucked the cigarette from Claudette's fingers and took a drag.

"But they missed," Claudette said. "And anyway, Dante was my boyfriend. Or was about to be." She turned her head to the side. "Now I've got no one. I never should have taken you with me."

Bonnie handed the cigarette back to Claudette. "You ought to thank me for saving you the trouble of finding out too late that he's the wrong kind of bad."

Claudette's face collapsed into a frown, and she bit her lower lip. "You don't know nothing, you got a man looking after you."

Bonnie could tell she was close to crying.

On the run with Clyde, she never had much time to make women friends. Blanche—Clyde's brother's wife— was the only adult woman she'd spent much time with and she was a handful. Bonnie's patience wore thin when it came to gal pals, but Claudette was nice enough and Bonnie knew she had to at least pretend to fit in until they figured out who was trying to wreck the dam. Plus, if she was honest, she was growing fond of Claudette.

"You got me now, honey," she said. "And there's literally thousands of single men here and only a handful of single ladies. You're so pretty, you can have your pick of them."

"You know I like bad boys," Claudette said, black liner leaking from the edges of her eyes. She sniffled. "I can't help myself. My mother said it would be the ruin of me."

"It will. But here's a little secret. It will also be your salvation. Clarence isn't nearly as good as he lets on," she said with a wink.

She pulled a handkerchief from her skirt pocket and dabbed Claudette's cheeks. Claudette took her hands in hers and squeezed. "No wonder you're so happy. Do you think Clarence could find me someone like him, you know, the good kind of bad?"

"It'll be our number one job," she said, feeling a flash of sympathy for Claudette. What would happen to her once the dam was finished? Where would she go? Life wasn't easy—or fair—for single women, and only got harder with the passing years.

"Say, what about Jimmy?" Bonnie said. "Didn't he try anything when he walked you home last night?"

"He is cute, but he ain't bad," Claudette said.

"The right woman can turn any man bad," Bonnie said.

Claudette gave up on being mad and they fell into laughing, but stopped short when Fitzsimmons walked up the sidewalk toward the office.

"Good morning, girls," he said, not meaning it. "Isn't it a little early for a smoke break?"

"Good morning, Mr. Fitzsimmons," they said in a fake sing-song unison, following him inside.

After a long morning of filing, pouring coffee, filing and more filing, at lunch, Bonnie walked to the company store to pick up a few groceries and a new alarm clock.

"Good day to you, Mrs. Prentiss," the grocer said. "Was there something wrong with the first one I sold you? Sometimes people wind them too tight?"

"No, sir," she said. "The clock is fine. I think it's my husband who's wound a little tight."

CHAPTER 19

Circular logic

The transport truck slowed as it rounded the corner and Clyde leapt off, swatting the dust from his pants as he made his way to the house.

"Honey, I'm home," he shouted, as he opened the front door.

Bonnie was in the kitchen, an apron on over a sleeveless red taffeta dress, pouring sweet iced tea. The table was set with tin plates overflowing with thick slices of ham, deviled eggs and canned pole beans.

"Oh ma'am," he said, stammering. "I'm sorry. These houses all look the same. Please don't tell your husband I barged in here."

Bonnie shot a disapproving look his way. "Take a good look at it, mister. It's the first, and now the last, meal I ever cook for you."

"This may be my last supper, but I'm the happiest man alive," he said, sweeping her up in his arms for a kiss.

"Just don't get used to it," she said. "Don't take me for granted."

After they ate, they were sitting on the stoop when Jimmy walked up.

"Hey you two, we're holding a make-up union meeting tonight. And this time we're inviting everyone, even women. Y'all interested? After last night, I sure hope the answer is yes. Could use the extra muscle."

Clyde laughed. "Any sign of a fellow with a busted face? Curious who was behind that mask."

"Not yet," Jimmy said. "But my boys are on the lookout."

"Or hiding him," Bonnie whispered just loud enough for Clyde to hear. "Sure, we'll come," she said, more loudly. "And I'll bring a friend. Go on, we'll catch up with you."

"See you down at the mess hall," Jimmy called.

Twenty minutes later, Bonnie and Clyde, and Claudette, slipped in the side door of the mess hall. The last wave of workers had finished supper and tables had been rearranged to accommodate the gathering men and women.

About a dozen union members were in attendance, and they looked serious and ready for trouble. There were twenty or so other workers, along with a handful of wives, wanting to learn more about labor unions.

At the front of the room, Jimmy stood before a gray chalkboard he borrowed from the school. He had drawn three circles of roughly equal size on it, and a letter in the center of each: I, G and W.

Bonnie and Claudette took seats up front, but Clyde caught Bonnie's eye, touched the side of his nose and walked back to stand by the side door in case any hoodlums decided to crash the meeting again.

"Okay everybody, let's get started," Jimmy said. "Tonight, we're going to talk about why unions are important for everyone, not just for working men, but for families too."

Jimmy's voice was strong and clear, radiating warmth and confidence. Claudette sat up a little straighter in her seat.

"Let me tell you about these three circles," Jimmy said, pointing to the chalkboard. "This one here with the 'I' stands for the bosses, or industry. The second one with the 'G' represents the government. And the third with the 'W' stands for you—workers and their families. What we want is for the circles to all be about the same size, which means nobody can put nothing over on no one else."

He paused for effect. "Do you think they're all the same right now?"

"Hell no," a man said.

Jimmy swiped at the circle representing industry with his hand, erasing it, then redrawing it twice as big as the other two. "That's exactly right. The boss side of things is much bigger than us, even bigger than the government and that means the banks and the bosses are calling the shots and they don't give a plugged nickel about what's best for us, or the country. What we have now, ladies and gentleman, is a situation in dire need of rebalancing."

There were murmurs of assent.

"When bosses, or to say it another way, industrialists and capitalists—"

"They're fat cats, call it like it is," shouted a young man wearing a straw hat in the second row. Clyde figured the kid for a union plant, saying what others were thinking but too fearful to say out loud. Smart move, he thought.

Jimmy smiled and kept going. "Call 'em what you like, but when this industrialist circle gets real big, they control the government, buying and selling politicians to do their bidding."

"Ain't that the truth," said a middle-aged man in overalls by the side of the group, chewing on a toothpick.

The door opened and Chief Hoskins walked in, taking a seat up front in the first row. "Don't mind me. Just curious about what you got to say. Unions are a hobby of mine," he said.

The men and women went still, like sculpted ice.

"Glad to have you here, Chief, everyone is welcome," Jimmy said, determined to keep things moving along. "We want bosses to hear what we're talking about. It's in their best interest to have loyal, highly-trained workers who ain't forever trying to slow down or put one over on them."

"Or sabotage the job site," the chief said.

"You know that ain't us," Jimmy said. "There's no reason bosses and workers need to be enemies. What we need to be is equals."

Two men came to the side door, both dressed in standard worker dungaree overalls and brown boots. They were both tall and dark-skinned. A young woman, her skin a softer shade of brown, wearing a pearl-colored dress, stood between them. Silently waiting in the doorway, they looked at Jimmy. He nodded, motioning them inside.

The chief's eyes, as well as most people at the meeting, followed as the three walked to the back of the room. Clyde moved aside and made space next to where he was standing, and then pulled a chair over and offered it to the woman, who smiled and sat.

Claudette whispered to Bonnie. "What are *they* doing here?"

"Don't they work at the dam?"

"Yeah, but, you know, they're colored," Claudette said.

"Divide and conquer, the oldest trick in the book of bosses," Bonnie said. "We're all in this together, right?"

Claudette looked puzzled, as if she had never thought things through in that way before.

The chief turned back to look at Jimmy, stretching out his long legs, laughing. "You rabble will never be my equal," he said, folding his arms defiantly across his chest, unconsciously resting them on top of his pot belly like a shelf.

A flash of anger lit up Jimmy's eyes, but he tamped it down, and then broke into a grin, thinking the man looked like a pink-skinned bridge troll.

"We are already your equal," Jimmy said. "Every single one of us."

"Damn, that boy's a real pip, real brave," Claudette whispered in Bonnie's ear, "He's got a smile so hot it could melt my underthings plumb away." Bonnie laughed, covering her mouth with her hand to hide the noise.

Jimmy erased the government circle with his hand, leaving behind ghost chalk markings, and then redrew it with thick lines as big as the business circle, but kept the workers' circle small. "When both of these two circles are big, what do you think that means?"

"That we get screwed," shouted a man sitting behind Bonnie. She could smell the whiskey on his breath.

"That's right," Jimmy said. "Because government is just as likely as any of us to fall under the sway of too much money. The way we keep companies providing living wages, and the way we keep the government from tilting things in the favor of big money, is by coming together for common cause."

He let the words sink in, not wanting to get ahead of the crowd, then tossed the chalk to the floor where it shattered. "It is up to us to make sure the workers' circle is as big as the other two, and the only way to do that is to band together in a union and have our own leaders as powerful as the bosses and the politicians."

"But how can we do that?" a man asked. He was older and agitated. "We organize and they bust our skulls. We strike and they bring in scabs. We protest and they machine gun us down." He looked around after he shouted, nervous that the sentiment of his outburst wouldn't be shared. But others quickly joined in.

"Yeah, unions are a good idea, but they get us in trouble," added another man.

"Workers were fired during the strike of thirty-one because there were ten thousand other men waiting to take the jobs," Jimmy said. "But why were jobs so hard to come by? Because the government and the bosses had gotten too big for their britches, and our circle broke all into pieces, just like that chalk. Now imagine if those men had stood in solidarity with us. If we all talked with the same voice. Our circle would get big mighty fast."

"We had mouths to feed, we had no choice," a tan man said, quietly. "Had to get my family outta Ragtown."

Jimmy nodded, sympathetic. "There's no blame here. Back then, they had us over a barrel, it was every man for himself. But President Roosevelt understands these three circles have to be in balance, keeping a check on each other, if we're gonna get through this rough patch as a country. He got new laws passed so we can build our circle up, legally and all."

He looked directly at the chief. "The bosses can't throw us out or keep us from talking. If they do, the government is going to fine them, and making money is their religion."

Jimmy pressed on, knowing he would have their attention for only a little while longer, sensing now was the time to stoke the fire. "Who built this dam?" he said, his voice lowered purposefully so that the men and women had to lean in to hear him.

"What did you say?" asked one.

"Who built this dam?" Jimmy said, a little louder.

"We did," a few voices called back.

"Tell me again, who built this dam?"

"We did," more voices shouted.

"Goddamn right we did," Jimmy said.

"I hate to interrupt your little socialist revival meeting, but it was the government paid for it," the chief said. "And Big Six Companies' expertise that's building it."

"No," Jimmy said. He banged his hand against a nearby table so hard it startled everyone. The chief leaned forward, and Clyde had one of his .45s half way out of the shoulder holster before he realized it was just stage theatrics.

"We built this dam," Jimmy yelled. "All of you. Without you, there is no dam, no matter what the government or the bosses say or do. Your labor is the bedrock of capitalism, of the economy, but they don't want you to know that, they want to keep us divided. Keep us fighting amongst ourselves."

A low murmur of approval swept across the room.

"We have got to claim our power. The workers—" he said, stabbing his finger into the heart of the smaller ghost of a circle on the chalkboard. "The workers are just as important as the other two circles. We've got a chance now to build ourselves into a single powerful voice."

"But we're doing all right here," one man said. "Got a roof over our heads, food in our bellies and a place for our kids to go to school. Why upset the apple cart?"

"What are you gonna do when this one here is finished?" Jimmy asked, smoothing back his hair, bringing his voice down to normal levels.

"Reckon I'll move on to the Bonneville Dam job up north," the man said.

"Maybe they'll have a job for you, maybe not. Maybe they'll pay you a fair wage, maybe not, but definitely not if a hundred other men are waiting to take that job. Why do we let them make all the decisions about who gets jobs and who doesn't, who gets to live in a house and who lives in Ragtown, even who lives and dies?" he yelled. "Now, who built this dam?"

"We built the dam," the group yelled back at him.

"You know what else? When this dam is finished, a hell of a lot of money is going into the pockets of a few men. They're going to close down this job, make you move your families, and maybe or maybe not give you a fair wage. But we built the dam, so why isn't some of that profit being shared with us?"

He dramatically flipped the chalkboard around, and showed another drawing with the workers' circle now the same size as the other two.

"Imagine what's inside this circle. A million men speaking with one voice and demanding secure jobs. Certainty about wages. Bonuses when the job gets finished on time. Sharing profits so we can have good schools, help for the sick and injured," he said. He looked at the two workers with the woman in the back near Clyde. "For all of us, everyone, working men, women, people looking for work and them that can't work no more but did more than their share. The more we all stand together, the more security we'll have for ourselves and our families."

A few hear-hears came from the crowd, egging him on. Clyde looked around, fearful that the growing enthusiasm would be checked by the chief at any second.

"If the bosses care about this country, wouldn't they see that united workers is a good thing? Why do you think they fight us?" Jimmy said, dropping his voice dramatically to a near whisper again.

"They're the enemy," someone said.

"When we're organized, we are equal, and then they ain't the enemy. When we're equal, they have to work with us. When these three circles are the same size, it works out best for everyone. The dam gets built. The workers are treated fairly. We vote in the politicians who favor that balance. The fat cats in Big Six still get rich, but maybe just a little bit less rich. There's enough profit to go around for everyone, but nobody is going share it with us unless we are their equal, and we make them share."

A muffled voice called out, "We tried this before, and other unions, like the auto workers, they keep on trying, but they break us. Don't see how your plan works."

"That's because it's not all of us. It's just a few small circles each looking out for themselves, like mosquitoes, buzzing and making little bites, but still easy to swat away. The bosses need us to be fighting against each other, always thinking that if anyone else gets a slice of pie there won't be nothing left, but we're only fighting over one tiny slice. We have to band together to demand a bigger piece of the pie."

He paused, and looked out over the crowd, like a preacher coming to the end of his sermon.

"President Roosevelt is giving us a chance to have a voice, and we have got to take it," he said. "It's a once in a lifetime opportunity and we can't mess it up. When we organize, we can ask for whatever we want. Is it right that all the profits go to fat cats in their big fancy houses up on the bluff looking down at our sweat and suffering?"

"No," shouted the room.

"Tell me why not!"

"Because we built that dam," the group yelled.

CHAPTER 20

Frayed edges

The next morning when the new alarm clock sounded, Clyde was so tired and sore from two days of work, he barely had the energy to throw it into the next room. But he managed, and it slammed against the wall and whirred and clattered ineffectively.

"Dammit, Clyde, I'm not buying another one of those," Bonnie said sleepily.

After wolfing down a couple of leftover deviled eggs and pulling on his clothes, Clyde kissed Bonnie and chased down the transport truck. This morning, some of the men had taken bets about how long it would take Clyde to run out of the house, half-dressed, and now were hooting and hollering as he finally caught up.

"Hand it over, boys," said Dino. "A nickel each."

At the dam, Clyde climbed out of the truck along with dozens of men and they all walked in lockstep toward the punch-clock, following the worn path of thousands of footsteps planted one after the other in line over the past five years.

Dino filled him on the logistics of the timekeeping as they walked. "The pay week ends today. You need to drop off your old card with Gerald, the paymaster over in the shack." He gestured at a little structure with bars over the windows.

"Thanks for the tip, Dino, and let me know what the bet is tomorrow and I'll time my chase better," he said. "Maybe up the wager and we can split the winnings?"

Dino grinned and walked off.

Clyde walked over to hand in his time card and when he saw the paymaster, he laughed. Gerald had a broken nose covered by gauze that hid a pencil-thin mustache, and two swollen, plum-colored eyes.

"Well, now," Clyde said with a smile. "You look like you got kicked in the face by a Georgia mule, or maybe it was a Louisville slugger." He leaned in close. "You ought not to get that close to danger."

Gerald glowered at him. "You'll get yours for this, Prentiss. And you won't be the only one who gets hurt."

Clyde leaned in even closer to the little bank teller style window. "Anything happens to Brenda, you even say her name, and you'll think our last set-to was a love tap."

"She'll be fine," Gerald snarled. "She'll have widow's benefits. Hope she took a long look at your sorry ass this morning, because there won't be nothing left of your body. They'll have to bury you in a soup can."

"You talk plenty tough for a man who I've only ever seen crying like a colicky baby."

Gerald slid a new time card across the counter and then jabbed his finger toward the cable car. "Don't miss your ride, Prentiss, or I'll have to dock you."

Clyde pantomimed a lunge, and Gerald flinched. Laughing, Clyde walked toward the departure area.

The flat dawn was still struggling to pierce a layer of brilliant white clouds hanging low over the canyon and Clyde was grateful for the morning coolness. Workers milled around the monkey-slide, organizing themselves silently and instinctively into groups large enough to fill the cable car that would ferry them down to the canyon floor. Clyde nervously watched the square metal cab creaking up the rock face, carrying grateful workers from the bottom, their labors ended for the night, thinking only of getting some much-needed shut-eye.

Suddenly, a deep, muffled report rolled up from the bottom of the canyon. Puffs of dirty smoke erupted from the right corner of the dam base. Within seconds, a siren wailed, broadcast from loudspeakers on wooden poles set up at major points across the site.

The workers swarmed to the canyon's edge to see what the fuss was about. In the distance, the smoke cleared, and they could see men rushing around; from far away, it looked to Clyde like an ant hill busted up by a firecracker.

On the landing, a foreman yelled into a radio, holding his finger in the open ear, struggling to hear the crackling voice over the sirens. "Yeah, looks like more sabotage," he yelled. A crackle of static followed, along with a series of shouted instructions.

The cable car plunged into the metal port, connecting to the brake pads and holds. "Come on, get out of that bucket, go on, unload. They're going to need help down there. The rest of you, load on up," the boss shouted.

As the day shift men, anxious to help, pushed toward the slide, Clyde noticed a man swimming against the tide of bodies. He held a hack saw and seemed to have come from under the transport.

Clyde joined the flow of men onto the open-air gondola, and looked back to see Gerald on the porch of the pay shack, watching the scene. The cable car pulled out of the docking station heading down the canyon with a lurch, then froze for a second, jolted and the car tipped a few degrees, and then righted itself.

A few men shouted their concern.

"Hold on girls, it's nothing," the operator yelled at them. "You'll be down in a second." He adjusted the gears and reached for the brake.

Clyde, already nervous, pushed his way to the edge of the car. "Not today," he said, and hopped over the metal edge, landing on the cut-out in the canyon wall underneath the carriage.

The operator yelled for him to get back in. Standing below the car, he could see into the underside guts of the machine. One of the cables had been sawed almost in half, the remaining strands stretched and some already broken. Clyde waved to Dino, who was watching him intently. "The cable's broke," he yelled. "Get the men off!"

Dino spread the word and men began leaping off, hitting the ground and rolling out of the way even as the operator disabled the brake.

Just as the last man fell free, the car lurched down the canyon and the cable broke. The twist of metal cracked like a whip and snapped a few inches over Clyde's head in a vicious, whining blur, and then the car came loose and clattered down the canyon wall.

The men, spared from a certain mangled death, cheered for Clyde—Clarence to them—and helped hoist him back up to the top. Clyde looked behind him at the paymaster's hut, but it was dark and shuttered over. Gerald was gone.

The foreman shook his hand, then called for a welder to begin work repairing the cable, and for trucks to carry the men to the bottom, the long way around.

But not Clyde. He was told to wait in the manager's office. When the door finally opened, a tall man—at least a foot and half taller than Clyde—stepped inside. He was thin as a shadow, but muscular, and built tough as whip steel, Clyde thought. When he stuck his hand out, he had a grip to match.

"I'm Henry Byrd," the man said. "Site boss here at Boulder Dam. You're new here, aren't you?"

"Yes, sir, third day on the job," Clyde said. "Name's Clarence Prentiss."

"Prentiss, thank you for what you did out there. You saved a lot of lives, and most important, kept us from falling behind schedule."

"It wasn't nothing. Glad I could help."

Byrd wore a suitcoat over a starched white shirt. Rumor had it he kept a closet full of pressed white shirts and changed them out every day, sometimes twice a day.

Looking now at this tall man, Clyde wondered how Henry Byrd ended up being the boss of thousands of men, and why had Clyde never been able to get himself on that kind of road? He guessed that golden road didn't exist in Dallas where he lived most of the time in his parents' car and sometimes camped out under a bridge as a kid. Maybe them roads were only for people who were already on third base when they got born. Hell, he hadn't even been near the baseball field when he popped out of his momma.

Well, neither of them had any control over their birth. One got lucky, the other not so much. That was no reason to resent a man, Clyde thought.

"How'd you know that cable was coming apart?" Byrd asked. "I don't want to seem overly suspicious, but we've had some setbacks on this job, and I'm curious."

"Blame it on my cowardly nature. Never been real good with heights and when we hit that little bump, I chickened out and made a leap for it. And I'm glad I did."

"Guess we're lucky you're not the bravest," Byrd said. "I want you to take tomorrow off. My way of saying thanks. It's New Year's Day. You married?"

"Yes, sir."

"Do something nice for your wife then. And Prentiss, I've got a good feeling about you. We need smart men to help keep this job site running well. Stop by the main office and let them know I want you trained up to be a manager."

Back at Boulder City, Bonnie was surprised to see Clyde sitting on the stoop when she finished her day of filing and being leered at by Fitzsimmons.

"Did you get fired already?" she asked, running up the steps and into his arms.

"Nope. The opposite. I was asked to be a manager."

"A manager? You?" Bonnie started laughing so hard she fell out of his embrace.

"Yeah, ain't that the damnedest thing?" Clyde asked. "I'm half flattered and half insulted."

He told her about the events of the morning and the thought of his imminent death made her angry and protective.

She led him to the bedroom and fussed over him, taking his boots off and stroking his hair at the temples. "We need to figure out who's behind all this and be shut of this place before you get hurt serious."

"I just can't puzzle it out," Clyde said. "The anarchists don't seem to be good for it, they've got the passion but lack the skills. The Vegas mob could be good for it, but it doesn't seem they'd risk killing the goose with the golden egg. And the unions could be good for it, but I can't figure the angle, unless it's just revenge for being treated so rough. There's too many biscuits and not enough pan."

"Maybe it's time to turn the heat up a little in the kitchen," she said.

"Sounds like you've got a plan."

"Let's rob a bank," Bonnie said.

CHAPTER 21

Predictable ways and means

They sat in their car pulled out of sight on a red sandstone bluff overlooking the new two-lane road to Las Vegas.

"Working for a living might not be so bad if we still got to do stuff like this on our days off," Clyde said. He fished a piece of cold fried chicken out of the basket on the car seat between them and tore off a bite.

"I think most people use their days off for having a picnic or maybe going to the movie," Bonnie said. "Not robbing an armored car."

"This is kind of like a picnic," Clyde said. "Only with more guns." He tapped the BAR next to his leg, took another bite of chicken and looked at the road through the binoculars.

"How'd you know they'd be coming today?" he asked.

"First thing I did when I had the office to myself was figure out when they move the money," she said.

"What's bred in the bone—" Clyde said.

"Comes out in the flesh," she finished. Bonnie held a mason jar filled with sweet iced tea, alternating between slow sips and lazy drags from a cigarette.

"I still don't know why we can't just run 'em off the road and take the money at gun point."

"If we pull a good old fashioned Bonnie and Clyde style hold up and then head back to our little house, we'll be in leg irons before the sun goes down tomorrow," she said. "We need to pull this off without a single shot fired."

Clyde tossed the chicken bone out the window. A vulture—little more than a dark speck with crescent wings—circled high above, impossible to miss against the bright blue sky.

"I don't like anyone leering at you," Clyde said.

"Make your peace with it fast," she said, peering through the binoculars. "The truck is coming. And Clyde, don't hurt them, otherwise this will all be for nothing."

She slipped out of the car and ran down the hill below the main road, stopping next to a banged up wooden water tower that collected rain for sheep herders on the long treks to and from California. The water tower was visible for just a heartbeat to drivers passing by. Earlier, she and Clyde tested the pull chain that would release enough water for a convincing outdoor shower. Bonnie peeled off her blouse and wriggled out of her dress, spreading her clothes out on a flat rock in the sun, and then, taking a breath to steel herself against the chill, stood under the spout and pulled the chain.

The water was cold, and took her breath away, but in the bright sun and out of the wind, it was bearable. She let it flow through her hair, and then looked down to see her soaked camisole and bra underneath, pulling them tighter so the fabric would cling to her breasts and show through to her hardened nipples pushing against the cloth.

She chanced a quick look toward the road where it curved, the only spot where cars had an unobstructed view. The armored car would be there any second and she hoped one of the guards was watching, otherwise she was freezing for nothing. The flowing water drowned out the road noise and she couldn't risk staring too long.

They saw her.

At least the driver did. He happened to look to the right as the truck took the turn and saw a flash of white undergarments and pink skin.

He slammed on the brakes, bringing the truck to a shuddering stop in the middle of the road. "Jesus H. Christ, did you see that, Derek?" he asked.

Derek shook his head and reached for the shotgun at his feet. "What is it, Earl?"

"Don't get your dander all up," Earl said. "There's a little gal bathing down there in nothing but her dainties."

"Shut the hell up," Derek said. "Quit yanking my chain."

"Hand to god," Earl said. He checked the rearview mirror and then peered all around. "And we owe it to ourselves to take a quick look. You know, to make sure she's okay." He backed the truck up, pulling off the road.

"I don't know Earl, this seems suspicious. Ain't it too cold for a bath?"

"Probably one of them Okies living in their car hoping for a job. They still ain't used to running water and all the appurtenances of modern living. 'Sides, there ain't no one around for miles. We'll just take a quick peek over the edge here."

"Is she pretty?" Derek asked.

"Let's find out," he said, pulling the hand brake. They left the doors open so as not to startle her off and crept closer to the little rise. At the last minute, they got down on their bellies and wriggled forward to peek over the edge.

Down below, fifty yards away, Bonnie let the water splash down her front. She tossed her hair back and shook her head, then splashed water on her legs, smoothing away the excess.

"Holy shit, she is a fine-looking piece of ass," Earl said.

"Like a goddamned angel," Derek said.

They were both so transfixed, neither saw Clyde walking up to the armored car, cradling his BAR. The sight of them splayed out ogling Bonnie made him want to put a bullet in each of them and dump their bodies in a mine shaft, but he promised Bonnie he'd stick to the plan.

He slipped into the driver's side, tossed his gun on the seat and quietly released the brake. Gravity pulled the truck downhill and he watched them getting smaller and smaller in the rearview mirror until he turned the corner and was gone.

"I can damn near see her titties right through her little slip," Earl whispered hoarsely.

Bonnie, not hearing any gunshots or screams, started winding the show down. She stood next to her clothes, letting the sun warm her and keeping her face turned from the vantage of the road. She was so cold, she was practically shivering, but wanted to sell the moment.

"She's almost done," Derek said. "I'm gonna grab the binoculars from the truck for a better look." He scooted back and sat up, then swore softly. "Earl, the blessed truck is gone."

"Stop screwing around," Earl said, not taking his eyes off of Bonnie.

"No, I mean it, Earl, the truck is gone."

Earl jumped up, swore and looked at the empty road. A distant horn blast sounded, Bonnie's signal to high tail it back to the car, and when the two men turned to look again, all they saw was a muddy puddle beneath the water tower.

"Son of a bitch!" Earl swore, throwing his hat on the ground and kicking it. He grabbed Derek by the collar. "We been set up," he said. "God dammit." He looked around wildly. "We can't tell them we was out here ogling some half-naked gal," he said. He grabbed his pistol and shot it into the air, emptying it.

"Why you shooting at the clouds?" Derek yelled.

"We got jumped by a gang of hoods," he said. "We tried to fight them off but they got away. Empty your shotgun too."

Derek shot into the air, the boom rolling off the hills, then shot it again and again.

"We sure don't look jumped," he said.

"I'm real sorry about this," Earl said, punching his partner in the eye.

"Ouch, dammit Earl, what was that for?"

"We need to look like we was on the receiving end of a beating," he said.

"Oughtn't I hit you then?" Derek asked, rubbing his eye, which was already starting to swell.

"Well, we don't want to oversell it," Earl said. "Come on, let's flag down a ride and get back to camp. Jesus, they're going to skin us alive."

"You sure you don't want a bruise or two?" Derek asked, trying to catch up to Earl.

Across a small canyon and far from the sight of the two guards, Bonnie wound her way back toward the main road and met up with Clyde in a gravel quarry out of sight from prying eyes. He had the back door of the armored car shot open and six bank bags of cash stacked up just above the bumper.

She was still chilled from the outdoor shower but warmed up at the sight of the loot.

"Looks like everything went according to plan," she said, pulling up beside him.

"Those two idiots were so busy gawking at you, they didn't even know the truck was gone," Clyde said. He started tossing the bags into the back of their car. "They're probably still laying there hoping you'll come back for a repeat show."

"Something tells me they are regretting their degenerate ways right about now," Bonnie said. "How much do you reckon is in there?"

Clyde shrugged. "Don't know but it's a lot. Payroll for the whole damn town." He tossed his BAR in on top of the bags and covered them with a quilt. Then he reached in the backseat and pulled out the old pistol the anarchist Dante had dropped and tossed it into the back of the truck. "Figured that old gun might come in handy."

"You were right, as always," she said.

"Let's get on with cranking up the heat by lighting things up in Las Vegas with booze and stolen loot."

CHAPTER 22

Choosing sides

Royce took a circuitous route back to the hotel, starting on foot and getting lost twice, which he took as a good omen, and then hailed a cab to another hotel, walked through the lobby and out the side door and then caught a second cab back to the Algonquin.

From his hotel room, he looked down at the bustling street, still congested and active even at this late hour, as he talked to Bonnie by phone. "The ring was pulled out of the auction at the last minute."

"That sounds suspicious," Bonnie said.

"It gets worse. Those two fellows in the fancy car, I saw them here."

There was a long pause. "Are you sure it was them?"

"There's not too many men in black suits and cowboy hats in New York," he said.

"Best be careful, Royce. Get on back here."

"My flight leaves at the crack of dawn, and I aim to be on it."

After he hung up, he headed down for a meal, taking a small table in the far corner of the Blue Bar, sitting with his back against the wall.

The waiter stopped by. "I'll take a filet, medium, with a baked potato," Royce said.

"And to drink?"

"A Dalmore. No, wait. What was that famous thing Dorothy Parker used to say?"

"I like to have a martini, two at the very most, after three I'm under the table, after four I'm under the host," the waiter said, with a dull mechanical tone, no doubt asked this same question at least hourly by the boatload of tourists looking to rub elbows with famous ghosts.

"Exactly. A martini then. Very dry. In honor of writers, of which I am one."

"Very good, sir," the waiter said, taking the menu.

"No really, I am. A journalist."

"A noble profession indeed. Mrs. Parker would be very proud."

After the meal and a second martini, he began to calm down. New York is a huge place, he thought. There was no way those men could know where he was staying.

As the bar began to fill with more tourists and after-theater drinkers, Royce pulled out the envelope from Percy to look at the photos again. Inside were seven color shots of the wedding band ostensibly worn by Bonnie Parker when she was shot to hell in 1934.

Each photo showed the ring from a different angle. A plain gold band with three small blue gems on either side, set between a delicate braid forming the mount. On one photo, he could just make out the inscription. *Together forever. April 29, 1934.*

On the opposite side of the band's interior there was a faint but distinctive "u" shaped imprint with an "x" above it that Royce was pretty sure was the jeweler's mark. Finally, something tangible, a thread to pull.

He was so engrossed, he failed to notice two men enter from the street. Two men in dark suits, wearing cowboy hats.

"May we join you?" one of them asked, jolting him from his reveries.

Royce slipped the photos back into the envelope, put it on his lap out of sight and then thought about making a run for it. But Bonnie's advice about riling things up came back to him.

"There are plenty of open tables," he said. "But it's a free country, and I like to make new friends."

They pulled two chairs from a neighboring table and sat down next to Royce, effectively trapping him. The taller man removed his felt cowboy hat and laid it crown down on the table. He had pale white skin and blonde hair slicked back; he sat so close, Royce could smell his lemony aftershave. The second man was dark-skinned, and shorter with coarse hair, and a sprinkle of scars high on his cheeks, the kind produced by childhood chicken pox. He left his hat on.

Both men wore expensive suits and even more expensive boots. Snakeskin. Or ostrich. Maybe alligator.

"Something to drink?" Royce asked. "My treat. I can recommend the Dalmore. And the martinis."

"That's mighty kind of you," the blonde man said. "But we are here on business."

"Who are 'we,' exactly?" Royce asked.

"Where are our manners?" the shorter of the two said. "I'm Mr. Hall. And my friend here is Mr. Oates."

"Wait," Royce said. "You're Hall and Oates? Like the—"

"The singers, yes," Hall said. "It never gets old. Ever. And truthfully, I think our business could accommodate some of the finest whiskey Scotland has ever produced if the offer still stands."

Royce waved for the waiter and ordered their drinks. They were silent until the whiskey arrived.

"A toast then," Hall said. "To discretion, the better part of valor."

They clinked glasses.

"Oh, that's smooth," Oates said.

Royce nodded. "My new favorite. But it requires a certain financial latitude that I generally find lacking. Still, you only live once."

"Precisely why we are here," Hall said. "It has to do with your longevity. You need to stop pursuing the story."

Royce bristled with a surge of martini courage. "I'm not sure what you're talking about. But I'm a journalist, a member of the free press, and I will pursue any damn story I choose, and you can take that to the bank."

He downed the remnants of his drink and set the glass down too hard, and was surprised to see the shadow of a second glass there, along with four hands. He shook his head back into normal vision, and the refrain from Dorothy Parker about being under the table after three martinis stumbled through his thoughts.

"We're not talking about just any story," Oates said. "We are talking about the story you are writing regarding Bonnie Parker, otherwise known as Brenda Prentiss—at least in certain circles."

"How could you know that? Who are you?"

"Who we are is irrelevant," Hall said. "Just know that we have resources at our disposal, and we are concerned about your safety, and the safety of Mrs. Prentiss."

"Is that...are you threatening me?" Adrenaline associated with fear began to clear the alcohol effects.

"We don't make threats. We make suggestions. And we are suggesting, enthusiastically, that you don't stir up old ghosts."

"Are you with the FBI?"

"Do we look like we're with the FBI?" Oates asked, as he downed the whiskey.

"Maybe the agricultural division, what with the boots and cowboy hats," Royce said.

"If that helps you listen to what we're saying, then yes, we're with the FBI," Hall said. "Leave the past where it belongs. We won't warn you again."

Royce felt his cheeks flush. "If our government is lying or doing things behind our back, and forcing people like Bon...I mean Brenda and Clarence Prentiss, regular folks, to do stuff, kill people, don't you think the public has a right to know?"

"They were not regular folks," Hall said. He leaned in, and Royce smelled the whiskey on his breath, mixed with what might be Juicy Fruit gum. "People don't need, or even want, to know how the sausage gets made. In the end, it's just a lot of raw, bloody meat going into the machine." He drained his glass and stood. "Thanks for the drink."

Oates stood too, putting his hat on. "Nice chatting with you Royce. Remember what we said."

"You damn well better leave Brenda alone," Royce said. Heart pounding, he watched them leave.

The waiter stopped at his table. "Care for another martini?"

Royce shook his head and left for his room. He called the office, not surprised when Terrence answered the phone. "Kid, I need you to find something for me. A jeweler's mark."

CHAPTER 23

What happens in Vegas

Clyde pulled over in front of a neon sign shaped like an arrow at the Comanche Restaurant and Lounge. Reaching into the back, he grabbed two stacks of bills from the armored car heist and stuffed them into his jacket pockets. "Let's have an early supper and then see if we can rile things up and make some new friends."

"I know what that generally means," Bonnie said, slipping the .25 auto into her purse, and smoothing her dress, still damp from the water tower theatrics.

"I keep telling you, that gun is too small," Clyde said.

"And I keep telling you, I don't need a cannon to get things done."

Inside, the club was crowded with drinkers and gamblers and working girls trying to separate Boulder Dam laborers from their pay. Bonnie and Clyde took a table in the dining area and a harried waiter rushed over.

"Something to drink?" he asked, and then looked down at Clyde's dirty work boots. "You're from Boulder City, so of course you want something to drink."

"Let's get something fun and refreshing," Bonnie said.

"Whatcha got?" Clyde asked, waving a dollar.

The waiter paused, not used to extravagant tips. "We make a mean gin gimlet."

"Sold," Clyde said. "We'll take two each."

The combination of lime and gin hit the spot. Then, feeling keen from the gin, they ordered food and lots of it—fried chicken, mashed potatoes and milk gravy, and canned sweet corn.

Bonnie ate a few forkfuls from the plate then slid it over to Clyde, lighting a smoke while he polished off the rest and then ordered a slice of banana cake and a cup of black coffee.

"I don't think I could eat another bite," Clyde said, scraping the last bit of frosting from the plate, and then licking the sweet remnants from his fingers.

"Good," she said. "Because you're about to run them out of food."

"Working for a living is hard," Clyde said. "I'm hungry all the time. And tired."

The waiter returned and Clyde paid the tab, adding another dollar to the tip, and then caught him by the arm. "Hey mister, got a tip for the hottest casino?"

"Yeah, here's my tip. Don't go into one," the man said. "The house always wins."

"Not tonight, friend," Clyde said. He slipped him another dollar. "Just tell me the most popular spot in town."

The waiter sighed and shook his head. "That'd be the Boulder Rapids Club. But seriously, don't get in too deep there. You'll lose your shirt and they'll take it out of your hide."

"I'm counting on them trying," Clyde said.

Arm in arm, Bonnie and Clyde headed down Fremont Street until they reached the Boulder Rapids Club. The place was smoky and loud, with blackjack tables and roulette wheels and craps. A three-man band played swing in the corner. Booze was flowing and people were yelling and arguing and flirting with local girls and some who were imports.

"What should we play tonight?" Clyde asked.

"Given what we're trying to accomplish, I'd say probably craps or roulette."

He settled for the craps table and waited until he could take over the dice. Once he started rolling, Bonnie stayed behind him with her arm draped over his shoulder—indistinguishable from any of the working girls, her dress, finally dried, clinging tightly.

Whenever Clyde made a bet, he'd hold the dice up to Bonnie and say, "blow on these for good luck, darling." She obliged, hamming it up for effect, puckering her lips into a kissy face. He played poorly on purpose, making risky bets and grumbling every time he lost as if it was his last dollar, and even complaining when he won.

"It's these damn low stakes games," he kept saying. "How can I win anything when we're playing for chump change?"

"Maybe we should go find a high stakes table, baby," Bonnie said with a pout. "Or play roulette? I like roulette."

"Good idea, doll face," Clyde said. "Any place in town got a little higher stakes table?" he asked the croupier. "We're getting bored playing for poor man's stakes."

The man smiled and fiddled with his cuff links. "You in such a hurry to lose your shirt?" he asked.

"You're the second man tonight to worry about my laundry," Clyde said. "I'm good for more than one paycheck."

The croupier nodded at the floor boss, who walked over. "This gentleman would like to see the stakes lifted a little."

"I'd like to see them done away with all together," Clyde said. "And let's switch games. Roulette. Make my little lady happy."

"How much do you have on you?" the pit boss asked.

"How much does the house have to cover my bet?" Bonnie laughed.

"It don't work like that," the man said. "You don't need to worry about our finances."

"Then you don't need to worry about mine," Clyde said. "Come on darling, let's go find some place where they ain't so square-headed."

"Wait, hold on," the pit boss said. "No need to run off." He eyed Clyde's rumpled clothes and recently sunburnt neck and forearms, taking him for a roughneck from Boulder City. "Fine, one spin, no limit, you're all in—winner take all."

He pointed to the neighboring roulette table, currently dark, and nodded for the croupier to set it up, as another bow-tied casino employee sidled up to take over the craps table. Grinning, Clyde and Bonnie sauntered over to the roulette table and the crowd of admirers shuffled behind them, following Clyde's every move.

Clyde nodded and fished into his pocket for some loose bills and dropped them on the table, then reached into this jacket for two stacks of twenty dollar bills and plunked them on the table. A rumble of excitement went up from the gamblers surrounding nearby tables, drawing more onlookers.

"Let's put this all on zero," Clyde said.

He saw the pit boss' eyes widen at the stack of money, but the man held his discomfort in check and nodded.

"Last call for bets," the croupier said, but no one dared come forward, and he spun the wheel with a practiced flourish, starting the ball around the outside track. Everyone watched in breathless fascination as the ball spun around, dropped and hopped and skittered, hitting in black 35, then red 12, then zero—causing a roar of excitement—then settling into red 32 at the last second.

"Red thirty-two," the croupier said. Without making eye contact, and holding back a grin, he slid the stack of bills into his drawer. "Next roller please."

"Huh," Clyde said. "I really thought that was going to land."

"It's okay, baby," Bonnie said. "You've got more, right?"

"Sure, I do, just not on me," he said. "Come on, let's get out of here."

As they walked toward the door, three men blocked their way. Clyde recognized one of them from the dam site on his first day of work when he and his partner tried to cut the brakes on his truck.

"Hey, I know you," Clyde said. "Lefty, ain't it? How's your buddy's head?"

"He's still not right," Lefty said. "Can't seem to walk in a straight line or keep food down."

"Real sorry about that," Clyde said.

Lefty shrugged. "It's a tough line of work we're in. But this ain't about that. The boss wants to talk to you."

"Yeah, and why would I want to talk to him?"

"Let's just say it's in your mutual best interest." He fished out a handful of chips and handed them to Bonnie. "Make yourself scarce, doll. The men have things to talk about."

"I don't go nowhere without her," Clyde said.

"Suit yourself, but don't say I didn't warn you if things get unpleasant."

Bonnie smiled, casually lit a cigarette and then blew the smoke in Lefty's direction.

Clyde laughed. "If things get unpleasant, trust me when I say you don't want to be next to her."

CHAPTER 24

The neon desert

Lefty and his two companions escorted Bonnie and Clyde upstairs to the third floor of the Boulder Rapids Club game room and a small office overlooking Fremont Street. Outside, night was falling, so the top of the neon club sign—a stylized river that ran toward a waterfall that turned into money—blinked on and off, lighting the room in bursts of blue, white and green.

A pale older man—anomalous in the desert—sat behind a beat-up desk, studying budget sheets. He had a worried, nervous energy, pausing often to stare distractedly into space while sounding out silent words. He looked right past—or through—his men and the two strangers, but Bonnie had a suspicion he saw much more than most. After a long minute, one of his men cleared his throat and the man focused on the present.

"Good, you found them," he said, looking up. He stood, causing everyone to take a step back. He offered his hand to Bonnie first. "I'm Roger Calhoun, I'm the, uh, owner of this club."

"I'm Brenda Prentiss," she said.

"Yes, of course, and you must be?" he extended his hand to Clyde.

"I must be Clarence," Clyde said. "Her husband."

"Yes, good."

Calhoun sat back down and shuffled through his papers, smiling when a particular figure caught his eye. "Exactly right," he said, underlining it with a worn-down pencil stub.

"Mr. Calhoun," Clyde said, but Lefty shushed him.

"Mr. Calhoun don't like to be interrupted," Lefty said.

"It's all right, Lefty," Calhoun said. "Guests are exempt from the rule, especially guests with such lovely companions." He smiled in the direction of Bonnie without meeting her eyes.

"Not to be disrespectful, Mr. Calhoun, but I'm curious why you wanted to talk to us," Clyde said. "I'm just a working stiff trying to show my gal a good time and lost a little more than I should have at your roulette wheel."

"That's not exactly true," Calhoun said. "According to Lefty here, a man whose opinion I trust, you are a bit cagier than the average roughneck. I'm paying the medical bills of an employee, likely for life, and that suggests you know how to handle yourself around danger."

"Sorry about your man," Clyde said. "I didn't want to end up in a fiery wreck and make Brenda here a widow before her time."

"I don't begrudge you clobbering Cantrell," Calhoun said. "Nor would I expect you to be in a big rush to die. I hope you can also appreciate my position. Like a general on the battlefield, I can't afford the luxury of thinking of other people with rich, full lives. It clouds my thinking and prevents decisive action."

"What sorts of decisive actions are you thinking about?" Bonnie asked.

"My associates in New York City had interesting things to say about you both," he said, moving to the window, leaving Bonnie's question hanging unanswered for a few beats, but then he continued. "We are on the precipice, the very brink, of creating something amazing here in the desert. A town that exists against all odds solely to cater to the dark side of human nature. Forget about utopias and god-fearing villages clustered around churches, Las Vegas will emerge from the sand as a temple to greed and hedonism."

He spun around. "But we're not quite ready to walk on our own without the presence of all your grubby compatriots spending their hard-earned paychecks on booze, women and gambling. We need water, power and another year or two before we become self-sufficient."

"And that's why you've been sabotaging the dam?"

"Such a strong word," Calhoun said, evenly. "A few accidents here and there, a few delays, a few broken bones and maybe a death or two—for a greater good."

"Why are you telling us this?" Bonnie asked.

Calhoun smiled. "I tend to make informed assumptions about people," he said. "I find it awfully suspicious that on the same day an armored car gets held up and sacks full of crisp twenty dollar bills go missing, you lose hundreds of dollars, all in crisp new twenties, on my roulette table."

"Word travels fast," Bonnie said, looking at her nails, with practiced nonchalance.

"Seems like things that happen in Las Vegas ought to stay here," Clyde said.

"Brenda and Clarence Prentiss. You show up here out of thin air, get good jobs and then ingratiate yourself with the bosses. My guess is you're running a con that ended today with a successful heist. And I approve. In fact, I encourage entrepreneurs. But I'm a businessman, first and foremost, and I would like to count you as, if not partners, at least leveraged allies."

"May we sit?" Bonnie asked.

"There won't be time," he said.

"Excuse me?"

"You'll be leaving in a minute, one way or the other." He clapped his hands together and held them together as if in prayer. "I'd like to hire you to be our eyes and ears, and mischievous hands, on the inside. You'll work with Lefty to make sure we can slow the work down to a pleasant, lasting pace. In exchange, you get to keep the haul from the payroll heist."

"We get to keep the money we already stole?" Clyde asked, sarcasm dripping from his words. "I don't like the rules of this game. What happens if we politely decline?"

Calhoun nodded thoughtfully, pointed toward the window and moved out of the way.

"I took the liberty of asking Chief Hoskins from Boulder City to drop by and discuss the appearance of company money on my roulette table. Tarry much longer, and you can explain your losing streak to him."

Clyde looked out the window and saw Hoskins getting out of a car directly below with two deputies in tow.

Clyde shot a look at Bonnie and she nodded. "You got yourself a deal, Mr. Calhoun," he said. "We're pleased to join your team."

The sound of boots thumping up the stairs got louder.

"Would you happen to have a back way out of this joint?" Bonnie asked.

Lefty stepped to the right and kicked the bottom wall, revealing a hidden door set against the patterned wallpaper.

"This leads down to the street," he said. "I'll stop by Boulder City in a day or two and we'll figure out the next little slowdown."

"I promise not to clobber you with a rock," Clyde said, pulling Bonnie into the narrow stairway as a heavy fist knocked on the office door.

CHAPTER 25

Chow-chow

When the alarm went off at sunrise, Clyde swore and reached for it, but this time Bonnie had moved it to the dresser on the far side of the room.

"God dammit, I hate working for a living," he grumbled. Clyde got out of bed in his boxers and undershirt, grabbed the clock and stomped to the front door. He jerked the door open and flung the clock out into the street.

As he crawled back into bed, Bonnie shook her head. "Honey, that's the fourth clock you've broken since we've been here."

"We robbed a damn payroll truck," he said, face pressed into the pillow. "Spend some of the heist money on a new clock down at the store later."

"We ought to give that money back," she said. "Now that we accomplished what we set out to accomplish, doesn't seem right to keep it to ourselves."

He raised his head to look at her incredulously. "Bonnie Parker, have you lost your ever-loving mind? We don't ever give money back to the people we steal it from. That's like the first rule of bank robbing."

"Come on, get up," she said, shaking him by the shoulder. "Today we're not criminals, we're just working stiffs."

She stood and stretched, and he rolled over so he could watch the sun shining through her undergarments and lighting up her lithe limbs.

"Something sure is getting stiff," he said.

"You are insatiable," she said.

"You're the one who keeps giving me pornography," he said, tapping the *Tropic of Cancer* on the bedside table. "I can't help it if I'm easily impressioned."

"Save it for tonight, tiger."

"Only if we go twice," he said. He pulled on his dungarees while she rummaged around in the kitchen. When he came in, she slipped a plate in front of him with two fried eggs over a square of leftover cornbread.

He sat down and looked at it suspiciously. "What is this, exactly?"

"It's an old family recipe," she said. "Called all-we-got."

He poked the eggs so the yolks bled down onto the cornbread. "My momma's version of all-we-got always had a little chow-chow with it."

She poured them each a cup of coffee from the pot on the stove. "Just eat it," she said. "I never said I was a cook."

"What about lunch?" he asked hopefully.

She folded another piece of cornbread into a napkin and handed it to him, along with a wrinkled apple.

"You gonna call Sal today?"

"Yeah. Now that we know the mob is behind the slowdown, we can get out of here," she said.

"Think I need to go up to the dam site to work then?"

"Best keep up appearances for now," Bonnie said, watching his shoulders sag as he heard the opposite of what he was hoping for. "Sorry, baby," she said.

"Shit, here's the truck," Clyde said, shoving the last bit of food in his mouth and heading for the door as he heard Big Bertha rumbling down the road. He knocked over the baseball bat leaning behind the door on his way out.

"Be careful out there today," Bonnie said, propping the bat against the wall again.

On the stoop outside of the house, Clyde pulled her into his arms and kissed her, bending her over under the force of his affection. The truck idled out front and the men whooped and hollered, and she blushed, pulling her robe closer together when he disentangled himself.

"Love you, Brenda Prentiss," he called, stuffing the cornbread in his pocket and running down the steps.

"I love you too, Clarence Prentiss," she called after him.

After he was gone, she dressed and walked to the main office. Claudette waited for her outside.

"Brenda, did you hear?" she asked, taking her by the arm. "Somebody robbed the payroll."

"Oh, goodness," Bonnie said, holding her hand to her throat. "That's awful. What happened?"

"Apparently, a gang of armed desperadoes ran it off the road and even though the guards tried to fight them off, they got overwhelmed."

"Is that so?" Bonnie said, fighting a smile.

"And they think Dante was the leader," she said, shocked and also a little pleased that she had once kissed such a reckless man. "With a whole crew of anarchists. They found a gun in the truck, some old Italian job. The anarchists got away with more than a hundred thousand dollars," she said. "Fitzsimmons is furious."

"A hundred thousand?" Bonnie said, "There's no way—" she said, catching herself mid-sentence. "There's no way that kind of money should have been in there. I looked at the budget, and that's twice the current pay cycle."

"They said they were going to give New Year's bonuses to all the workers as a way to say thanks," Claudette whispered, as they sat behind their desks. "But Jimmy thinks it's all a lie. He thinks the company stole the money so they could stretch out paying people, talk about pretend bonuses, and soften up the crew so they don't go on strike. He thinks they're going to try to pin it on the union."

"Oh, so that's what Jimmy says," Bonnie said, teasing Claudette.

Claudette giggled. "You were right about him, he's dreamy."

"Stop chattering immediately," Fitzsimmons said as he walked up to the building. "This is a place of business, not a Sunday school social."

"Yes, Mr. Fitzsimmons," they said, rolling their eyes behind his back, as they followed him into the office.

Bonnie was already pouring a cup of coffee when he called out, "And bring me a cup of coffee."

She contemplated dumping it on his crotch, but fought the urge, deciding to postpone it until she and Clyde were leaving for good. "Close the door after you leave," he said. "And then ring me through to the main office of Pacific Bridge in Portland."

At her desk, Bonnie flipped through the card file until she found the number "What is Pacific Bridge?" she asked Claudette.

"They're part of the Six Companies, the group of well, six companies, that banded together to bid on this project. Guess it was too big for any one of them to put up the bond, but together, they cobbled it," Claudette said. "Fitzsimmons works for Pacific Bridge, or he did.

Now he's kind of on loan to manage the hiring and the contracts here for the whole shebang."

Claudette turned to answer a ringing phone.

Bonnie figured this would be as good a cover as any to place the call to Sal. She began to get nervous after the fifth ring. Just as she was about to hang up, Sal answered.

"Good morning, this is Six Companies at Boulder City with a call for Pacific Bridge," Bonnie said.

"What's wrong?" Sal asked.

"What was that you said? Something about an item being located?"

"You know who's sabotaging the dam?"

Bonnie took a chance and turned her body away from the working ladies, and whispered. "The mob admitted it. Said they need to slow things down so the workers keep buying booze and gambling."

She spun back around and sat up straight at her desk. "I'm sorry, our connection is poor, what was that you said?" Bonnie said, more loudly.

"That sounds like small potatoes to me, like locals trying to line their pockets with graft, not someone trying to take down the whole thing," Sal said. "Stay on it. I'm coming out."

"Is this call coming from Mexico?" Bonnie asked.

"Don't you dare go back to Mexico," Sal said. "I don't believe it's the mob. Keep investigating until you are dead certain. Or dead." She hung up.

"Well?" Fitzsimmons asked. He was standing behind her, looming over her like an ocean wave about to break.

"I'm sorry sir, there was a bad connection, let me try again," Bonnie said.

Fitzsimmons fixed an angry stare at her. "Stop wasting my time and the company's money." He walked back into the office and slammed the door.

"He's a pompous little jerk," Bonnie said, placing the call and transferring it to his private line.

"Oh, they all are," Claudette said. "He's very good at his job though. At least he was."

"What does that mean?" Bonnie asked.

Claudette rolled her chair closer. "His invoices have been a little loosey-goosey lately. Underpaying for things, or else items not showing up. And that's not like him. And I noticed the employment records aren't up to his normal standards. Some of the folks he's hired don't seem to have any experience at all. I suppose it's just the stress of things as the project gets close to the end."

"Maybe," Bonnie said.

Bonnie was disappointed with Sal's directive and distracted herself by carrying a stack of filing to the drawers and began flipping through, looking for some of the invoices Claudette mentioned. By lunchtime, she could see a trend, but couldn't quite put it together.

"Come have something to eat with me," Claudette said

"Nah, I need to walk down the store," Bonnie said. "Next time."

At the store, she picked up a few items of food to charge against her paycheck to avoid arousing suspicion of paying with a crisp new stolen twenty. But searching the aisles, she couldn't find any alarm clocks.

"We're all out," the clerk said.

"How can a company store on the country's biggest job site be out of alarm clocks?"

"It's the darnedest thing," the man said. "There was a run on them last week. Must've sold forty of them. But I may have one more in the back. Wait here, please."

He bustled into the storeroom and returned with a single wind up. "Had a little ding on it, so I was going to send it back. You can have it for free."

"That's kind of you," she said. "And save one for me when the next shipment comes in, would you?" she asked. "Name's Brenda Prentiss. Actually, save two. No, three." Bonnie hoped they would be out of Boulder City long before the next shipment or before Clyde could destroy three more clocks, but better to get them now, just in case.

"Of course," he said, jotting her name down on a scrap of paper. "Just this?" he asked, pointing at the few items on the counter.

"Hold on," she said. "Let me grab a jar of chow-chow."

CHAPTER 26

King of the jungle

"I want to do something fun tonight," Bonnie said. They were in bed, clothes strewn from the front door to the bedroom, tired and sweaty from making love.

Clyde cracked one eye and gave her a sideways look. "What do you call what we just did?"

"That was real fun, but now I want to go out."

"Aww, Bon, can't we just have something to eat and rest up for round two? I'm worn out from driving that truck round and round all day. And now you tell me Sal says we got to stay, and I got to keep working for who knows how long. Honest work will be the death of me."

"Don't think of it as working," she said, already sitting up. "Think of it as cover for the spying. And plus, we've got a trunk full of stolen money and a closet full of guns, there's nothing honest about that."

Clyde knew the argument was already lost so he sat on the edge of the bed and pulled on a clean pair of pants. "How about we go see a movie? I heard they have a popcorn machine."

She ran her hands down his back and then circled his waist and hugged him. "That sounds real nice," she said. "And I promise to make round two extra special."

He shrugged into his shirt, tucked it into his pants and then slipped on a shoulder holster. "I wish the movie was already over," he said.

She pulled on her last pair of silk stockings and then buttoned on a colorful skirt—her favorite—she bought in Mexico, pairing it with a white blouse. She smoothed back her hair, put on red lipstick and tucked a pearl-handled dagger into her garter. "Ready," she said.

As they walked to the theater, she squeezed his arm when she saw the marquee. "It's Tarzan and His Mate," she said excitedly. "With Johnny Weissmuller. He's so handsome and brave."

"It's all acting," Clyde said. "Like some old half-naked fella could do all that stuff."

"Don't get all wound up," she said. "You're my Tarzan. And I've seen you without your loin cloth."

"You're prettier than Maureen O'Sullivan any day of the week and twice on Sunday."

She leaned in closer. "You keep talking like that, and we are gonna have to skip the movie."

"Kind of in the mood to see it now," he said. "Besides, I want them two fellows who been shadowing us to have to wait around until we're done to try and jump us."

"I wondered if you saw them," she said, ribbing him. "Was thinking maybe all this hard, honest labor had made you soft."

Clyde thumped his fist against his chest. "You can't put one over on the king of the jungle, baby."

"You big goof," she said. "Who do you think it is?"

"Haven't got a good look yet," he said. "So, either they're real good, or they're a little on the timid side."

Outside the theater, the short line to buy tickets was moving quickly.

"In other words, it's either the mob or the anarchists," Bonnie said. "What did we do to them?"

"One's wondering if maybe they spilled too much or maybe is testing us, and the other is likely thinking we had something to do with framing 'em for the payroll heist."

She nodded. "Let's hope they don't mess up the movie. These tickets are expensive," she said, as Clyde shelled out two quarters for the movie, and another for the popcorn.

The theater was full mostly with workers, some of them already sleeping, along with a few families—the kids quietly playing in the aisles. As they walked in, Bonnie nudged Clyde and nodded her head to the row of seats near the back of the theater. Claudette and Jimmy were sitting side by side, leaning against each other.

"Looks like she found her King Kong," Bonnie whispered. She and Clyde took seats near the front and watched the show, laughing and holding hands.

When the credits rolled, they walked back up the aisle, before the lights came on, hoping to get a head start on whoever was tailing them, and they were almost to the door, when they heard muffled voices speaking Italian as two men stood and shoved their way out of their seats, climbing over the laps of other movie-goers, who yelled at them to shut up and wait their turn.

"Well, that answers that," Bonnie said. "Our anarchists are about to make a run at us."

"I was kind of hoping it was the mob," Clyde said. "Guns and icepicks I can deal with, bombs are so, I don't know, loud and messy."

"Come on," Bonnie said, dragging him down the street and back to their house. "Safer for everyone else if we're inside. Let's not get blown to smithereens out here yacking about it."

Down the street, Dante and Mateo watched Bonnie and Clyde enter their house. They stopped running and waited for a minute to catch their breath.

"Now they will pay for getting us fired," Dante said.

"And for framing us," Mateo said. "You were right all along, she is working for Six Companies. How else would our gun end up at the armored car heist? They must have picked it up."

"We may be forced to flee, but we will have our revenge," Dante said.

They crept up silently, hugging the shadows of the street line and watching for witnesses.

When they were satisfied at last, Mateo stood in the street, knife drawn, while Dante stealthily approached the house. At the door, he produced a grenade from his pocket and pulled the pin.

Dante said a prayer, pulled the door open and lobbed the bomb inside. "Death to the oppressors," he yelled, before stepping back into the shadows.

CHAPTER 27

Family jewels

"Those things will kill you."

Royce looked at his seatmate, a woman old enough to still dress in her Sunday best for air travel, and smiled, waiting for the no-smoking light to blink off with a cigarette in one hand and a lighter in the other.

"But what a way to go," he said, lighting up and reclining the seat.

Within minutes, a thin layer of blue haze hovered above the jet's rear smoking section, as the back-half of passengers—all except the unfortunately seated woman— lit up simultaneously.

After the visit from the cowboy-spooks at the bar, Royce couldn't sleep—wired on a mix of adrenaline, paranoia and alcohol.

Instead, he lay in the dark and listened to the ceiling fan and let his mind race through spy movie clichés and the potential gruesome deaths awaiting him. When the phone rang at midnight, his mind was still speeding along at a hundred miles an hour and he almost jumped through the ceiling.

It was Terrence. He had tracked down the jeweler's mark to a shop in Chicago. A shop that, improbably, still had an active business license but no phone number.

Royce wanted to reach through the receiver and hug the boy. Instead he told him to call the airlines and change his flight to the Windy City. And to feed his cat.

The flight attendant wheeled the drink cart by and Royce asked for a Bloody Mary and a black coffee.

"Certainly, sir," she said with a smile, then noticed the notebook in his lap. "You some kind of writer?"

"Some kind," he said. "The worst kind. A journalist."

She smoothed the hem of her burgundy mini-skirt and leaned over to set the coffee, Bloody Mary mix and a complimentary single-serving bottle of Smirnoff on the tray.

"Think I could talk you out of another bottle?"

She gave him two more. "I've got a thing for writers. If you wrote poetry, I'd probably be making plans with you for after we land."

"Maybe I'm a poet and don't even know it."

"I *will* take the vodka back," she said with a teasing smile.

He watched her rolling down the aisle, then poured two of the bottles over the ice and left the can of tomato mix unopened.

The woman beside him had fallen asleep, her hat askew and bottom denture partially extended, and Royce looked past her and out the tiny window at the tops of a lumpy continent of clouds.

Three hours later, after more flirting with the stewardess and a bumpy landing, a cab dropped him off at a brick building sandwiched between a dry cleaner and a shuttered diner. The place gave no outward sign of being a business. He checked to be sure he was at the right address.

Royce rang the bell and heard its croaking echo from inside. He waited a minute, and then pulled on the rusted doorknocker, giving it two firm raps. After another long silent minute—during which he was convinced his trail of clues had run cold—the door creaked open a few inches, anchored by a curve of chain. A pair of milky blue eyes peered out from behind dusty spectacles.

"Hello," Royce said, trying to hide his eagerness behind a friendly voice. "Is this Solomon Jewelers?"

The door crept open a little wider, as far as the chain would allow, revealing a man so stooped by age, he had trouble keeping his eyes level with the door. "Who wants to know?"

"My name is Royce Jenkins, I'm a reporter and I'm investigating a death. The person who died was wearing a ring with the mark of Solomon Jewelers on it."

The door closed abruptly.

"Mr. Solomon," Royce called. "Hello? Mr. Solomon?"

The chain rattled and the door opened all the way.

"I'm Theodore Solomon," he said. His face was a warren of wrinkles, and a thin layer of white hair dotted parts of his otherwise bald head, like peach fuzz, in between a geography of dark age spots. "But I've been retired for more than a decade."

"If I show you photos of the ring, do you think you can help me identify who it belonged to?" Royce asked.

"You don't know the jewelry business very well, do you?" Solomon asked, his voice unsteady and wavering.

"What do you mean?"

He tugged on the suspenders holding up ill-fitting plaid pants two sizes too big and struggled to look Royce in the chin by angling his head to the right.

"I made hundreds of rings, hundreds, maybe thousands, thousands, and most of them have likely changed hands, no pun intended, many times. Or were melted down into something else."

"Could you at least look at the photo?"

"It's a mighty small chance, but come on in," Solomon said. His shirt, once white, was now more of a grimy gray with what looked like dried egg yolk spatter on the front. "Been awhile since I had any people company."

Inside, Royce stepped over a yellow tabby—napping in a square of sunlight and followed the old man into a sitting room to the right of the main hallway.

Piles of newspapers and boxes of all sizes lined the room, reaching to the tall ceiling where cobwebs fluttered. Stacks of sweatshirts, mimeograph sheets, a bag full of what looked like receipts and invoices, and a small trashcan overflowing with paper clips and packages of yellow post-it notes covered the tables and chairs and filled the bookshelves.

Dozens of green woolen army surplus blankets were piled in a corner, on top of which three more intertwined cats quietly slept. A cat in the doorway to the kitchen let out a long, lazy meow. It was met by a hiss from another cat bristling inside an overturned cardboard box.

Royce lost count of the number of cats.

A pathway carved through the mess led to a round antique wooden table, cracked down the center, where Solomon sat down. Next to a brown-stained teacup with a fly slowly drowning in the amber liquid was a bowl full of what appeared to be loose diamonds and other gems.

Royce remained standing—there was only one chair. He had never witnessed a hoarder before, though he'd written once about one. He wondered if he should call social services or something. "Do you live alone?"

"Are you blind? I have cats."

Royce nodded. "Yeah, but, do you have any family around here?"

Solomon shook his head. "Nope. Outlived them all. Ain't that the damnedest thing?"

"How about friends or neighbors?"

"Are you here about my social calendar, or did you want me to look at your ring?"

"The ring, for sure," Royce said, pulling out the photos from his briefcase. Solomon picked up a jeweler's loupe from a box under the table containing dozens of them. He held the loupe close to his right eye and, head bowed so that his chin touched his chest, scanned the grainy images one by one, muttering to himself.

"Any chance I could use your bathroom?" Royce asked.

Even as the words came out of his mouth, he knew it was a mistake. But he had been unable to stop anywhere on the ride here, and the vodka and coffee were running through.

"Down the hall to your left," Solomon said.

Royce didn't move.

"Do you have to go or not?" Solomon asked. "I get false alarms too. It gets worse, trust me."

"I have to go," Royce said. He walked down the corridor. The hallway walls were covered in old wedding photographs, with the gaze of the camera focused on the left hands of a parade of women in white. Engagement rings, wedding bands, happy faces and glowing smiles, elaborate high-necked frilly dresses and sharp tuxedos. The pictures chronicled the evolution of bridal style across five decades.

When he opened the door to the bathroom, the floor was crowded with four overflowing litter boxes and a mouse, a goddamned mouse, perched on the edge of one. How the fuck could that be, Royce wondered, given all the cats? He made a deal with his bladder and closed the door, standing in the hall, trying to ignore the stench of ammonia.

"You're in luck," Solomon called from the junkyard parlor.

Royce walked back into the room. "Yeah? How so?"

"I do remember this little beauty," he said, pulling the loupe away from his eye. "I designed and cast this one, must be about fifty years ago. I remember it well."

Royce felt his breath shorten and heartbeat speed up, but remained silent. Years of interviewing taught him the hard lesson that unless you were angling for good quotes, silence encouraged people to talk more than direct questions.

"Tell me again why you want to know about this ring?" Solomon asked.

He decided to tell the truth. "The ring is part of an investigation I'm working on. If I can find out who originally owned this ring, I might be able to learn something important about Bonnie and Clyde."

"The Bonnie and Clyde?"

"Yes," Royce said. "You know of them?"

"Don't be a jackass," Solomon said. "Everybody my age remembers Bonnie and Clyde." He took a sip from the teacup, hopefully—Royce thought with a shudder—straining out the fly. He didn't. The fly was gone when he set the cup back down.

"They got shot to hell," Solomon said.

Royce pulled out his notebook, wanting to capture the details of this surreal situation—the mouse, the tea fly, the loose diamonds. "What do you remember?"

"She was real pretty," he said. "I was young then, but I remember thinking I might be willing to die for a woman like that." He wiped his watery eyes. "But that kind of thinking comes from the underside of the body, if you know what I mean." He chuckled, a dry cross between a cackle and the hiccups, then succumbed to a coughing fit.

After catching his breath, Solomon smiled, his eyes watering even more. He stroked the cat stretched across the table.

Royce waited. In his mind, he was already writing this chapter of the book. This hoarder-jeweler was colorful, and might have a whole chapter to himself. But only if what he had to say helped him figure out who actually died in that car back in 1934.

A gray tabby rubbed against the old man's leg. "They were shot down without any trial. Vigilante justice, mob rule. Haven't thought about them in a month of Sundays. She was a looker. Just like the little gal who I made this ring for," he said, pointing at the photos of the wedding band. "Like I said, I made thousands of rings. But she was real pretty so I remember her. But it was the stones that really got my attention."

He tapped one photo with his knuckle. "See those? The blue stones. Called Arkansas sodalites. First time I'd seen 'em. Last time too. The little lady brought them in with her, and told me that they were from her grandma's ring, asked me to put them into a ring for her."

Royce pulled up an empty bucket, flipped it over, and an avalanche of dust poured out. He sat down.

"She was a slight thing, a tiny brunette. It was a hard ring to make, the stones were small and brittle but I managed. Gave it to her, and never saw her or the ring again."

"You remember her name?"

"I can do you one better. Her photo is on my wall."

Royce felt time stop all together, then speed up so much his hands started trembling.

"She and her fiancé were up here visiting his folks, which is how she came to use my services to begin with, and they stopped in. I asked them for an engagement picture for my advertisements."

"Can you show me?"

Royce followed Solomon back into the hallway, toppling over a stack of newspapers and sending three cats yowling for the kitchen. He stopped in front of an old black and white photo that had been colorized.

"That's them. Her name was Ebbon. Stan Ebbon. Or Dan Ebbon. Or something like that. Wasn't a girl's name. Sounded more like a man."

"I would like to buy this picture from you, Mr. Solomon," Royce said.

Solomon shook his head. "No, I wouldn't want to part with it. Wouldn't want a bare spot on the wall."

There was a yowl and a crash from the front room as a cat fell from something high and glass broke. "Now, dammit," he said, turning and shuffling off.

Royce slipped the framed photo off the wall, then hung another that had fallen onto to the floor, one of many, in its place. "No, you wouldn't want a bare spot," he whispered.

CHAPTER 28

Batter up

The grenade sailed in through the open door in a graceful, deadly arc.

Clyde stood squared up in the middle of hall, baseball bat held up behind this head like he was facing down Dizzy Dean in the World Series. He eyed the deadly pitch carefully and then eased into a fluid swing as the bomb began to drop out of its arc, connecting with the grenade solidly, right in the thickest part of the bat—the belly of the wood. The force jarred him, but he committed to the follow through and it was enough to drive the grenade right back at Dante's head.

Dante shrieked and ducked as the bomb traveled over him and back out the door, bounced once at the edge of the little yard, and then rolled to where his brother Mateo stood. Mateo shrieked as well, dropped his knife, and turned to run.

Bonnie, standing behind the door with one of Clyde's .45s in her hand, kicked the door shut and slammed the lock into place.

"Did you see that?" Clyde asked, dropping the bat and shaking his tingling hands, "Just like the Bambino."

"We should probably get down," Bonnie said.

He nodded and pulled her down to the floor as a blast rattled the floorboards. There were screams of pain, followed in short order by shouts of alarm. Bonnie tossed the gun to Clyde who caught it and tucked it out of sight into his shoulder holster.

She opened the door and saw the crumpled form of Dante in the yard. The concussion had knocked him sprawling, and he was addled and groaning. In the street, Mateo was bloodied and tattered, unmoving. There was a small crater near him where the grenade exploded.

Squatting down beside Dante, Bonnie caught him by his thick hair and lifted his head so that he was staring, dazed, into her eyes. "You're the worst anarchists in the history of the world," she said. "I'm surprised you were able to do any of this sabotage, much less kill a man."

"We killed no one," he said. "You ruined everything before we could even start our plan."

"All those explosions at the dam, you had nothing to do with them?" she asked.

"No!"

Bonnie sighed. "Well, you'll be planning your revolution from behind bars now."

Bonnie moved beside Clyde, pretending to be flustered as a crowd of people began to assemble. Henry Byrd himself walked up, followed by Chief Hoskins—hand on the butt of his revolver—and a deputy in tow.

"Prentiss," Hoskins said. "I should have known if there was trouble, you'd be at the center of it."

"I'm as surprised as you, Chief," Clyde said. "Me and Brenda here was just settling in for a little, well, a little prayer session, if you know what I mean, when we heard an explosion. We ran out here and found these two shady looking fellows all blown to hell."

"Why would two bomb-throwing radicals try to blow you up?" the chief asked.

"You think they were coming after us?" Bonnie said, lapsing into her damsel-in-distress theatrics. "Clarence, what is going on? I'm so frightened."

"Don't you worry darling," he said, giving her a squeeze. "The chief don't know what he's talking about." He turned to face Hoskins. "You're scaring my wife. I'm sure it was all some kind of coincidence."

"Let's play this one safe, Prentiss," Byrd said. "I don't mean to scare your missus, but you did stop their last little attempt at slowing down Six Companies when someone cut the wires on the monkey-slide. Could be someone's got it in for you."

Clyde put on a slightly surprised, serious expression. "I guess I hadn't thought of it that way."

"Trouble does seem to follow you around," Byrd said. "I don't know whether to have the chief escort you out of town or give you a promotion."

"Are them my only two choices?" Clyde asked.

Byrd laughed. "A promotion it is. Anyone who saves lives and earns himself a target on account of standing up to anarchists is okay in my book." He stuck his hand out. "I want you to manage the secondary vehicle fleet on the canyon floor. We may have seen the last of these jokers, but then again, anarchists are like rats—you see one or two, chances are the whole place is lousy with them."

"Thank you, sir," Clyde said. "I appreciate the vote of confidence."

"I'm so proud of you, baby," Bonnie said, hamming it up for his sake. "Just four days on the job and you already got a promotion."

After the chief dragged off Dante and Mateo and the crowd dispersed, Bonnie and Clyde settled into bed.

"Hon, we got lucky they threw a bomb at us," Bonnie said. "What if it had been a bottle of nitroglycerine?"

"I reckon I would have bunted," Clyde said.

CHAPTER 29

All caught up

"Baby, it's time to get up," Bonnie said, shaking his shoulder and then ducking under the blanket to build a small fortress of covers against the chill of the dawn air.

Clyde brushed her hand away. "It can't be. I didn't even hear the alarm."

"That's because this new little clock the grocer gave sounds like a sick cricket," she said, holding the barely whirring timepiece in her hand. "We slept right through."

He plucked it from her hand and threw it into the kitchen. "Damn you clock, you had but one job to do."

"Aww Clyde, now I'll have to borrow a clock from Claudette." She got up and pulled the blanket around her naked body, checking her watch on the side table. "Come on, you'll be late. The truck will be rolling by in a few minutes, and you're a manager now."

Clyde sat up on the side of the bed and pulled on his clothes, shaking his head. "Not even time for a little early morning loving. I don't know how people live like this."

"You have a one-track mind," she said, silently grateful, and glad it kept him from dwelling on the fact there was no breakfast. Or lunch.

Bonnie stood on the stoop and watched as Clyde swung on board Big Bertha, keeping eye contact with her

177

until it turned the corner and disappeared. Dino was laughing from the back, and waving a dollar.

After a cup of coffee and a smoke, she got ready, grabbed her beret—it was a chilly morning—and walked to the office.

Even at this early hour, the office buzzed with an unusual amount of activity.

Claudette stood by the telegraph machine, pulling off the messages that came in overnight, sorting them into piles based on which manager needed to see the information. She smiled at Bonnie with a curious look on her face, half guilt and half exuberance.

Bonnie recognized it instantly. "You wicked little tomato. You and Jimmy?"

Claudette nodded, beaming. "It's official, he's courting me now. We've been taking long walks, and he's been blowing on his harmonica, playing sweet songs for me."

"And what have you been blowing?" Bonnie asked.

Claudette blushed, but didn't deny it.

The telephone jangled and Bonnie sighed. "I want to hear all the sordid details, but let me get this before Fitzie flips his shitzie." She tossed her beret on the desk and picked up the receiver. "Good morning, Six Companies headquarters. How may I help you?"

"Good morning, Brenda. This is the front gate. Could you let Mr. Fitzsimmons know his guests are here?"

"Of course," Bonnie said. "Who is it?"

"He'll know," the guard said, breaking the connection.

"That was the guard house," Bonnie said. "Some guests are here. I wonder who?"

"There are always people dropping in for tours," Claudette said. "Congressmen, reporters, architects, engineers—even movie stars. Did I tell you about the time I talked to Bette Davis?"

"Only twice before," Bonnie said.

Claudette stuck her tongue out at Bonnie. "Well, I thought it was keen."

The door to Fitzsimmons's office opened and he stepped out. "We have a meeting at nine and it's important. I need someone who can take shorthand." He looked at Bonnie. "Do you know shorthand?"

"Yes, sir," Bonnie lied, not even sure what he was talking about.

"Good. You," he said, pointing at Claudette, "type out five copies of this agenda." He handed her a sheet of paper with scribbles. "And make sure the conference room is ready. Have the mess hall send over coffee and donuts."

Claudette nodded and hurried to the typewriter. She threaded in two clean sheets with carbon paper in between and started typing while Bonnie called the mess hall.

"This doesn't sound good," Claudette whispered, as she filled out the paper. "They're bringing in the Pinks."

"The Pinks?"

"The Pinkertons," Claudette said. "Surely you've heard of them. Private police force. They're like an attack dog the big bosses turn loose on the workers."

Bonnie smiled. "Sounds like Jimmy might be rubbing off on you."

"He's rubbing me just the right way," she said, her eyes turning dreamy and distant. "So smart, and kind, and just enough angry." She blew a bubble with her gum and the pop snapped her back to reality. "This is not going to go well for him." She looked at the agenda more closely. "They're going to try and break the union before they announce layoffs so they can't organize to protect themselves or get new jobs."

There was a knock and one of the young workers from the mess hall came in carrying a tray of donuts. He grinned lopsidedly at Claudette. "You're looking real pretty today," he said.

"Thank you, Curtis," she said, sending a smile his way without ever breaking her rapid-fire typing. "Please set them down on the table there and get on out of here before I lose my self-control and throw myself in your arms."

"That sounds all right to me," he said, blushing.

"You know if I was five years younger, we'd already be married," she said, winking at Bonnie. And still typing.

"Oh gosh, Miss Claudette, I can't ever tell if you're joking," Curtis said.

"I never joke about marriage or religion," she said, snatching the papers out of the typewriter and threading fresh ones.

Bonnie pulled out coffee cups. "What is this shorthand thing Fitzie was talking about?"

Claudette shook her head. "You're a terrible secretary. It's a way of writing in code so you can take notes real fast. You'd better let me do it." She looked up at the clock. "They'll be here any minute. Take over typing up the agenda here."

Bonnie settled in behind the typewriter and a half-typed agenda. A name in the bulleted list caught her eye. A security consultant would be giving remarks about his experiences dealing with criminal activities. Hank Black.

Car doors slammed outside and male voices could be heard approaching the door.

"Oh shit," Bonnie said, standing suddenly, knowing she had about a minute before he entered the office. She could feel her face getting hot. "Claudette, I need you to cover for me, and not ask any questions. I have to go. Right now."

"What do I tell Fitzie?"

"Anything," Bonnie said. "Tell him I have lady problems, that tends to shut men up quick."

She bolted for the back door just as the front door opened and Hank Black walked in with four Pinkertons.

Halfway home, she remembered the beret she left on the desk, the same beret she was wearing in the photographs of Bonnie and Clyde that were splashed on every newspaper in the world.

CHAPTER 30

Confessions

Hours later, the desert sun began to sink and brilliant oranges and pinks lit up the cloudless sky. Dirty, tired and hungry, Clyde slid up the canyon wall inside the crowded cable car, eager to see Bonnie.

After the teeth-rattling ride back to Boulder City, he hopped off the truck and walked to the front door. He was surprised to see the lights out, the house dark and shuttered. He opened the door, hand on the switchblade in his pocket, and tossed his hat on the back of a chair.

"Brenda, you home?"

He turned on the light, thinking there might be a note on the kitchen table. Nothing.

Odd, he thought, maybe she had to work late. Or maybe she was with Claudette. Still holding the knife, he walked into the bedroom and flipped on the light. Bonnie was sitting on the bed, his BAR leveled at the door and her finger on the trigger.

"Hey there, darling, rough day at the office?" he said, hands in the air.

"I wasn't sure you'd be alone," she said, easing the safety back on. "Hank Black is here."

"That ain't good," he said, taking the gun from her and laying it on the bed. "I don't suppose you went to the store today? I'm starving."

"All you ever think about is food. Didn't you hear me? Hank Black is here."

He sat down beside her and put his hand on her thigh. "I heard you, but it's not true. Sometimes I think about lying here naked and spooning with you. Been thinking hard on that all day."

"Be serious," she said. "This is a real problem."

"I don't see it that way," he said. "He ain't interested in boring old Brenda and Clarence Prentiss, only outlaws like Bonnie and Clyde. Long as we keep our noses clean and don't ever get too close, we'll be fine. Must be a coincidence he's out here."

She shook her head, tortured by the consequences of her moment of weakness and the phone call to her mother from the Arizona hotel.

"I don't think it's a coincidence. I think he…shit, Clyde, it's my fault."

He gave her a curious look, and then slipped on his shoulder holster and twin .45s. "Maybe you'd best tell me what's going on."

Bonnie was on the verge of tears. "I didn't mean to sell us out. I just wanted to hear her voice."

"Who's voice?"

"My momma," she said.

"Oh, Bon," he said quietly, drawing her into his arms. "What have you done?"

"I called her. I know I shouldn't have. But I just wanted to hear her, to know she was okay." Her words picked up speed, carried along by a flash flood of emotions tumbling down a once-dry riverbed and uprooting everything in their path. "I didn't say anything, not a word, but I think she knew, and I think Hank Black was in her house. He took the phone from her. Somehow, he traced it back to that hotel, that La Posada place. He must have stayed on the line until the operator came back on."

Clyde stroked her hair, trying to calm her. "Even if he did go to the hotel, he wouldn't be able to track us down here." And then he paused, and his face took on a grim expression. "That damn map," he said.

"What map?"

"The one where we traced out our route from La Posada to Boulder City," he said.

"Isn't it in the car?"

"No, I never found it and you were sleeping so I just flipped a coin and turned right at Kingman. Luckily, the coin fell our way."

"I must have left the map at the hotel," she whispered. "He's like a goddamn hell hound when it comes to tracking. He knows I called my momma from the hotel and now he's here. Clyde, I'm so sorry."

"But Bon, he don't know our names. There's a whole city full of people here. He'll have to spend some time snooping around."

"No," she said. "We have to get out of here. We have to pack up and leave tonight. I don't want to be the ruin of us, of this second chance. Let's just get in the car and get the hell out of here before we wind up in a real ambush."

"But I just got promoted," he said, his face dropping. Bonnie could not believe what she just heard. She stared wordlessly at Clyde, and then he started laughing. "Gotcha!" he said, slapping his knee.

She punched him in the arm.

"You're right, leaving is the smart play," he said. "We can tell Sal our covers might be blown. If anything, she's the understanding sort."

"If that woman does anything to my family, I swear by all that's holy I'll put her in the ground and burn Texas down until they're free," Bonnie said.

"We busted folks out of the pokey once, we'll do it again if it comes to that, but for now, let's think for once instead of just reacting."

A hurried knock on the front door startled them both.

"So much for that plan," Clyde said.

Bonnie slipped a gun from Clyde's holster and cocked the hammer, and he swung the BAR up off the bed and flicked off the safety.

"We may have to dangle," he said. "Keys are in the car, we'll make a run for it. Don't stop, no matter what happens."

She nodded and they cautiously approached the front door, guns leveled, and then she jerked it wide open. Clyde swung the heavy gun up, but it was Claudette— frantic and frazzled, almost hysterical.

"There's been an accident. Jimmy's hurt real bad," Claudette said.

Clyde hid the gun in the broom closet and took the pistol out of Bonnie's hand as she hugged Claudette with one arm.

Claudette sobbed. "He may not make it."

"Oh, honey, where is he?" Bonnie asked, holding her hand.

"He's in the hospital, on the other side of town. A bunch of guys got hurt. The brakes went out on the transport bus."

Clyde's jaw tightened and he pulled his jacket on over his guns. "Let's go see him."

"What about that other thing, the thing we were just talking about?" Bonnie asked.

Clyde tapped his shoulder holster. "I like Jimmy, and this puts me in a rotten mood. If anything comes up, I'll take care of it permanent like."

A feeling of dread passed over Bonnie, and she wondered if there really were no second chances in life, that they were simply put on this earth to kill or be killed, and that fate could never be outrun.

CHAPTER 31

Hanging by a thread

The Boulder City Hospital was just south of chaos. A dozen men stretched out on medical cots, and a half a dozen more sat in chairs, or else walked around dazed. Four were not so lucky—their bodies were under sheets. A call went out to Las Vegas and beyond for all the medical staff they could muster, to help the overwhelmed doctors and nurses onsite at the hospital.

Clyde saw Dino, his right arm in a splint, and put his hand on his good shoulder. "Dino, what happened?"

"A bus crashed."

"And all you broke was your arm?" Clyde asked, looking around at the injured and dead. "You're one lucky son of a biscuit."

"Nah, I wasn't in the crash. I got hurt earlier in the day, in the supply room by the pay house. Someone must've been monkeying with the shelves. I went to grab a bucket of tar this morning and the whole thing collapsed on top of me. I'll be fine, but the same can't be said for some of these poor saps."

"What about Jimmy?"

Dino tipped his head toward a room at the end of the hall. Jimmy was in a bed near the back, head wrapped in bandages, face swollen and bruised, blood seeping from gauze wrapped around his upper arm. Claudette, at the sight of him, let out a choking gasp and fell to her knees beside the bed, laying her hands on his chest.

At the sound of her voice, Jimmy struggled to open his eyes and tried to smile. "Claudette," he whispered, with great difficulty. "Sorry to put you through this."

She took his good hand, tears dripping down her cheeks. "Don't you dare worry about me right now," she said. Bonnie dragged a chair around so Claudette could sit next to him, and then stood behind her, hands resting on Claudette's shoulders.

"What happened?" Clyde asked.

"I don't rightly know," Jimmy said, haltingly. "One minute we were driving down south of the generator houses, heading down that big hill toward the mix plant, and then it just didn't stop, the driver yelled that he didn't have no brakes. Did his best, but it tipped over at that last little hairpin turn. You know the turn, the tight one."

Clyde nodded. "Yeah, I know that turn real well."

"I jumped out just before it tumbled over, but most of these guys weren't so lucky," Jimmy said.

Jimmy coughed and winced at the pain, then slipped into unconsciousness. Claudette closed her eyes too, holding back the wail that wanted to be released from deep in her heart.

"He's going to get through this," Bonnie said.

"How could you possibly know that?" Claudette asked, tortured but desperate for hope.

"I've been around the dying," Bonnie said. "More than you might expect. He's a long way from that. Jimmy's tough, and he's got you to help him pull through."

When Jimmy opened his eyes again, Clyde leaned in close. "Jimmy, we're going to go take a look at the truck and make sure this was an accident. Anything you want to tell us in the meantime? Like who is behind all this sabotaging nonsense?"

"I don't know nothing about that, Clarence. But if I don't make it, will you make sure my momma gets my last paycheck?"

"You're gonna be fine. Pretty sure Claudette wouldn't have it any other way."

He nodded to Bonnie and she hugged Claudette and then they left the hospital.

"What are you thinking?" Bonnie asked.

"That somebody cut the brakes," Clyde said. "And since them old boys from Las Vegas already tried it on me once, I'm a little suspicious that maybe they ain't relying on us near as much as we'd hoped. Maybe that little dance from Calhoun up at his club was just to throw us off on the scent, keep us out of the way."

They drove the long way around to the bottom of the crash site, turning off the headlights and taking the last part slowly and with the door open as Clyde navigated the road as much by memory as sight.

"I'm glad I can't see right now," Bonnie whispered, staring stone-faced into the darkness.

"We'll be fine," he said, watching the texture of the road. "I've drove up and down this old thing near fifty times this week, I could probably drive it with my eyes closed."

"Don't you dare close your eyes," she said.

"That last little hairpin turn is up ahead," he said. "Let's park here and walk the rest of the way so we don't end up trapped."

He pulled the car out of sight behind a mound of gravel and they walked the last half mile down to the wrecked transport bus.

It was late and dark and no one was around the crash area, although the spotlights from the construction crews working even now at this late hour at the south side of the dam lit up the far canyon wall like a theatrical spectacle.

The bus was mangled and scorched from a fire that warped the hood and damaged the interior. The stumps of a few emergency flares sputtered, casting flickering shadows on the rock wall behind the wreckage.

"Jesus," Clyde said. "It's a wonder anybody made it out of this alive."

The metal was still hot to the touch and shooting off steam from the drenching it got from fire hoses. Clyde pulled out a flashlight, got down on his back and scooted under the wheel well as best he could, coughing and waving away the smoke. Bonnie nervously watched the road and strained to listen into the darkness.

"It's a mess under here," he said. "But it sure looks like the brakes were cut."

"Clyde," she whispered. "A car's coming."

He pulled himself back out and sat up, watching as headlights flashed up over the rock walls and the sound of a motor drowned out the constant hum of machinery at the dam site. "It's okay," he said. "I'm boss over vehicles now. I should be here." He crawled out and stood in front of the approaching car, shielding his eyes from the glare. The car came to a stop at the bottom of the winding canyon road, below the spot where Clyde had hidden their car.

"What the hell are you doing?" a voice called out, a decidedly southern voice. "This is an active investigation scene, boy. Come away from there."

Clyde was about to call out, when the man moved in front of the lights and they could make out the silhouette of a cowboy hat.

"Shit," Bonnie said. "It's Hank Black." She shrank back behind the bus.

"Who is that with you?" Black yelled.

Clyde killed his flashlight and scrambled behind the banged-up bus too. "Dammit, the one person in the entire world who don't care that I just got a promotion."

"I am Hank Black," the man yelled. "I'm a Texas Ranger and a duly sworn officer of the security forces, here by the authority of the Six Companies and the Bureau of Reclamation. You come out here right now, or I'll assume you are acting with hostile intent."

There was a long pause and then the cock of a gun hammer. "Have it your way."

"We've got to get around him and back up to our car, otherwise we're going to be trapped down here in the canyon," Bonnie said.

"Guess we have to kill him," Clyde said, reaching for his .45. "Don't see no other choice."

"No, we're not killing him," Bonnie said. "Not unless it comes right down to it."

"Why not? He sure didn't mind killing us when he had the chance," Clyde said, pushing his gun back in place. "The papers said they shot two hundred rounds into our car without so much as a how-do-you-do."

"Two wrongs don't make a right," she said. "You've been working here long enough to know the lay of this land. How can we get past his car?"

He thought about the topography of the canyon in this section. "There's a ledge about twenty feet straight up above us, ain't more than six inches wide, built years ago by the money boys when they were blowing rock. Still got the cables hanging from it. If we get up there to the ledge, it'll cut right across to where our car is parked."

"Let's get going then," she said.

"There's two problems," he said. "We need to make sure his car stays put."

"I didn't say you couldn't kill his car. What's the second problem?"

"You know I ain't real good with heights. And there's one stretch where a ledge crosses a drop off of at least a hundred feet."

"Don't make me come over there," Black yelled. "I've got a shotgun and plenty of ammo, and you ain't going nowhere. I can wait here all night if I need to. And I reckon Chief Hoskins will be along soon enough to check on me."

"We can't be sitting here when the sun comes up," Bonnie said. "And you can't tell me that the man who played baseball with a grenade is too much of scaredy-cat to stand on top of a little old wall."

"I'm fine with being up high," Clyde said, "And I ain't even afraid of falling. That's just like flying, and who don't like that? It's the landing I take issue with."

"Come on, tough guy," she said. "Take me for a dangle."

Clyde pulled one of his .45s, aimed at the car and emptied the clip in rapid sequence. Black swore and ducked down as bullets shattered his headlights and cast the scene in darkness. In the ringing silence, they heard the ratchet of a shotgun and ducked down behind the wreck as he shot in their direction. The big gun belched out a tongue of fire and sent a spray of buckshot clattering around them.

Black shot four more times then, swearing and muttering, paused to reload.

"Now, "Clyde whispered and they ran toward the canyon wall behind them. It was pitch black and he had to pat around until he found a cable leading up into the darkness. He gave it a yank to make sure it would hold, and then put Bonnie's hand on it.

"Use the cable to crawl up on my shoulders and pull yourself up until you get to the ledge," he whispered. "Then grab ahold of the anchor line drilled across the whole wall and wait until I can get up there."

She clambered up, with Clyde helping to push, caressing her bottom as she passed. She swatted at his hand, then hoisted herself onto the thin ledge, gripping the anchor rope for dear life.

He joined her minutes later. He could barely make out her face, worried but fixed with that peculiar look of defiance and determination she always wore when things got tough.

"We just got to stick to the wall here, take it nice and slow, and make our way past one tricky part where the road curves around," he said. "Like I said, it's a pretty big drop, but it won't look like nothing in the dark."

She nodded and, hugging the wall, inched her way forward. Clyde, distracted by concerns about her safety, was able to fight back the instincts screaming in his gut to freeze, motionless. Below them, the beam of a flashlight cut through the night as Black moved closer to the wrecked bus. He was shouting and shooting, cautiously moving forward.

As they inched along in the darkness, trying not dislodge any stones to alert Black that his quarry was above him, Bonnie paused.

"I think we got this," she whispered.

"Just be careful," he said. "We're at the worst stretch now. One wrong step and there won't even be enough of you left to bury."

"Worry about your own self," she said. A rock rolled out from under her foot and she tugged at the anchor line to steady herself, but it pulled free.

With a choking cry, she fell into the darkness, taking one last, lonely look at Clyde.

CHAPTER 32

Interviewing ghosts

"Bonnie, are you there?"

Royce tapped on the front door again and when she still didn't answer, he walked back to the greenhouse out back. He heard music through the open door. He knocked and called out.

"Come on in," she said. She sat facing the door at a card table, her pen poised over a notebook. A pot of tea and a cup were on one side of the table and a small automatic handgun on the other.

He pointed at the gun. "Expecting trouble?"

"I never stopped expecting it," she said. "But after your phone call, I figured it was time to be a bit more mindful."

Royce pulled up a chair. "What are you writing?"

She closed the book and smiled. "Poetry. You'll forgive an old woman her indulgences."

"Oh, that's right," he said, pulling out his own notebook and the recorder. "You wrote poetry. Write poetry, I should say."

"Kept me occupied all these years," she said. "I've probably got a hundred journals by this point."

"Are you any good?"

"Not in the least," she said. "I was terrible then, and only barely improved all these years later. I even joined a writer's group, but it just makes me realize how sad and pathetic writers are."

"I'd take offense, but you're right, of course. Would you let me take a look? One writer to another."

She flipped the notebook open and turned it around. "Be kind."

"When you are out of road," he started to read, but she raised her hand.

"Read it out loud and I'll shoot you in the arm."

He laughed, hoping she was kidding. He scanned the lines. "It's really good. Once we get your story told, you should think about publishing some of these."

"That is never going to happen," she said, reaching across the table and catching his arm, her grip tighter than he expected. Her eyes blazed. "You promise me right now, Royce Jenkins, you promise me that you'll burn every goddamn one of these journals when I'm gone. I don't care if you read them, but they're private—between me and Clyde."

He nodded. "Okay, I will. No problem. I promise."

"Sorry," she said, leaning back. "It's just that some of it is personal and kind of weepy and dumb, especially after Clyde got shot and landed in that wheelchair. It sort of took the starch out of both of us for a while." She took a sip of tea.

Royce turned on the tape recorder. "Do you want to talk about that now? How he ended up in a wheelchair, I mean."

Bonnie took a sip of her tea. "No. I want to keep things in the right order. Turn that off for a minute and tell me what happened after New York."

Royce pulled the photos of the ring from his satchel, filled her in on the details of his visit to Solomon Jewelers, and then showed her the photo he slipped off the old jeweler's wall in Chicago.

"They look young and sweet and in love. You think they're the ones that died in the car?"

Royce nodded.

She sighed, and leaned back into her chair, handing the photo back to him. "You'll figure out who they were and how they came to be in that car?"

"I'll do my best."

"Do it faster," she said. "The fact that you kicked over some rocks and snakes are slithering out means we're running out of time. Anything happens to me, you'll have what you need to tell the story. But I want to make amends for what happened to those two kids while I'm still alive and kicking."

Royce flipped open his notebook. "Speaking of that, the last time we talked, you had just fallen off a cliff face in the dark. What happened?"

"I died, of course," she said. "You're interviewing a ghost."

Then she laughed, and Royce wondered how such a tiny old woman could laugh with such depth and percussion and joy.

He supposed that, just like the saying went, everyone gets the face they deserve in old age—the years etching, in wrinkles, a roadmap to a life's experiences. So too, it seemed, one got the laugh they deserved. It was a retrospective that revealed, in tones, how much you compromised and how much life beat you down or, conversely, how much you extracted from it.

Bonnie's laugh revealed, he realized, a woman who lived—if nothing else for all those years—true to herself, and to Clyde.

He wondered what his own laugh would be like when he was rounding the bend to eighty years old.

CHAPTER 33

Head over heels

As Bonnie fell into the darkness, time slowed to a crawl and the air beneath her felt thick, like old cotton candy. An image of her mother flashed before her eyes, sitting by her bed when Bonnie was little and had the croup, singing her a sweet, comforting lullaby.

And then, without conscious control or regret, Bonnie let go of her life, and in that instant, was catapulted outside of herself, watching her body fall into the darkness—hands reaching toward Clyde—and already thinking it was probably for the best.

Her life on the road rushed before her eyes, and she felt peaceful thinking about the love they shared, felt buoyed by how many folks had seen them as something special, but saw as well the anguish they caused through the years, and then heard a clear voice saying it was not her time, her purpose had not been realized, yet.

All that happened in the space of seconds.

Then something bit into her ankle and pinned her in midair, arresting the fall and transferring all that force into pain that swung her upside down and into the rock face.

The back of her head bounced off the canyon wall, her vision flared with red comets and yellow sparklers. She was upside down, her left leg stretched to the point it seemed ready to tear loose from her hip socket.

"Bonnie!" Clyde yelled, and she heard the primal fear in his voice, the melody of panic.

"Clyde," she said, trying to keep her voice low as she got her bearings. "I'm mostly all right, but I'm in a bit of a pickle."

"What's happening?" he yelled, the panic still flooding his voice.

She watched the bobbing beam of Black's flashlight as he looked around the wreckage for them. "I'm tangled up in something, and I don't know how long it's going to hold." She felt around in the dark. "Some kind of metal net."

"It's the wire netting to keep the rocks from falling onto the road," Clyde said. He held on to one of the cables and tipped out over the ledge, trying to locate her by the sound of her voice.

"I hear you, you sons of bitches," Black called from below. "Where the hell are you?" He swept the flashlight across the rocks. Luckily, the beam traveled below them, but they both knew Black wouldn't give up.

"I'm going to try to get myself right side up," she said.

She wrapped her fingers around the netting, the wire digging into her flesh, and pulled herself up, straining her stomach muscles until she was curled up on the side of the cliff like a pill bug. She carefully freed her trapped ankle and, holding tight to the netting, repositioned herself, digging the tips of her shoes into the mesh.

"I can't see you," Clyde said. "Keep talking so I can get down to you."

"What should I talk about?" One of the wires she was standing on snapped, and she dropped down several inches. "The wires are breaking," she said. "Should I talk about that?"

Clyde yanked on the old cable to test it. Satisfied, he twined it around his waist and started lowering himself down the rock face.

"Hold on, Bon," he said. "I'm coming." They were sitting ducks for Hank Black if he saw them, but there was no going back now.

Another square of wire broke, this time in her left hand and she struggled to keep her balance while scrabbling to find a new grip. "Hurry, Clyde. This whole damn thing is starting to unravel."

"I still can't see you," Clyde said, lowering himself farther down. "We got one chance," he said. "Your lighter."

"He'll see us."

"Me and that bastard will each have one shot. I bet I can get ahold of you faster than he can pull the trigger."

Another length of wire broke under her foot, and her leg scraped down the cliff. She fumbled in her jacket pocket for the lighter. "You ready?"

"As I'll ever be."

She flicked the flame to life. Three things happened almost simultaneously: down on the canyon floor, a gun roared; under Bonnie's feet, the wire snapped and—still holding the lighter—she began to fall again; Clyde ran sideways down the rock wall and kicked off hard with both legs, swinging out into space then curving around.

The lighter blinked out, shotgun pellets peppered the wall below them and Clyde collided with Bonnie, catching her in his open arm.

She hugged on tight as he let the momentum swing them up toward the ledge. More gunshots echoed up and down the canyon, and distant, muffled swearing, but it was dark again and they were safe.

Holding on to the guideline, he kept his arm around her waist. "Baby, are you all right?"

"I'm a little banged up," she said.

His hands shook from the strain of holding them both and from the fear of losing her to gravity.

After pulling her back onto the ledge, they traversed the rest of the way quickly and quietly, leaving a cursing, mumbling Hank Black behind still scouring the darkness. Back near the mound of gravel, the ledge petered out onto the level ground of the canyon road and they hurried to the car.

"Another daring escape," she said as he turned over the ignition and roared off toward town. "I thought you were afraid of heights, but you were swinging around up there like a Flying Wallenda."

He puffed out his chest a little. "I guess heights ain't as scary when you can't see how far you'll fall."

CHAPTER 34

The most important meal

When the alarm went off, Clyde groaned, every muscle aching from the effort of holding them against the cliff the night before. "Throw that goddamn thing against the wall for me. I'm too tired to do it myself."

Bonnie wasn't feeling much better. Her banged up head pounded and the muscles in her leg felt like they'd been doused in kerosene and set on fire. "Don't you dare break Claudette's clock."

He yawned and sat up, then slowly, methodically bashed the clock into the top of the dresser. "We'll buy her a new one. We still have stacks of money from the payroll heist."

Clyde stretched, winced at the pain in his shoulders, and then scratched his stomach and watched as Bonnie walked to the kitchen.

"Besides, we're done now," he said. "We know for sure the mob is behind the sabotage since they cut the brakes. I say we pack up the guns and loot, head to Las Vegas and put a bullet in Calhoun's head—and anybody else who looks cross ways at us—then get on back down to Mexico. Case closed." He stood up and peeked out the window.

Bonnie gripped the side of the table and fought against the nausea from her headache. A wave of dizziness washed over her and she thought back on that instant, convinced she was falling to her death, when she was jolted outside of her own body. She still didn't know what the hell that was all about, but it filled her with a calm certainty about what came next.

She took a deep breath and steadied herself, filling the coffee pot with water. "Something still doesn't smell right. The mob might be behind it, but I'm not quite ready to declare them our only suspect."

"Listen to you, Nancy Drew," he said, turning around, standing to look out the window. "Hank Black on our tail and me working myself to death, and you want to take your sweet time."

She started the coffee percolating on the stove, then rummaged around in the cupboards.

"There's not much for breakfast," she said. "Some cornflakes, but they're pretty old. I think they might have been left behind. And we're out of milk. And pretty much everything else. But we have some orangeade. Pour some orangeade on the flakes, maybe?"

"Let's walk down the store and buy a couple hardboiled eggs and a loaf of bread and anything else that sounds good. Be a shame to let all that money go to waste right before we crack this case wide open. And we can see how Jimmy is doing," Clyde said.

"Look at all the things we get done when you get out of bed on time," she said.

Later, holding hands, they neared the hospital and tensed when a man stepped out of the shadows and whistled. "Psst, Prentiss." Lefty gestured at Clyde.

"Son of a bitch," Clyde murmured. "I'm gonna fix his wagon."

"Hold on," Bonnie said, squeezing his arm. "I'm not sure running off half-cocked makes the most sense."

"I'm fully-cocked. Hell, I'm double-cocked. Those bastards shouldn't have hurt Jimmy, or any of those men on that transport bus."

Bonnie put her hand on his arm, felt the muscles clenched tighter than the steel cables they'd been dangling from the night before. "Let's get all the facts before we jump ahead to the reckoning," she said. "And make sure we have a play before you start swinging."

"Prentiss, seriously," Lefty hissed. "Stop fussing around with the skirt. This is serious."

"Skirt?" she said, spitting the word out. "Oh, we'll fix his wagon all right. Fix it but good. Soon as we can."

They walked up to Lefty and he looked around nervously. "Mr. Calhoun wants to see you. Right now."

"What the hell were you thinking?" Clyde asked, jaw clenched. "You were supposed to run things through us before you did any more damage."

"That was your misunderstanding then," Lefty said.

"People got hurt," Clyde said. "People I call friends."

"And he doesn't make friends easily," Bonnie said. "So, that's kind of a big deal."

"We'll spring for a nice bouquet," Lefty said.

Clyde balled his fist up and Bonnie caught it in her hand, holding it tight to her side.

"Like I said, Mr. Calhoun wants to see you, which is also kind of a big deal," Lefty said. "And he don't ever make friends. Just business acquaintances, and also corpses. You should be honored to be in the former category. For the time being."

"We're kind of busy, you know, punching the clock."

"Here's the thing," Lefty said. "Mr. Calhoun is at the Crossroads Diner up the road. He'll be there for an hour.

If you get there before he leaves, he'll pitch an idea to you. If you're not, well, we'll assume you no longer want to be acquaintances."

"We'll be there," Bonnie said.

They watched him leave.

"I guess this is as good a time as any to get them all in one place and close this down for good," Clyde said. "But how we gonna get out of going to work so's we can hear him out?"

"I can weasel out of my job if you can weasel out of yours," she said.

"I guess I need to check on a new truck in Las Vegas," Clyde said.

"And I'm having lady problems again," she said.

Twenty minutes later, they pulled up to the Crossroads Diner. There was one other car in the parking lot.

Inside, Calhoun sat at a booth at the back. Lefty stood nearby with his hand in his jacket pocket. Three triggermen were strategically located, holding shotguns. The place was empty of patrons.

Clyde smelled something wonderful, maybe apple pies, coming from the ovens, but even with the heat from the kitchen, he kept on his jacket to hide the pair of .45s in his shoulder holster.

Bonnie had wrapped a lavender scarf around her neck, and clutched a little beaded purse with her favorite .25 auto in it, glad to be out of the office, thinking that even if the morning ended in gunfire, it was preferable to that monotony.

"Mrs. Prentiss, you look very fine," Calhoun said, again, not quite making direct eye contact with her. "Mr. Prentiss, glad you could make it as well."

Clyde slipped in beside Bonnie at the booth. "Mr. Calhoun, I have to say, I am a little disappointed to think you acted without warning me."

"Yes, about that," he said. "Plans were in motion and Lefty felt it prudent to not betray our confidences by introducing complexity."

"That complexity got some people hurt."

"From now on, you can run point," Calhoun said. "Slow the progress however you see fit," he said, drumming his fingertips on the table. "That is, if you see fit to help me this afternoon."

"What can we help you with?" Bonnie asked, hoping to get a bead on the full size of their operation.

"Unexpectedly, some business associates are arriving from Los Angeles after lunch," Calhoun said. "They are interested in investing in my little concern. And by that, I mean take it over. And I am not overly fond of partners."

"When it comes to unwanted suitors, I've found it helpful to firmly decline so as to clear up any confusion," Bonnie said.

"And if that don't help, busting them in the mouth with a hammer works too," Clyde said.

"I prefer a middle ground," Calhoun said. "The number of people I can trust with my life is currently limited to the people in this room, minus the waitress. I'd like to think our arrangement, our understanding, puts you both in that category as well."

"I'd feel a lot better about being on your payroll if you hadn't pulled that stunt at the job site," Clyde said. "And also, weren't threatening to turn us over to the coppers for the armored car heist."

"We'll give you five grand cold hard cash to side with us today."

"And breakfast," Bonnie said, thinking that Clyde was likely hungry. Calhoun looked at her curiously. "What?" she said. "We haven't eaten yet."

CHAPTER 35

Running out of gumption

"Who are these torpedoes you're expecting?" Clyde asked. He pushed away his plate, any trace of the three-egg farmer's breakfast sopped up by the fat piece of toast he just finished.

The diner was still empty—Calhoun made sure of it—and Lefty thumbed rounds into a spare clip for his .38 Super. "Have you ever heard of Murder, Incorporated?"

Bonnie watched the sun heat up the highway connecting Boulder City to Las Vegas, tapping cigarette ashes into the remains of her breakfast, a scooped-out half of a grapefruit. "Who hasn't? Contract killers. They operate on the east coast."

"Turns out they know how to buy airplane tickets, and apparently, are intrigued by the climate in Las Vegas," Lefty said.

"You boys seem tough enough, setting aside your little lady guns," Clyde said, eyeing the slim automatic in Lefty's hand. "Why take on Murder, Inc.?"

Calhoun nodded, and Lefty answered. "First, anybody who knows his way around heaters knows these little babies will punch holes right through bullet proof vests or car doors or anything," Lefty said. "Your big old forty-fives run out of gumption the second they encounter anything stout. Second, we're not taking on Murder, Inc. Mr. Calhoun wants to persuade them the stakes here are too low for them to bother."

"Who in their right mind would think the desert a place to linger and carouse?" Calhoun asked. "We will be doing our utmost to steer them toward that conclusion."

"And what will we be doing, Mr. C.?" Bonnie asked.

He tried to smile at the familiarity, but it came off as a grimace. "If they are interested in us, they have done their homework. They know my men, they know my town and they likely have sent an advance guard. They don't know either of you, however. You'll be following the proceedings from close by, and providing assistance, terminal assistance, should the need arise."

"Sounds very cautious of you," Clyde said.

"Let me be crystal clear, we only need your assistance if a threat is imminent," Calhoun said. "The last thing we need is negative attention from the least ethically-constrained and most enthusiastic group of professional murderers in the country."

"Count on us to be quiet like little armed church mice," Bonnie said.

"We meet them at the Boulder Rapids in two hours," he said. "Wait fifteen minutes here, then follow us into town and act like you are there to gamble." He slid an envelope across the table. "Here's your payment and enough cash to spend some time in the casino without dipping into your pay."

"You're assuming we won't win," Clyde said.

"The house always wins, Mr. Prentiss," Calhoun said.

"I wouldn't bet against us, Mr. Calhoun," Clyde said.

Two hours later, Bonnie and Clyde sat at the bar in the Boulder Rapids with a beer and a gin fizz.

"How do you think we should play this?" Clyde asked, wiping some dark smudges of grease from his hand onto a crisp white linen napkin.

She looked at his hands curiously.

"I had trouble parking the car after I dropped you off," he said.

She took a sip of her drink. "If we want the sabotage to stop, we need Calhoun and all his mob boys run out of town. To do that, we need the Murder, Inc. goons to put the whole operation in their sights."

"They have to think this place is already turning a profit, the opposite of what Calhoun wants," he said.

She nodded. "I have a plan."

"That brain of yours is something special to behold," Clyde said, leaning across and kissing her, letting his hand snake down to her waist and lower. "And that behind of yours is something special to hold."

She ran her hand up his neck, almost dislodging his fedora, pulling him in close until the heat sucked the breath out of them both.

"You see that old fellow down there at the end of the bar, right?" she whispered in his ear.

"The one that looks hard as a six-penny nail? Yeah, I saw him."

Bonnie sat back and smoothed her hair. "He sure ain't here for the gambling or the girls or the drinking. Hasn't taken so much as one sip of that beer. Does he strike you as a local or a tourist?"

"Pretty sure that's a plane ticket sticking up out of his jacket pocket. Right next to the bulge from a heater."

"He's from Murder, Inc.," she said, whispering again in Clyde's ear. He grinned and pulled out the envelope with the cash and ripped it open so the money was visible.

"Now we wait for Calhoun and the rest of the Murder, Inc. goons to walk by and make our play," she said.

Clyde, watching the upstairs railing in the bar mirror, tilted his head. "Won't be waiting long. Here they come."

Bonnie looked in the mirror behind the bar and saw Calhoun and Lefty, along with three well-dressed men, their eyes darting left and right as they descended the stairs. "Show time." She sauntered toward the end of the bar where the muscle sat, Clyde a few steps behind.

"Hey there, handsome, looking for a good time?" she asked the man.

He looked up, caught off guard, and clipped out a response. "Beat it, sister, I'm on the clock."

"You don't know what you're missing," Bonnie said with a pout, then sashayed off.

Clyde, using her distraction as a screen, tossed the envelope full of money on the bar and then motioned the bartender over.

"You got today's take?" Clyde asked the bartender loudly.

The muscle man perked up and watched the interaction surreptitiously as Clyde picked up the envelope and fanned through the cash. "Seems light," Clyde said.

"I don't know what's going on," the bartender stammered, looking nervously in Calhoun's direction.

"Well, I'll just have to talk to Mr. Calhoun about that," Clyde said. He put the money in his pocket and then, turning to go, bumped into the man on the barstool hard enough to jolt him to his feet.

"Watch it, pal," the man snarled, reaching instinctively for the gun in his shoulder holster.

"Mr. Calhoun, he's got a gun," Clyde shouted, causing Calhoun and the group to pause in the middle of the casino floor. Clyde snatched a whiskey bottle from the bar and crashed it over the man's head, but not hard enough to do any lasting damage. The man staggered and dropped to his knees.

"It's a set up," the man yelled as he fell. "They're setting us up. This place is flush." He fumbled for his gun but Clyde kicked it out his hand.

Bonnie slipped her little .25 out. "Don't worry, Mr. Calhoun, we'll take care of these big city Brunos." She popped off six rounds at the three men, aiming wide intentionally, and the men scattered and drew .45s.

"No, no, no," Calhoun yelled. "You got it all wrong."

Another hired gun from Murder, Inc. stood up in the back of the room, pulling a Tommy gun out from under the table.

He began spraying bullets toward Calhoun, the heavy slugs chewing up the felt tables and sending card-players and gamblers under the tables and cards and poker chips flying.

One of Calhoun's men took a slug in the ass, another in the arm. Lefty dragged Calhoun to the ground. Clyde caught Bonnie by the hand and, ducking low, they ran toward the door.

Outside on the street, people crouched and hid in doorways. Clyde jerked the car door open and Bonnie dove inside and then he hopped across the hood and slid behind the wheel. As he ground the key to start it, the front door of the club burst open and Lefty, a splatter of blood on his cheek, caught sight of them. He glowered and swapped out a clip in his .38 Super.

"Shit," Clyde said. "That's the hot little shooter he's so proud of. It'll zip right through the doorframe. We need to scoot."

"You sold us out, Prentiss," Lefty yelled. "But by god, we'll punch your ticket before Murder, Inc. takes over this town."

He ran toward the car, arm outstretched and the pistol blossoming flashes as a full clip of bullets zinged toward Bonnie and Clyde.

Clyde draped himself over her as the rounds shattered the windows and cored through the back door and fenders.

Clyde, swearing, threw the car in reverse and tromped on the gas. It crashed into the car behind them and, engine still whining, he slammed it into drive and hit the car in front, dislodging the fender in the process.

"Stay down," he yelled at Bonnie and ground the gears into reverse again.

With a roar, Lefty towered in the window, gun extended. "Just tell me why, Prentiss. Tell me why you had to fuck up everything before I put a bullet in you?"

Clyde glared up at him, right into the barrel of the gun. "Because your last little stunt put a friend and a bunch of other men in the hospital."

"From a falling shelf?" Lefty asked.

"No, from cutting the brakes on the transport rig!"

"We didn't touch the fucking brakes," Lefty said.

"Really," Clyde said with a grin. "This was all a terrible misunderstanding then."

"And your death warrant," Lefty said, squeezing the trigger.

There was a deafening roar and Lefty staggered back a half step, his gun discharging into the sidewalk. Clyde looked down to see Bonnie holding one of Clyde's .45s, smoke curling out of the barrel and through a hole shot through the door. The big slug grazed Lefty's thigh and spun him sideways.

"Guess my forty-five was up to the task after all," Clyde said as he stomped on the accelerator and squealed backward out into the street.

Lefty fell to the ground, and started shooting again from the sidewalk, the high-speed slugs punching through the glass and the seat. Clyde felt a burning sizzle and swore as blood sprayed the inside of the driver's window.

"Oh god, baby, you're hit," Bonnie said.

CHAPTER 36

Splattered

Royce held a dusky copy of a microfiche article from a Dallas newspaper dated June 1934. The headline read: *Young Couple Missing, Feared Victims of Foul Play.* Royce stared at the grainy black and white photo of a man and woman, smiling, attractive, in their twenties.

He compared the photo to the framed one he lifted from the ancient jeweler in Chicago. There was no doubt it was the same man and woman. Their resemblance to Bonnie and Clyde in their day was noticeable, but not overwhelming.

"I have more," Terrence said.

"Of course, you do. What else did you find out, kid?"

He wondered how the hell the intern managed to keep those white shirts so crisp. The benefits, he guessed, of still living at home with Mom. Terrence handed him the folder, and Royce tossed it unopened on the desk. "It looks long, and also boring. Summarize it for me."

"Yes, sir," Terrence said, a flush of pride coloring his voice. "The woman is, was, Samantha Ebbon. Went by Sam."

That fits, Royce thought, with what the old jeweler half remembered. A man's name, he said.

"What about the fellow?"

"Roy Spinner. College sweethearts, engaged to be married. It was announced in the papers. They met at Louisiana State University sometime in the early 1930s. Birth records show Samantha was born here, of all places, in Lubbock, and his family was from Chicago. Both lived in Dallas after college, but went missing in May 1934."

"Any speculation about what happened?"

"Very little, except for one Dallas neighbor saying they eloped, on account of the family of Miss Ebbon being none too happy about the match," Terrence said. He cleared his throat. "Apparently, Roy had some trouble with the law. I found some police reports, it was mostly small time stuff, stealing and fighting."

"Where were they last seen?"

"I couldn't find anything about that," Terrence said.

"Where are the families now?" Royce asked.

"There's no trace of the Spinner family, although I have calls out to the Chicago newspapers," Terrence said. "But the Ebbon family is still here in Lubbock."

"Ah, Royce, you do still work here," Larry said, leaving his office to lean against the door sill. "I was thinking about giving young Terrence here your job for good. What's so all-fired important about the Ebbon family?"

"You know them?" Royce asked.

"I do, and so do you. Well, at least one of them," Larry said.

"I don't think so," Royce said, searching his memory.

Larry smiled. "Sure, you do. Remember that art show you wrote up a couple years ago, the artist working over in the restored railroad depot?"

"The one with the terrible drip painting art? Her name wasn't Ebbon."

"Nope, but her mother was an Ebbon before she married," Larry said. "Her name is Lisa Devlin. A real pretty gal, if I remember correctly. And I'm sure she remembers you."

Royce remembered her well. She was a knockout, but she rubbed him the wrong way—came off as arrogant and a little pretentious. He might have let some of that come out in the article. Her father was a big shot and he raised high, holy hell. Larry took Royce off the art beat after that.

"What's so important about the Ebbon family? And can I come along just to see the look on her face when you show up again?" Larry asked.

"No," Royce said. "But if I'm not back in two hours, tell my sister she can have all of my stuff. Except for my girlie magazines, which I bequeath to you, Terrence."

Twenty minutes later, Royce pulled up to a two-story brick building, an old depot—the only occupied building in a warren of abandoned warehouses on either side of a set of rusty train tracks.

No one answered his knock. He slid open the unlocked hanging wooden door, and walked down the corridor.

Lisa Devlin's studio was at the far end of the building. The door was cracked open and he walked in. She was bent over a car windshield propped up on wooden sawhorses. Dozens of open cans of paint lined the floor around her. The old walls of the depot were busted down, sunlight poured through skylights into the cavernous room. Pink Floyd blared out of a boom box.

She had her back to him, swaying to the music, her long brown hair pulled into a ponytail. The windshield was spattered with drips of red and orange paint, and the legs, arms and hairless heads of plastic dolls were pasted around its jagged edge.

The music was so loud, she didn't hear him call to her, so he walked closer and tapped her shoulder. Startled, she spun around, paintbrush in her hand, and whipped streams of red paint across his face and shoulders.

"Crap," she said. Globs of paint dripped off his face and, as she stood there, from the brush onto the tips of his cowboy boots. She dropped the brush to the floor, grabbed him by the hand and led him into a side room with a battered old ceramic work sink.

"I'm sorry." She handed him a towel. It smelled of turpentine. "Oil paint, tough to get off," she said, matter-of-factly.

Lisa pointed to a grimy mirror above the sink. He rubbed his face with the towel, and got some of the paint off but smeared more of it in deeper. In the reflection, behind him, Royce watched as she tilted her head to the right. And then to the left.

From the counter, she grabbed a Polaroid camera, holding it up. "Do you mind?"

Without waiting for an answer, she began taking photos, getting close to his face, then his collar, as the camera whirred and spit out image after image, and then she pointed the camera at his boots, where the red paint mixed with water and turpentine puddled.

Royce wasn't quite sure how to respond, so he just stood there.

"You look like a cowboy who's been attacked by a vampire," she said.

She lined the photos out on the counter and contemplated them. Royce continued toweling off the paint as best he could, waiting for her to finish with whatever artistic moment was possessing her. "Okay," she said, finally turning. "Why are you here?"

"You may not remember me, but I'm—"

"I remember you," she said. "Royce Jenkins. The handsome journalist. You wrote that god-awful article two years ago. Said I would fail, said the Lubbock Art Collective would fail."

"I'm sorry about that," he said. "Truly."

"Don't worry about it," she said. "You were half right. They say even bad publicity is good, and I suppose I owe you since your article did get the attention of some local artists. But it was a shitty article, and I assumed that's why you never showed your face here again, which is a shame."

He felt a prickle of heat blush through his cheeks. "I'm here on another story now."

"Yeah? What's that?" She held up the photo of the paint-splattered cowboy boots, scraped the still drying colors with her fingernail, examined the effect, opened the door and walked back into the studio. Royce followed her. The music was still blaring. There, she pasted the photo on the center of the windshield, next to a Barbie leg, and then softly hit it with a hammer so a slight crack formed around the image.

"It's about Samantha Ebbon," Royce yelled.

"Who?" she yelled back over the music.

"Samantha Ebbon!"

"My aunt?" Lisa looked up. She turned the music off. "Has there been a break in her case?"

"Maybe," he said.

"What have you found?"

"I can't say yet, but I promise you it's something real."

She studied his face, and Royce could tell she was sizing him up and wondering if he was worth trusting. She shrugged. "What do you want to know?"

"Did anyone ever hear from her again after May 1934?"

"No. She disappeared."

"The papers said she may have eloped," Royce said.

"I didn't know her, of course, but my mother was certain she wouldn't have left without any word. They were very close. My mother always said, to anyone who would listen, that her sister was murdered."

"What about the man, Roy? Was he a bad seed?"

"Things were rough in those days. There were no jobs. He made some mistakes, way I understand it, but who doesn't." When she tucked a flyaway strand of hair behind her ear. Royce's gaze unconsciously followed the trace of her finger. "His family never heard from him again either. One day, the two of them were in love and planning their wedding. The next day, they were just gone."

"Where were they last seen?"

"In Sailes. It was the summer, and Roy had a line on a job there. Aunt Samantha drove up to see him, and they never came back. Her car was found parked in the center of town. Nothing odd, no signs of foul play."

"In Sailes, Louisiana?" Royce asked. "Where Bonnie and Clyde were ambushed?"

"Yeah. And around the same time," Lisa said. "My mother said it made it harder to get anyone to pay attention to help find her sister. The town was all crazy because of the ambush and crowded with people. It wasn't until that all died down that anyone was willing to look into their disappearance."

Shit, this is it, he thought. This is fucking it.

"Okay, well, I think that gives me what I need," he said, masking his excitement. "Does your mother still live around here?"

"Yep, outside of town. Same little ranch house I grew up in. Dad died last year, but you knew that since you or someone in your office wrote his obituary. I've been trying to get Mom to move in with me, but she's stubborn. Likes her memories."

"I appreciate your time, you've really helped. Do you mind if I contact your mother?"

"There's a lot of hurt in my family about what happened, they never really got over it. My grandmother died a few years after Aunt Sam disappeared, of a broken heart, my mother always said. So, maybe don't visit my mother unless you have something concrete."

Royce nodded. "Hey, if you don't mind me asking, how is it that you got enough money to buy this place here?"

"I'm a classic trust fund baby," she said, putting her hand on her hip.

"Really? How did your family make their money?"

"We didn't. My family has been the recipient of a monthly stipend from an anonymous benefactor going on fifty years now."

"Anonymous?"

"Lucky for me they just keep doling out the money."

"You don't find it odd that the mysterious money started rolling in about the time your aunt disappeared?"

"Of course, but after hiring too many detectives to count, we finally gave up. Don't really give it much thought anymore," she said. "Even the fund administrators say they have no idea where the money comes from."

"Who administers the fund?"

"The National Grange," she said. "Heard of them?"

CHAPTER 37

Off the rails

"Son of a bitch, I think he shot my ear off," Clyde said. He had one hand clapped over his ear, blood seeping between his fingers and running down his neck onto the starched collar of his only white shirt. The other hand was on the steering wheel, eyes glued to the rearview mirror as they rocketed down Fremont Street backward.

"Let me see," Bonnie said, pulling his hand away and leaning around to look. She winced. "It's not so bad, just the lobe. But you're bleeding like a stuck pig. You keep losing parts of yourself on every mission, pretty soon there won't be enough left for the spying."

"If we don't shake them gunsels, they're gonna put paid to our future as government agents," he said, gritting his teeth as she pressed a clean handkerchief to the wound.

Calhoun and two others stumbled out the front door of the Boulder Rapids, shooting back inside at the killers from Murder, Inc. They saw Lefty on the sidewalk swapping out the clip in his gun and pointing angrily at Bonnie and Clyde, as they sped backward and away from the scene.

"You thinking about turning around any time soon?" Bonnie asked.

"Kind of like looking at who's chasing us," Clyde said, navigating backward past surprised drivers.

Calhoun and his men helped Lefty up, piled into their car and roared out in pursuit of the outlaws. Calhoun—his face twisted with rage—and another torpedo leaned out the passenger windows and fired at the retreating car. Bonnie and Clyde ducked as bullets slammed into the grill and windshield, and both front tires blew out with a pop.

Clyde kept his foot on the gas as they raced backward on the rims, creating a horrible screeching sound and leaving a trail of sparks skipping up behind them.

"Dammit," Bonnie said.

"Don't worry," Clyde said. "We've been in tougher spots than this."

"It's not that," Bonnie said. "It's just that if it wasn't the mob that cut those transport truck brakes, our days of working for a living aren't over yet."

"Nope," Clyde said, as he swerved into oncoming traffic—the drivers honking and swearing—on the main street. "Ain't that the damnedest thing? The anarchists in jail and the mob sidelined. Think Jimmy is good for it?"

Bonnie rolled her window down and emptied her .25 at Calhoun. "I hope not. He's nice, and sweet on Claudette."

"We're running out of suspects," Clyde said.

She looked over her shoulder. "Seems like we're running out of getaway road, too," she said, nervously eyeing a freight train crossing the road a hundred feet behind them.

"We're gonna be just fine," Clyde said. He looked at the remnants of grease on his fingertips. "While I was parking the car, I took the liberty of cutting their brakes. I was pretty sore about the way I thought they treated Jimmy and the gang."

"I've never been prouder of you," she said.

They sped directly toward the moving train, with Calhoun and his boys gaining.

"Hang on," Clyde said at the last second, cranking the steering wheel hard to the left and sending their car crashing trunk first through the window of an ice cream and sweet shop.

Lefty was in the front seat of the pursuing car and smiled triumphantly, gun extended, but it was short lived. The driver was stomping the brakes but the car didn't slow, just kept rumbling toward the train.

Lefty mouthed one last "fuck you" at Clyde, who was waving at him, as the driver swerved straight into a parked car to avoid being crushed under the train.

"Come on, darling," Clyde said, scrambling out. Stunned patrons and employees in the store stared at the steaming car and the battered man and woman climbing out. Bonnie smoothed down her dress and smiled.

"Sorry about that, folks," Clyde said, dropping a wad of twenties on the dash. He looked at the barrels full of hard candy and dropped another twenty, then filled his pocket with butterscotch.

He popped one of the candies in his mouth. Blood flowed onto his collar and he squeezed his handkerchief, dribbling blood out of it, and clapped it back to his ear. "I got us out of the lead tango, but how in the hell are we supposed get away from Calhoun and Murder, Inc. without a car?"

"On the hobo chariot," Bonnie said, pointing at the train.

They sprinted out of the sweet shop and past Calhoun's car—it was totaled and upside down, the passengers sprawled and out cold but coming to—and ran alongside the slow-moving train. When a boxcar with an open door rolled by, Clyde caught Bonnie around her waist, hoisted her in, and then scrambled up after her.

Once inside, she turned her attention to his ear, unwrapping the scarf around her own neck and pressing it over his wound and then wrapping it tight around his head to hold it in place. "My poor baby," she said.

"You love birds better move away from the door before the bulls see you," a gravelly voice said from the shadows. "Or it'll be trouble for us all."

Clyde ducked and pulled his .45, cocking the hammer and aiming it toward the voice.

"Take it easy, Jesse James," the voice said. "They check as it leaves town. They see you and they'll stop the train and roust us all."

Bonnie grabbed Clyde by the arm and pulled him deeper into the car just as they passed a man peering into the doors.

"You wild boys better be gone by Boulder City," the man shouted into the car. "If you're still on when this iron horse rolls into town, we're going throw you in front of the train."

As the train picked up speed, Clyde kept his gun aimed into the shadows.

"We don't want any trouble," Bonnie said.

"But we ain't averse to it, neither," Clyde said.

A young man stepped forward out of the darkness and advanced toward them.

"Why, you're just a boy," Bonnie said, looking at the young man.

He had a constellation of freckles across his cheeks and forehead, and blushed when she spoke, but stuck his chin out defiantly. "I ain't no boy, lady."

"Are you all hoboes?" Clyde asked. "Like the ones in that movie, you know, Wild Boys?"

"Guess that's what they're calling us now, but we're not movie stars or nothing. I'm hunting for work. Potatoes in Idaho, apples in Washington, hops in Oregon. Last month I was picking in California. Started out in Ohio. Name's Walter."

"I'm Brenda, and this here is Clarence. You're a long way from home, Walter," Bonnie said.

"Reckon the rails are my home," Walter said. "I been back and forth across this country three times now."

"A train don't seem like no place for anyone to be living," Clyde said.

"Depends on the bull," Walter said. He noticed Bonnie's confused expression, and explained. "The bulls are the guards Union Pacific pays to keep us off the trains. Some of 'em look the other way, some throw us off. You get to know which ones to steer clear of. Mostly." He nodded down at a man sleeping near the wall. "He weren't so lucky."

Walter lifted up the blanket covering the man. The smell of gangrene overpowered the stink of urine, and they saw the bloodied nub at the end of his leg. Walter put the blanket back down.

"He lost his foot after one of them bulls threw him off. Tried to get back on, but got caught under the wheel."

"That's terrible," Bonnie said, turning her head away. "Will he be okay?"

"Probably not. Drinking to avoid the pain, but he's all out of hooch now," Walter said.

"How do you eat?" Bonnie said, yelling over the noise of metallic wheels screeching against tracks as the train braked through a curve.

"Steal a little here and there from farmers," Walter asked, sitting down on a hay bale. "Throw ourselves on the mercy of church folk. Y'all got real jobs?"

"In Boulder City, working on the dam. And I'd give it to you in a heartbeat if I could," Clyde said.

"You're soft in the head then. I'm on my way to Flagstaff. I heard there's work getting fields ready to plant pintos. If that don't play out, mind if I look you up on the way back through to see if you're still offering to give up your job?"

"If I'm still there to look up, you can have my job, if I got any say over it," Clyde said.

"Why ain't you all riding up in the passenger car like the regular folk?" Walter asked.

"We had a little car trouble," Clyde said, tucking his gun away.

"Ain't my business anyway," Walter said.

They settled into the silence and rhythm of the train, Bonnie resting her head on Clyde's shoulder and lulled into uneasy sleep. Thirty minutes later, the train whistle woke her up and Clyde stood and stretched. "Don't want to get spotted at the station."

"I've made the jump off at Boulder City lots of times," Walter said. "I'll tell you when to bail and how to land proper for a dollar."

Clyde pulled Bonnie to her feet and handed Walter a five.

"Get ready, it's coming up soon," Walter said. "The key is to make sure you get good and clear of the train and try and keep your feet moving when you hit for as long as you can. It'll make the fall easier."

"I don't plan on falling," Clyde said.

"Well, if you do, tuck your shoulder and roll into it so as not to snap your neck."

"Ready, baby?" Clyde asked Bonnie. She nodded.

"Go now!" Walter ordered.

Bonnie hopped off and took a few stuttering steps before she got tangled in some tumbleweeds and fell, but rolled and stood, waving at Clyde that she was all right.

"Your turn," Walter said, giving Clyde a nudge for encouragement.

Clyde hit too hard, planted his feet and sprawled awkwardly, face first. He popped up, swearing. The scarf protecting his ear came undone and was flapping behind him now. "Little shit pushed me."

"That was real graceful, Miss," Walter said, waving from the open door and then disappearing back inside.

Clyde patted his jacket. "And he lifted the rest of the cash."

CHAPTER 38

Choked

When Bonnie woke, sunlight was shining softly through the window and birds were singing. It was the picture of domestic bliss, until she looked over at Clyde and saw his pillow and the sheets under it soaked red with blood.

She checked her watch. "Shit," she said, shaking his shoulder. "Clyde, Clarence, you bled a lot last night. And also, you're late for work."

He sat up, blinking slowly, paler than usual. "Why didn't I hear the alarm?"

"Because you smashed it yesterday, remember? I'll pick up a new one today and set it on the other side of the room so you can't get your mitts on it, but you've got to get going. You need to twist some arms today and figure out if the union is behind all this."

Bonnie dabbed iodine on his ragged ear lobe, drawing an overly dramatic howl of pain from Clyde, then a grin to see what Bonnie would make of his theatrics. She shook her head, and put some tape over the wound. Clyde got dressed as she rustled up a lunch—a half empty bag of Saltine crackers twisted closed, a tin of sardines and another withered apple.

He looked at it mournfully. "Not sure this is the kind of lunch I need to do any serious arm twisting."

She kissed him lightly. "You're meaner when you're hungry. I'll make sure you get your fill tonight."

"Are we still talking about food?" Clyde asked.

"Depends how you play your cards," she said.

"I'm starting to like playing house with you," he said.

"Don't get used to it," Bonnie said. "I miss being on the road."

"I can't hardly wait to make a dishonest woman out of you again."

"You say the sweetest things," Bonnie said. "Now, get on out of here. Hopefully you can hitch a ride with the coffee boys."

After he was gone, she curled her hair and got dressed for work. By the time she arrived, the line of dour-faced workers waiting in the hallway was longer than she had ever seen.

Claudette waved when she walked in, snatching up the phone as it rang. "Good morning, Six Companies, Boulder City, how may I direct your call? Hold, please." She transferred the call. "Morning, Brenda."

"Morning, Claudette." Bonnie spoke cheerfully, feeling an unexpected sense of contentment that there was someone, however fleeting, in her life she could call a friend. "What's with all the men waiting? You putting on a peep show later?"

"Think there's money in that?" Claudette asked in mock seriousness, then laughed. "It's on account of them drawing down the workforce. Job is almost over and they're starting to cut some final checks."

The phone rang again and Claudette returned her attention to the phone. "Good morning, Six Companies, Boulder City, how may I direct your call?"

How was it possible people did these office secretarial jobs, any job, really, day in and day out for a lifetime,

Bonnie wondered. The maddening repetition, moving papers from one place to another all day, every day, or answering phones, tasks interrupted only by the even more demeaning job of filling coffee cups for men who mostly, if they even noticed the women around, tried to look down their shirts or up their skirts.

She had tried to broach the subject over lunch with the office girls a few days before.

"Why not ask the bosses to at least change up our assignments so we can do different jobs?" she asked. "It wouldn't be so damn boring and we'd learn more stuff so we could do a better job in the end. If we all asked together, we'd have a better chance."

"Like a ladies' union?" one girl asked. "They'd fire us on the spot."

"Brenda, I can't lose this job," another woman said, filing her nails. "We lived in our car for nearly a year. I can't go back to that."

Only Claudette—newly awoken to the power of unions by her growing attachment to Jimmy—agreed, but Bonnie promised to let it go for the sake of the rest. She had an escape from this drudgery, what did she care in the end?

Jimmy was right. It was a simple calculus—organize so all workers spoke with one powerful voice, rather than thousands of small, easily ignored voices.

She now understood why those three stuffed cabbages in New York wanted to keep the economy in their own pockets and do everything they could to bust strikes.

It was surely best for the captains of industry to keep the working class undereducated, suspicious of each other, and desperate for jobs, any job—whites fighting blacks, Irish fighting Poles, Italians against, well, maybe everyone, carmakers fighting janitors, always blaming each other, thinking that to get ahead meant some other worker had to fall behind, instead of thinking there was plenty of cornbread to go around.

Why in the world don't more people rob banks for a living, she wondered.

She poured a cup of coffee, dropped in two sugar cubes, stirred them away idly and carried the coffee over to the filing cabinets.

After a quick scan of the room—Claudette was on the phone again and Fitzsimmons had the door to his office closed—she returned to the task of pretending to file while skimming through papers.

She was up to the "L's" and a file labeled "lawsuit" caught her eye. She scanned the papers, which, if she understood the legal jargon—all the "whereby's" and "in accordance with's"—described an accident in the early days of construction when the diversion tunnels were still being blasted out. The papers said men in the tunnels had been "subject to excessive mechanical and automotive fumes, including carbon monoxide, suffering mental disability with lapses in memory and intelligence."

She guessed that meant the men ended up a little tetched in the head.

One of the men brought a lawsuit against Six Companies to compensate for his injuries, but apparently, he had a reputation as a cheating, lying bastard. And Six Companies made darn sure the jury knew that, even if he had been poisoned down in that tunnel. The jury ruled against him, but now his lawyer was looking to bring a new lawsuit.

At the bottom of the memo, there was a line that read: Plaintiff is known associate of Jimmy Hall, union agitator.

Bonnie took a quick look around to see if anyone was watching and then slipped the memo into her pocket. "Prentiss," Fitzsimmons barked from his office.

She froze, wondering if the jig was up. It was worse.

"There's been another sabotage. The union was behind it. Your husband is hurt. He's at the hospital. You're off the clock if you leave before your shift ends."

CHAPTER 39

Soaked

An hour earlier, a father and son stood next to the railing at the tourist overlook on the canyon's edge looking down at the dam gleaming in the mid-morning light. It was their first road trip in a new Station Wagon and the boy, who one day hoped to become an engineer, was thrilled. His uncle was a draftsman for Six Companies and they planned on having lunch with him later.

The dam was a stirring sight. The angle of the sun cast long shadows over the concrete monolith, rising up from the desert floor, the concave white slab reflecting the golden rays of the swelling day.

The tour guide held nothing back in his performance to a busload of tourists there to gawk at this symbol of American ingenuity, and the father and son were eavesdropping.

"After years of long work by thousands of men, and millions of taxpayer dollars, the dam and power plant are entering the last phase of construction," the guide said. "The small diversion dams have been removed, water is collecting behind the dam and the transformation of the primitive..."

He looked at his notes.

"...the primeval river that once flowed uncheckered, I mean, unchecked through the narrow canyons fettered only by the ragged and imposing cliffs honed over millennium is almost complete. Soon it will become a wide, placid lake, storing millions of gallons of once wasted water destined to be squandered in Mexico, now captured and remade into a place for boating and fishing, for nourishing farmlands and for electrifying the next century in the great United States of America."

The tour guide paused and looked up to measure his effect. Pleased at the wide-eyed silence of this group, he continued.

"The men whose daring and foresight made this all possible will control nature, releasing water at a timing determined by industrial needs for farming, electric power and flood control. This project is our own modern day version of the Egyptian ferals...pharaohs, who made the pyramids. And all thanks to the know-how and stick-to-it-ness of the leaders of industry who financed and built this monument out of the goodness of their hearts for the benefit of all."

"What's that, Pop?" the boy asked, pointing to a wisp of smoke near the base of the dam.

His father pulled up the binoculars hanging around his neck and aimed them in the direction of the smoke.

"I'm not sure, son, but something doesn't look right," he said. "It looks like a fire."

Down at the dam site, Clyde was tinkering on the engine of a water truck that was idling too fast when he heard the roar of the explosion. Flames ripped out of a concrete tunnel mouth leading down into one of the support structures for a generator house.

Men shouted and sirens wailed as emergency vehicles mobilized. Instructions began to blare through the loudspeaker system. "Explosion on spur sixteen. There's a fire. Stay alert. Help is on the way." The voice of the radio man was loud and garbled by static and panic.

Clyde saw Dino walk by, his arm still in a sling, and yelled, "What's going on?"

"Sabotage. Someone said one of the bosses was trapped in there. He was one of the worst during the strike of thirty-one. Getting a taste of his own medicine."

"Still don't deserve to die roasting like a pig," Clyde said. He hopped in the water truck, slammed it into reverse and rumbled toward the billowing smoke. He backed the truck right into the mouth of the tunnel and jumped out.

He heard a voice screaming for help.

"Back up friend," he yelled. "Flash flood coming through." With the flames licking at him, Clyde grabbed a sledgehammer and used it to smash the cap off the end of the tank nozzle, releasing a surge of water down into the tunnel. Within minutes, the flames sputtered out and a bedraggled looking man, scorched and half dead, came crawling out of the mud and wreckage.

Clyde helped him to his feet, then bent to pick up a scorched piece of battered brass almost buried in the mud. He wiped it clean and dropped it in his pocket.

"Goddamn union sons of bitches," the man screamed, loud enough for the gathering crowd to hear. "I found this on the wall just before the whole place went up." He uncurled his fist where he had held fast to a crumpled sheet of paper. Straightening it out, he revealed a sketch of the three circles from Jimmy's talk.

"Don't mean nothing," Clyde said. "Anybody could have put that there." He helped the man up into the front of the truck. "Come on. I can get you to the hospital faster than waiting for the ambulance."

At the hospital, the orderlies helped the boss onto a stretcher and carried him off. One of the nurses, a pretty brunette with worried green eyes, saw Clyde's ear dripping blood. The bandage had come off in the excitement.

"You brave man," she said. "You're hurt too."

"Aww, it's just a scratch," he said, but let her lead him back to a chair and fuss over the wound, taping it up with clean gauze. He was laughing at something she said when he saw Bonnie standing in the doorway, hands on her hips and jaw set.

"Brenda, I was just—"

"Save it," she said, voice icy. "There I was worried you'd been blown to pieces, but turns out you were just fine and in capable hands. I guess you don't need me worrying over you." She turned and walked away from the nurse's station at an angry clip.

Clyde hopped up. "Thanks for patching me up," he said to the nurse. "Don't go too far in case things get rough."

He ran after Bonnie and caught up at the front door, snaking his arm through hers to slow her down. "Don't be like that," Clyde said. "She was just doing her job."

"I'm not mad at her for doing her job," Bonnie said. "I'm mad at you for enjoying it so much." There was a crash and loud voices from inside the ward. "Don't think I'm forgetting about this," she said.

They walked back inside and saw Jimmy on his crutches, his right arm in a cast from his shoulder to his wrist, backed against the wall by the paymaster Gerald and two of his cronies. Jimmy's bed was tipped over and his clothes and belongings were strewn on the floor. The other patients in the ward cowered in their beds.

"You damn near killed one of our friends," Gerald said. His face was still puffy and bruised from the baseball bat beating, and his thin mustache bristled with indignation. "Your union nonsense ends now."

"I don't know what the hell you're talking about," Jimmy said. "I've been laid up right here."

"We've heard from the nurses you've been sneaking out on a regular basis, probably planning this all along, and we're going to fix your wagon."

"Boys," Clyde said, entering the room. "This here's a hospital. They have rules about wagon fixing and other forms of rough housing." He picked up a gleaming scalpel from a tray of surgical instruments and reversed it in his grip so the blade was poking out of the bottom of his fist.

Claudette walked in unaware of what was unfolding and saw Jimmy standing. "What are you doing up?" she asked, starting to rush toward him.

Bonnie caught her arm and pulled her back. "Hold on one second, sweetie."

Gerald glowered at Clyde, taking note of the razor-sharp spike in his hand. "I'm gonna settle things between us one day, Prentiss. This ain't over."

"I sure hope not," Clyde said. "I enjoy making you look like a milksop."

He pretended to lunge forward and Gerald shrank back, swore and ran for the back door, his friends in tow.

"Thanks for getting me out of a jam again," Jimmy said as Claudette helped gather his clothes and books.

Clyde looked at Bonnie to see if she'd calmed down any, relieved to see her glare had lost its intensity. "I ought to be thanking you for the diversion." He took Bonnie's hand and squeezed it. "I'd better get that truck back to the job site."

"This is the first time I've ever seen you anxious to get to work," Bonnie said.

He flashed what he hoped was his most charming smile.

"Well, get on with you," she said. "We'll settle up tonight. I need to punch back in before Fitzsimmons fires me too."

CHAPTER 40

Lighting the fuse

"Check the shed, check the shed," the man mumbled as he hurried toward the metal building at the far edge of the railroad terminus. Even his mumbles had a thick Scottish brogue.

The squat tin building had a bright red door and a sign that read: Danger. Explosives. Keep out. Underneath, someone had sketched a grinning skull.

The gravel crunched beneath his worn brown boots, drowning out the growl of his belly. "I'm gonna miss lunch, but every day I need to check the lock on a door that's been locked for..."

He stopped and squinted, swiped at his eyes with the back of his gloved hand, and then looked more closely at the door.

The padlock was slipped aside and the door was cracked open.

The heat was amplified inside the metal hut. Nervously, he pulled the clipboard from the nail behind the door, and looked over the inventory list. Now that the dam was almost finished, they had a truckload of dynamite ready to ship to the Bonneville Dam job on the Columbia River. They just had to keep it under lock and key so whoever kept blowing stuff up couldn't do any real damage.

He wiped the sweat from his brow and said a silent prayer to the goddamned lord of the working man for giving him a job next month in Oregon. A few years of rain, after five years in this Arizona sauna, sounded right.

But first he had to make sure the dynamite stayed in one place. He used a little nub of pencil to check off the boxes. It didn't add up though, so he checked it again. Then he felt something turn in his guts.

Six crates were missing.

Glancing down at the floor, soaked into the sawdust was an oily black outline of the missing crates, the lines of nitro sweat showing where the crates once stood.

Six crates. Enough to bring the dam down.

Lunch forgotten, he ran back to the office and snatched up the phone and called headquarters.

Claudette was outside when the phone rang, so Bonnie answered. "Good morning, Six Companies, Boulder City, how may I direct your call?"

"I need to talk wi' Mr. Fitzsimmons right now," a panicked voice said.

She glanced at Fitzsimmons poring over papers in his office and took a chance. "May I take a message?"

"Jaysus, yes, take a message, lassie. Tell him aboot the missing dynamite. A great lot of it. Six crates or mair. Tell him this is Mac. The dynamite is missing, missing, six crates gone. Woman, do ye understand me?"

His brogue was so thick, she really didn't understand much, but she heard "Jesus" and "six crates missing dynamite," inside what seemed like nothing more than a long series of vowels and grunts.

"Right away," she said, hanging up.

"Prentiss!" Fitzsimmons shouted from his office.

"Yes, sir?"

"How many times must I explain this to you. We thank our callers before we hang up."

"Yes, sir."

"Come in here, I have two special assignments. And bring me a fresh cup of coffee."

She filled a cup at the coffee pot and fantasized once again about pouring it over his bald head, washing the greasy comb over down over his eyes and scalding his angry mouth shut. Instead, she smiled demurely—a great effort—and delivered the beverage. She watched his eyes try to peek down her shirt, heard his breathing slow and tried not to think about how he was imagining her.

His desk was littered with papers, including what looked like a requisition for a goods transfer from Boulder City to Bonneville. He nodded toward the chair.

This is it, she thought. If he propositions me, if he says anything about my figure, I'm going to choke him with his natty tie.

"It seems you have fooled a number of people. We have a VIP from Washington attending today. She's asked for a tour. From you."

"From me? Why?"

"A very good question," he said. "Apparently, you worked for her at some point. In the typing pool. Sal something or other."

"Of course."

"With the completion date coming soon and all the trouble from the union, it's important we make the right impression. Please show her around town, but do not visit the dam site without an official Six Companies representative."

He returned his attention to the papers, tracing one of the twisty graphs and grimacing.

He looked up, annoyed to see her still sitting.

"Was there something else?"

"You said there were two assignments?"

"Yes, that's right," he said. "Our new security consultant Hank Black requested you personally to take some dictation. Please meet him at the hotel tomorrow morning."

"Yes, sir," she said. "Oh, and Mr. Fitzsimmons, a Mac called. He seemed anxious to hear from you."

CHAPTER 41

Terrible tour guides

Sal had arrived while Bonnie was in Fitzsimmons's office. Now, she sat in Bonnie's chair, pulling off a pair of gray gloves that matched her linen skirt and suit top. She wore a lilac blouse underneath, and balanced a matching clutch on her knee.

"I'm not accustomed to waiting," she said.

Always cool as a cellar cucumber, Bonnie thought.

Fitzsimmons walked out of his office, solicitous.

"Welcome to Boulder City," he said, extending his hand awkwardly, unused to taking a subservient position to a woman.

Sal shook his hand lightly. "I wish I could say it was a pleasure."

"What is your business here again, exactly?"

"Oh, enjoying the clean air. A constitutional, so to speak. And checking to make sure President Roosevelt's millions are being well spent."

"I assure you, we are on track and ahead of schedule," Fitzsimmons said.

"Even with the sabotage?" Sal asked. "That seems highly unlikely."

"I'll arrange a tour with head engineer Henry Byrd on the site tomorrow. You can see for yourself. We're confident we will meet all our milestones. Today, Mrs. Prentiss can show you and your man around Boulder City."

"Thank you for following my instructions. Come, Mrs. Prentiss." Sal said, turning her back to Fitzsimmons.

Carl was waiting outside in a chauffeur's uniform, the telltale bulge of a pistol under his arm. He held a driver's cap beneath the other arm and beads of sweat ringed his forehead. He looked hot and uncomfortable, but smiled at Bonnie and nodded.

"Hey Carl, nice monkey suit," Bonnie said.

"Thanks, Mrs. Prentiss. Beats plowing by mule." He opened the back door of the teal Buick Victoria to let Sal slide inside, followed by Bonnie.

Carl drove slowly down Main Street.

"Your boss seems horrid," Sal said.

"I have bad luck with bosses," Bonnie said.

"The town seems horrid."

"It grows on you," Bonnie said. "That's the movie theater where the anarchists started following us, and that's the company store that never has any alarm clocks. That's the corner where the mob tried to shake us down. And the church there? That's where the strike breakers tried to beat Clyde up. And you can almost see our little flop house from here, which is where we almost got blown up."

"That sounds like such a juicy radio drama" Sal said. "Pull over, Carl. What it also sounds like is that you still don't know who is behind the sabotage."

"We know who isn't behind it," Bonnie said. "The anarchists aren't behind it. They're all scorched and in jail. And the mob isn't behind it. They're all shot up and on the run."

Sal rolled her eyes and stared off into space. "I sent you on a mission to find who is trying to destroy Boulder Dam, not who isn't."

Bonnie sighed. "Spying is hard. Someone is trying their best to make it look like the unions are behind it, but the numbers don't quite add up."

"What does your esteemed partner in crime think?"

"Clyde? He thinks working for a living is a sin. He also thinks the big boss of the project is a pretty good guy."

Bonnie pulled out her cigarettes but Sal stopped her. "Not in the car."

She put them away. "Oh, and Clyde got his ear shot off. Well, not all of it, but a pretty good chunk."

"That sounds like another great story I'll never hear. Tell me about the payroll robbery. Any ideas who pulled that?"

"You heard about that all the way out in Washington?" Bonnie asked.

"Herman Daniels wasn't the only person I have on the inside. Did the robbery have anything to do with the sabotage?"

Bonnie shook her head. "No, not at all. Completely unrelated. Probably just a couple of criminals passing through, who happened to be real good at robbing, since they didn't get caught."

Sal sighed. "Old habits," she said. "I guess I don't need to give you more of a stake then."

"We lost our car in Las Vegas. Could use a new one."

"I'll figure something out. But first, I need to figure out this Hank Black thing."

Bonnie nodded. "Almost came down to it two days ago."

"That's the only reason I'm here," Sal said. "He's looking for you. Please tell me you haven't done anything stupid, like send a letter to your family?"

"I haven't said a word to anyone," Bonnie said. "And that's the god's honest truth."

"He's on your trail. And if he sees you, it's all over," Sal said. "He'll either shoot you on the spot or parade you back to Texas in ankle cuffs. And that will sorely inconvenience me."

"We're both fond of being alive and not in jail," Bonnie said. "Maybe we should just skedaddle on out of town tonight and let you take over."

Sal looked at Bonnie for a long pause, almost incredulous. "If you leave, the deal is off. I've already lost one inside man, the project is too close to completion and the nation can't afford for this to go south. We need this dam. We need a win. I'll take care of Black. You figure out who is trying to blow things up."

"You'd better hurry. I'm supposed to meet Black tomorrow morning. And I just found out that six crates of dynamite are missing."

Sal shook her head. "You make me so tired. Get out. Carl, get me back to the hotel. I need a drink."

"Can't you drop me off? It's a long walk, and it's dusty out here.

"No," Sal said.

"But it's right on the way."

"Did you think we're friends now?" Sal asked. "Because we're not. You're an asset, and apparently not a very good one. Don't forget that I've got you on a chain because you're a murderer in love with a murderer. Get out and do your job so I can go do mine."

Bonnie got out and glared at her. "You really ought to take one of those Dale Carnegie courses on improving your attitude," she said, slamming the door.

CHAPTER 42

Less than dead

"I do not like that woman," Bonnie said.

Clyde bent over the sink splashing cold water on his face. "Aww, she's not so bad. She's like hot sauce. Keeps things from getting too bland."

"And a little goes a long way," Bonnie said.

"Sounds like she hardly threatened to kill us at all this time." He slipped a bottle of whiskey into his jacket pocket. "Let's go see how Jimmy is doing and then maybe grab a bite to eat at the hotel."

When they walked into the hospital, Jimmy was holding court, laying out the case for the union to a dozen injured men who sat on the floor or on nearby beds, listening in rapt attention. Even one of the nurses had stopped her rounds and stood, hand on the bed frame, to listen.

Claudette sat beside him, and waved happily when she saw Bonnie. "I got something for you," Claudette whispered. She pulled Bonnie's beret out of her bag. "You left it in the office the other day. That fellow from Texas sure was interested in it."

"Hank Black? What did you tell him?"

"I told him it was mine, but I don't think he believed me. He said something about tracking someone, and needed to talk to every Bonnie on the site. I told him he was barking up the wrong tree, but then he went into Fitzsimmons's office and closed the door."

"Thanks for covering for me," Bonnie said, shooting a look at Clyde, then turned her attention back to Jimmy.

"I'm just saying we men need to organize, and when we do, there is nothing we can't accomplish," Jimmy said.

"Hey professor, mind if I ask you a particular?" Bonnie said.

"Of course not," he said, turning to her.

"What about the women?" She saw the nurse quickly nod in agreement. "You keep saying men have to organize, but what about women?"

"Women don't work," said a man on crutches. "You don't make no sense."

"Plenty of women work, son," Clyde said. "And watch your tone."

"Of course we work," Bonnie said. "And even if we don't, who do you think watches the kids so you can work? But that isn't the point. You said the union needs to represent everyone, including the unemployed, so that people aren't competing against each other. Women need to be part of that. We've got a lot to offer."

"And what about the coloreds?" Clyde said, following Bonnie's lead. "They're trying to get by, same as the rest of us."

"I ain't joining no union full of women and coloreds," one man said, getting up and limping back to his bed. The rest soon followed.

"Now you see the limits of common sense," Jimmy said, frustrated. "Of course, you're right. Everyone should be welcomed into the union of workers, employed or not, women or men, white or black, even the Irish. You've heard me say that before, at the last meeting."

"Got to say it more often," Bonnie said. "The unions will cannibalize themselves if they leave people out."

Jimmy shook his head. "Don't I know it. But we're battling against some narrow minds and tightly held convictions. I'm fearful if we can't convince folks to look beyond their own self-interest, to get beyond the idea that working class is only white folks, well, this whole thing might come crashing down. It'll be easy for the bosses to break us apart, like those rock walls where the dam is now. If you plant charges between the working and the unemployed, between men and women, between whites and colored, we're all reduced to shovel-ready gravel."

"I love that you're such a dreamer," Claudette said, taking his good hand in hers. "No matter how far-fetched it all sounds."

Jimmy laughed. "You have no idea. I want to see this country move to a system where there are no wages at all."

"How would people live?" Bonnie asked.

"We pool everything and make sure every man, woman and child has enough to get by, then we divvy up what's left. Bosses get a bigger share than workers, but they don't get everything. Workers get an ownership stake, and get payouts based on how the business does, with guaranteed minimums," he said. "Worker councils, with input from the bosses, decide how to invest and allocate profits. If you don't do something like that, the money will keep piling up in the pockets of the bosses, until workers have no money and no say at all."

"I like the sounds of your plan," Clyde said. "But I don't imagine many bosses look favorably." He pulled out the bottle and took a nip, then handed it to Jimmy.

Jimmy took a sip and shrugged. "We'll get through to them eventually. I'm excited for the future of this country. We're going lead the world in making a rip-roaring economy where workers and owners come together to use profits to create the best darn society ever seen on this old planet."

"He's talking child care, and health care, good job training, old age pensions—all kinds of stuff," Claudette said.

"There's more than enough money, if it's flowing fairly to both worker and boss alike, and not just to bosses," Jimmy said.

"You better not keep that vision under wraps for long," Bonnie said. "Or that dream is going get murderized before it takes its first baby steps."

"Are you still spinning out your wee communist pipe dreams?" a man asked in a thick Scottish brogue.

It was Mac, stopping by to visit his friend Ian, laid up in the same accident that leveled Jimmy. He reeked of whiskey, which thickened his brogue.

"Aye, Mac," Jimmy said. "I'm dreaming big enough for all of us."

"Well dream faster, we just had six crates of dynamite take a scamper."

"What did Fitzsimmons have to say about the dynamite?" Bonnie asked.

"That shoogly neep? Nae a word. Nae a hoot."

Bonnie looked helplessly at Clyde, then Mac.

"He didn't say nothing," they said simultaneously, translating.

She grabbed Clyde's hand. "We have to go right now."

"Why do I think this means no supper," he said. "Just keep the bottle," he yelled back at Jimmy, who was already passing it to Claudette.

"We have to get into the main office," Bonnie said, leading Clyde out into the darkness. "Mac called this morning to tell Fitzsimmons a bunch of dynamite was stolen, and Fitzsimmons never called back. Seems like if you're in charge of the ordering, that's the kind of thing that would make you nervous."

At the front door of the administration building, Clyde held the crown of his fedora against the glass, slipped on his brass knuckles and punched the pane out of the door.

Bonnie made a beeline for Fitzie's office, Clyde aiming his pocket flashlight at the desk as she started rustling through the papers until she found the requisition form. She held it up nodded. "See? He cancelled it. And after the dynamite turned up missing. That son of a bitch."

"I'm not tracking, Nancy Drew," Clyde said.

"Why would Fitzsimmons cancel a requisition to move so much dynamite? Unless he wanted to cover it up."

"The company is behind their own sabotage?"

"It gets worse," she said. She turned the requisition form around and tapped her finger against a signature the bottom. "Jimmy was the one who signed off on it at the job site."

"Dammit, don't tell me he's in cahoots with Six Companies," Clyde said.

"Sure starting to look that way. Or playing both sides." She sat her purse on the edge of the desk to slip the form inside, knocking a letter opener off in the process. She bent down to pick it up and saw a box pushed out of sight under the edge of the desk. "What is that?"

Clyde pulled the box out and opened it. It was half full of alarm clocks.

"No wonder they were always out of alarm clocks down at the store," Bonnie said. "What could they possibly be stockpiling all these clocks for?"

"Not clocks," Clyde said. He reached into this pocket and pulled out the scorched piece of brass from the latest explosion, a battered, misshapen version of one of the twin bells on each alarm clock. "Timers, for six crates of dynamite. We need to find that son of a bitch and fast."

"You need to drop your guns on the table," a voice called out from the shadows. A voice with a distinct Texas twang. It was Hank Black.

Clyde dropped the flashlight and had his .45s out in a heartbeat, but heard the ratcheting of a hammer being cocked.

"Drop it, Barrow, or I'll cut you and the lady in half with this double-barreled scatter gun."

Clyde hesitated, searching the shadows.

"I won't tell you again," Black said. "I pulled the trigger the first time. I don't know how you came to be standing here without a scratch on you, but you have to know I'll pull the trigger again."

With a snarl, Clyde released the hammer forward and dropped the gun on the desk.

"The other one too."

Clyde pulled the matching pistol out of his shoulder holster and set it beside the first.

"You too, Parker," he said. "I know you've got a little twenty-five auto on you somewhere."

"Maybe I left it at home," she said.

"Maybe I pat down your corpse," he said.

"Fine," she said, slipping her favorite pistol from her purse. She laid it beside Clyde's guns. "They look so cute together."

Black stepped out from behind the door with an ominous double-barreled shotgun in his hands. "I'm not sure what kind of scam you're pulling here, but I knew you'd come back. Once I saw the beret, I knew it was you, I knew you were back. You have to be patient if you want to catch rats out in the open. They're creatures of habit."

"I think you've got us confused with someone else," Clyde said.

Black shook his head. "Nope. You're a lot less dead than I'd been led to believe, and I still wouldn't believe it if not for my own two eyes. Bonnie and Clyde, still alive. I always thought something looked off about them bodies. I figured it was just the couple hundred high velocity rifle rounds messing things up."

He fished a pair of handcuffs out of his back pocket and tossed them toward the couple. "It's almost better this way. You should die in an electric chair, screaming and smoking and sparking."

"Not shot down in an ambush by cowards?" Clyde said.

"It ain't cowardly to put down a rabid dog from a distance," Black said. "Less chance of getting bit."

"Assuming you've got the right dogs," Bonnie said.

He gestured with the barrel of the shotgun. "Cuff yourselves together. Your second life is over."

He gestured toward the front of the building. "Walk to my car. We're driving to Las Vegas. You've got a date with a hanging judge."

CHAPTER 43

Rhyming schemes

Royce was early, and leaned against the wall near a table with two pitchers of sweet tea and a plate of ladyfingers. He gazed around the basement room, looking for Bonnie.

When he called earlier to say he had new information, she suggested they meet in town after the monthly poetry reading at the church.

"Poetry reading?" he asked. "Yours?"

"Don't be ridiculous," she said. "I'm an avid listener and the sole financial support for their monthly poetry journal, but don't let them know."

Looking across the basement room now, he saw her sitting in a metal folding chair, in a circle with about a dozen or so people. Most were old; two were ancient— both in wheelchairs and one with a plastic catheter bag hanging down precariously from beneath the seat. A teenager with spiky hair and a sullen scowl clutched a journal with a grinning skull painted on it.

Royce pulled a cigarette from his pocket and started to light it, then thought better of it and poured himself a Styrofoam cup of iced tea.

A stooped old man, bowlegged and with a broom for a mustache—long gone to gray—stood in the center of the group reciting his poem. His face was a dried-up riverbed of wrinkles, though illuminated by a kind of grace from the task at hand, and he had on stiff new jeans, a snap button, yoked work shirt and a bolo with a polished piece of agate in the center. His hat was off, this being indoors and the house of the Lord, and he held it in one hand as he read.

And so I rode slowly back to the Bar None ranch
The stars above my head did shine bright
The trees swayed, branch to branch
And oh, how I missed my dear Caroline.

Royce winced and looked toward Bonnie. She grinned, the smile lighting her face like a mischievous schoolgirl. He felt momentarily dumbstruck, watching her glow in this decaying place surrounded by such a motley crew, and after living such an incredible life. He marveled again at how joy still lived within her, and so close the surface.

Weak applause broke out and the old man bowed his head, sat down on his metal folding chair and perched his hat on his knee.

The minister stood, an earnest young man with thick blonde hair and heavy glasses, a bead of sweat in the furrow between his eyes. A transplant, Royce figured, probably from the Midwest.

"Well, Mr. Granger, that was mighty fine," he said, standing. "God bless you for sharing that poem. Anyone have any comments to offer?"

"Bright and Caroline don't rhyme," said the woman sitting next to the minister. She wore a tiny hat with a lace veil. Her shoes were black and sturdy, and she worked her dentures together with a wet clacking sound when she wasn't talking.

"Doesn't always have to rhyme," the old cowboy said, tugging at the crease in his jeans ironed to a peak. "That's modern."

"Cowboy poetry needs to rhyme," said another woman. "Or at the very least, it ought not be modern."

"Or maybe just take 'bright' off, then it would rhyme," the teenager said, blushing self-consciously.

"You know son, that's a damn fine idea," the old cowboy said.

The minister passed out blank white notecards and pencils. "We heard five poems today, take your time, but please vote now on which should be included in the church poetry journal next month. You can vote for one, or more, even all of them. Our anonymous donor provided funds for an expanded edition."

"What was the name of the second poem, the one this young fella wrote?" the cowboy asked.

"Harvester of Souls," the woman said, then clacked her dentures again.

The punk adolescent blushed even deeper. Bonnie handed her card to the minister.

"Mrs. Prentiss, how are you?" he asked, his voice emphasizing 'are' in the special pitch people instinctively used when addressing the ambiguity of grief.

"I've had better days," she said. "But thanks for asking."

"We sure miss Clarence," the reverend said.

"Not half as much as me," Bonnie said.

"God calls the best home to heaven early," the reverend said.

"I sure hope it's the good lord. Otherwise there's bound to be trouble in hell," she said.

"If you need anything, you know the church is here for you."

Bonnie nodded. "I appreciate that. But what I need right now is dinner. Royce, will you do me the honor?"

Later, in a booth at the Branding Iron Restaurant, the waitress took their order.

"Black coffee," Bonnie said.

"That's all?" Royce said. "You said you wanted something to eat."

"I just wanted out of there." Her face looked tired and drawn, as if all the energy stayed behind at the poetry reading.

Royce snapped the menu shut. "You should eat. Why don't you bring us two orders of chicken-fried steak with mashers?" he said to the waitress.

The waitress hung the order and then came back and poured two cups of black coffee. Steam tendrils swirled around the rim, and then disappeared. Bonnie stirred in two packets of sugar, and leaned back.

"I'm not sure old cowboys should be writing poetry," Royce said, trying and failing to be funny.

"His wife Caroline died in a car crash a few years back. Drunk driver. Sometimes poetry is about remembering, or working through things. Doesn't have to always be art for all eternity."

"Now I feel like an ass."

"It's all right, you were an ass before you said that."

He laughed, and took a sip, then winced. "I'm going to write a poem about drinking yesterday's coffee today."

He poured creamer into his cup and tried it again, then pushed it to the side. The waitress set down two plates of chicken fried steak with mashed potatoes and gravy and a homemade dinner roll.

"Go on, dig in," Bonnie said.

Royce spread the cloth napkin over his lap. He dipped the doughy white roll into the gravy and then bit into it. Bonnie sipped the coffee, but didn't pick up a fork.

"You don't know what you're missing," he said.

"What I'm missing is the information you said you had for me."

"I traced the ring and it led me to the niece of the woman who it belonged to."

"You know the identity of the couple who died for us in the ambush?"

"Almost everything fits. I mean, we can't be sure without the bodies, but it turns out there's a secret trust fund that benefits the woman's family," Royce said. "For fifty years, that family's been receiving money anonymously. Overseen by the folks at The Grange. I'm betting when we track down his kin, it'll be a similar story."

Bonnie helped herself to a cigarette from Royce's pack. She stared through the restaurant windows, her mind drifting back fifty-odd years to the night she and Clyde were snatched from their car before the ambush.

She imagined what had gone through their minds, those two innocents, as they lay bleeding out. Tears formed in the corners of her eyes and traced slow, lazy trails down her cheeks.

Royce stopped eating. He started to hand her his napkin, but saw that it was covered with swipes of gravy. She wiped her eyes with her finger, looked up and cocked her head.

"I'll be fine," she said. "I just got a little dust in my eye. From 1934."

She stubbed her cigarette out in the gravy pool congealing in her dollop of potatoes, looked out the window again into the parking lot, trying to gather her thoughts. "Um, Royce, those men seem mighty interested in your car out there. And no offense, but your LeBaron is kind of a turd on wheels."

Royce looked up and recognized Hall and Oates, the two men from New York. "What the hell? Those are the men I told you about. We've got to get out of here."

Bonnie fingered the little automatic in her beaded purse. Royce looked around the restaurant. "But there's only one way out," he said, pointing to the front door.

She tilted her head toward the kitchen. "No, there's two. You don't get to be this old by not knowing how to get away from trouble."

"We won't get far on foot," he said.

"I've got a plan," Bonnie said.

"A plan?"

"Trust me."

"Do I have a choice?"

"Only if you want to talk to those fellows out there again." She pulled out a wad of rolled up hundred dollar bills and set it on the placemat in front of her just as the waitress put the check on the table, startled by the cash.

"What's your name, honey?" Bonnie asked.

"Hazel."

"Hazel, do you have a car?"

She nodded. "Not much of one."

"Would you be willing to let us borrow it for a little while?" Bonnie asked. "Give us until the end of your shift, then report it stolen. The cops will find it with not so much as a new scratch on it."

"You all planning on getting up to no good?"

"What do we look like, Bonnie and Clyde?" Bonnie asked with a laugh.

Hazel slipped the roll of money into her apron, then pulled out her keys, worked her apartment key off the ring and tossed the rest on the table.

"It's the yellow Pacer out back."

"Mind if we—"

"Leave through the kitchen?" Hazel said, finishing her sentence. "Go on. You've got three hours until I get off work and call the cops."

CHAPTER 44

Ambushed, again

Hank Black was whistling, pleased with himself.

Bonnie and Clyde were sitting side by side in the back seat, handcuffed together—her right hand to his left—and the opposite wrist handcuffed to the doors in the back of his car. Black had their guns on the seat beside him—they would sell for a pretty penny to a collector.

"You've got the wrong folks, Mr. Black," Bonnie said. "Who even are Bonnie and Clyde? If you mean the outlaws, don't you know they died last year?"

"Shot down by your own hand," Clyde said. "Or so I heard."

"Save your breath," Black said, pulling out onto the highway. "Like I said, I knew something was off about them bodies. I'd been tracking you two no accounts for years. I knew it wasn't you then, and I know it is you now."

He took a chew and rolled his window down, then spit a long stream of tobacco juice out into the night. Brown saliva spattered the back window and Bonnie grimaced at the sight of it speckling the glass.

"Clarence and Brenda Prentiss my hairy ass," Black said. "How'd you pull of a stunt like that, anyway? Did you make some kind of deal with the devil?"

"She's a devil all right," Clyde muttered, and Bonnie elbowed him.

"I'm sure we don't know what you're talking about," Bonnie said. "This has all been a terrible mix up. It's like I was telling that nice lady from the government today—"

"You can keep blowing smoke up my ass all you want," Black said. "You put on a real sweet voice, pleasing to the ear. But I know it's you." He hummed happily, tapping his fingers on the wheel.

"Speaking of smoke, mind if I light up?" Bonnie asked.

"Go right ahead," Black said.

The way they were handcuffed together across the center of the seat, it was an awkward maneuver, but she lifted the pack of smokes from her purse, held it while Clyde extracted a single cigarette and pressed it to her lips. She pulled out the matches and held the box steady while Clyde struck one and lit the cigarette. She cracked the window and blew smoke out.

"I feel blessed in a way, I really do," Black said.

"How's that?" Clyde asked.

"I get to make my name with you twice. I'll be a true goddamn American hero when I bring Bonnie and Clyde to justice. Again."

"We're not Bonnie and Clyde," Clyde said. "And if this dam fails on account of your meddling, your name'll be mud."

"What are you on about?" Black said, squinting back at them in the rearview mirror.

"In case you hadn't noticed, there's something fishy going on here," Bonnie said. "We've been looking into it, official like."

"You mean something fishier than two dead murderers coming back to life?"

"Yeah, like sabotage," Clyde said. "And six missing crates of dynamite."

"Nothing a little union busting won't solve," Black said.

"It's not the union," Bonnie said. "They've been working real hard here to build it right, and to protect the working man, first by trying to get regular shifts, then to get some drinking water, and hold Six Companies accountable for poisoning people accidentally."

"You don't like the work, move on," Black said. "You don't strike and raise a ruckus and blow things up."

"You can't expect people to work for nothing, expose them to danger and death, do everything you can to keep them from advancing, and then get rid of them when it suits you," Clyde said. "That ain't how the system is supposed to function, and you know it. Workers ought not to be disposable."

"I never dreamed Bonnie and Clyde would turn out to be socialists," Black said, spitting tobacco juice out his window again.

"You can call us whoever or whatever you want," Clyde said. "But thinking a working man should be able to keep his job in good times and bad, afford a decent house and food for his kids, put a little away for when he can't work no more, to me that's just American."

"You're living in some kind of a socialist utopia, Barrow. I hope hell has work gangs when you get there."

Bonnie shook her head and slightly lifted her hand that was cuffed to Clyde, motioning at Black's head. She pantomimed getting the cuffs over him and using them as a chokehold.

Clyde nodded, watching the road to gauge the speed and anticipate how bad the crash was going to be.

But then Black slammed on the brakes at the sight of two stopped cars angled across the road, emergency lights flashing. "Police. Now why would they put up a road block here?" Black asked.

"Oh, shit," Clyde said. "It's an ambush. Don't stop, Black. Throw it in reverse."

"Nobody ambushes a Texas Ranger," Black said, looking out past the headlights. "I'm on official police business and they are official police."

"It's probably that son of a bitch Hoskins," Bonnie said. "It's Boulder City security, real cops don't have jurisdiction out here. Come on, you know this doesn't look right. Get out of here."

"The day I take advice from murderers is the day I turn in my badge," Black said, rolling down the window. Three shadowy figures stayed behind the cars.

"Howdy boys," Black called, waving his badge through the window. "I need to get on through to Las Vegas—"

A blossom of orange flame lit up the darkness as a Tommy gun started chattering, then another joined in. Bullets shattered the window and clanged into the grill and hood.

"Son of a bitch," Black said, jamming the car into reverse and stepping on the gas. Bonnie ducked and Clyde tried his best to shield her as the heavy slugs tore through the car. Black sagged as a bullet ripped through his hand on the steering wheel, knocking two fingers off at the knuckle before punching through his shoulder and into the back seat.

He slumped sideways and dragged the wheel down hard to the right, sending the car careening backward off the road. It rolled once and settled upside down in a dry creek bed.

Still handcuffed to the door and Clyde, Bonnie came to her senses first. "Clyde, baby, you all right?" she asked, then realized what she said. "Clarence, baby."

He didn't respond, hanging limp and half suspended by the cuffs, a trace of blood on the side of his head.

"Black, you alive?" Bonnie asked. She could see him crumpled on the roof, bloody and still.

Out ahead through the cracked windshield, she saw the three men advancing. "God dammit, Black, throw me the damn keys." He moaned.

One of Clyde's guns, tossed into the back by the force of the impact, was on the roof of the car—now the floor—just out of reach. She kicked it forward until she could walk her fingertips onto the checkered grip, then carefully pulled it close enough to grab.

When she had the gun, she tugged Clyde's arm to the left as far as she could—halfway across her body—and aimed the barrel at the cuffs holding her left hand to the door. It was all about instinct and angles, and she tried not to think about the heavy slug slamming into her wrist and blowing her hand off.

She cocked the hammer, prayed he had a round in the chamber—racking the slide was a two-hand job—and pulled the trigger.

The bullet punched into the car door, two inches above the handcuffs. She readjusted, hoping it wasn't by too much, and pulled the trigger again. This time, the slug nicked the cuffs and caused them to bite into her wrist.

The sound of the shots scared their assailants back into cover, and she could see muzzle flashes from up above the road as machine gun fire rained down onto the bottom of the overturned car.

She pulled the trigger again and the slug finally punched through the links holding the cuffs together. With her left hand free, she switched gun hands and pressed the muzzle of the gun into the middle of the cuffs tethering her to Clyde, pushing them down into the seat cushion and then pulling the trigger.

With both hands free at last, she kicked through the shattered glass of the window and dragged Black's shotgun out, leaned over the back of the car and sighted in at the machine gunners.

"You ought not to stand so close together," she said, letting both barrels fly. The recoil knocked her off balance, but the load of buckshot served its purpose. Even with her ears ringing, she heard howls of pain and the fusillade tailed off.

She got the keys out of Black's pocket and pulled Clyde out, checking him for bullet wounds. "What's going on, Bon?" he asked, groggy.

"It's Brenda. You must have hit your head. We got ambushed."

He found his guns and holstered them, then tossed Bonnie her .25.

"I sent them packing, but Black is shot up."

"That's my girl." He looked at the crumped body in the front of the car. "Serves him right. Hard-headed old cuss. And ain't it ironic, too. Shot down in an ambush. Let's scram."

"We're not those people anymore," she said.

"We ain't?"

"We have to try and save him. Help me get him out."

"What the? Save him? Why?" Clyde stammered, but he followed Bonnie's lead.

They pulled Black out of the car and Clyde stuck a rolled-up jacket under his head, then twisted his bandana around the stumps of his fingers. Bonnie tore off the bottom of her slip and pressed the fabric into the bloody wound in his shoulder. The pain jolted his eyes open and he struggled to make sense of his surroundings.

"What are you doing, Parker?" he asked, his words slow and thick.

"It's Prentiss, you old coot," she said. "And I'm saving your life."

At the sound of an approaching car, Clyde reloaded the shotgun and held it casually at his waist, aiming it toward the headlights washing over the edge of the road. They heard a car door slam, then saw movement behind the beams.

"You all look a fright," a woman called down. "If I give you a ride back to Boulder City, you are forbidden from bleeding in my car."

"Sal," Bonnie and Clyde said in unison.

CHAPTER 45

Heart to heart

Sitting shoulder to shoulder around an overturned crate, a group of men played dice at the end of the street, using a kerosene light to follow the action.

Shadows flickered across their drawn faces as they passed a bottle and laughed at the twists of fate in every roll. A few looked up curiously as an unfamiliar car ground to a stop in front of Brenda and Clarence's house.

"Okay, stick to the plan," Sal said. "Hurry. And Carl, take off the chauffeur hat and jacket."

Sal and Bonnie slipped out of the front seat. Sal put her head down, feigning upset.

"Come on now, honey," Bonnie said, loud enough to be overheard. "The boys will take care of your man, come on inside and let me get you some tea, don't you dare cry for him." Bonnie put her arm around Sal, and felt her stiffen at the touch, but she didn't break character, and they hurried into the house.

Carl and Clyde pulled Hank Black out of the back seat, still unconscious, and hoisted him between the two of them, his legs dragging behind, making a line in the gravel, as they pulled him up the walkway. Black moaned loudly.

"Prentiss, everything okay? You need some help?" one of the men yelled.

"Naw, but thanks. My cousin's boyfriend had too much fun in Las Vegas. Gonna let him sleep it off," Clyde said. The blood from Black's injured shoulder was soaking into Clyde's shirt, and he quickened his pace before the bleeding gave them away.

Bonnie held the door open and they dragged Black into the bedroom. The bed springs creaked loudly as they dropped his bulky body onto the thin mattress.

"Cuff him," Sal said. Carl lifted the dead weight of his arm and cuffed his left wrist to the metal headboard.

"Take his guns," Sal said, looking confident, even as she felt like the situation was spinning dangerously out of control. "And get me some hot water and towels."

Clyde took Black's sidearm, a hammerless .38 in an inside-the-pant holster in the small of his back. Bonnie rifled through the kitchen and brought Sal a pan of water and two dishtowels.

"Scram," Sal said.

"Scram?" Bonnie said.

"Beat it. Make yourselves scarce, get out," Sal said. "I can't be much clearer," she said, when they didn't move.

"You can't order us around in our own home," Bonnie said.

"You mean the fake home you are temporarily occupying at my bidding?"

Clyde slipped his arm through Bonnie's to keep her from jumping on Sal. "Maybe we could just skip the part where you insult and threaten us, and get to the part where you tell us what you're about to do," Bonnie said.

"We don't have many options here," Sal said.

"You're not killing him," Bonnie said. "We won't let you kill him."

"Won't let me?"

Clyde looked hard at Bonnie, saw the determination in her eyes, nodded, and took her hand.

"Our murdering days are over," Clyde said. "We'll take our chances on the run if need be."

Bonnie squeezed his hand.

Sal looked at them both, puzzled. "When did you grow a conscience?"

"Been creeping up on us," Bonnie said, feeling good about the surprised look on Sal's face.

"You're talking about executing a man for just doing his job," Clyde said. "Even though I don't much care for his line of work, we won't be part of that no more."

Carl looked nervously between them, thinking about the .38 Clyde was still holding.

"Your value to me, along with your freedom, will be short-lived if you give up on all your criminal ways," Sal said icily.

"We're not giving up on everything," Bonnie said. "Just evolving a little."

Sal stared at them, and Bonnie saw something in her eyes that reminded her of her own momma. On the rare occasion she did something her mother could take pride in, it earned a similar, short-lived look. And now, in Sal's eyes, she saw that look for what it was: hope, and a promise.

Black moaned again and narrowly opened his eyes, but only for a second before he was out again.

"My plan, not that I need you to approve it, is to patch him up and then try to talk some sense into him," Sal said. "That will be harder to do with the two of you standing there like ghosts of his worst mistake. If that fails, I'm going to have him thrown into some hellhole of a prison in India, or maybe Africa, so no one ever hears from him again."

Clyde nodded. "We're gonna sit on the porch. Keep your word, or things are going to get real strained between us."

They walked outside and Bonnie pulled Clyde close. "I'm proud of you Clyde Barrow," she whispered. "I'm proud of us."

When the door closed behind them, Sal pulled a chair up next to the bed and slapped Black lightly across the cheek, then harder. He sputtered and cursed and sat halfway up. He looked at the gauze wrapped around his hand and tried to flex his missing fingers. "Son of a bitch, they shot off my trigger finger."

"And put a bullet through your shoulder," she said.

He looked down at the bloody wound, and winced. "They were cops," he said, disbelief lingering as an echo in his words. "I saw the lights. Why would they shoot one of their own?"

Quietly, methodically, Sal used a small punch knife with a pearl handle to shred the dishtowels into smaller strips. "Cops are people too, motivated by the same things as the rest of us—greed and fear and hate. Often the desire to do good makes us better than our basest tendencies, but not always."

He watched her rip more pieces of the terrycloth. "Who the hell are you?"

"I'm the person who saved your life," Sal said. "Along with Brenda and Clarence Prentiss."

"You and I both know that those two are Bonnie and Clyde," Black said. "I don't know who you are, but unless you murder me right here, I aim to bring those two fugitives to justice. They're killers, and they will pay for their crimes."

Sal leaned forward and slid the tip of the dagger through the fabric of his shirt and jerked it up suddenly, splitting the cloth to reveal the wound. "Interesting that you think killers should be held accountable," she said.

"Why wouldn't I? I'm sworn to follow the law."

"You received a phone call the day before you ambushed Bonnie and Clyde," Sal said. "The caller warned you that the people in the car would not be the outlaws. Do you remember that call?"

His eyes widened, but he tried to tamp down his surprise, knowing it gave him away. "How do you know about that?"

"Because it was me," Sal said, leaning in closer. "But you didn't listen. And because of that, you murdered an innocent couple I paid to drive that car through Sailes."

Outside, Bonnie leaned in with her ear to the window.

"What's she saying?" Clyde asked. "What's happening in there?"

"All I can hear is you," she said, shushing him.

Inside, Black pulled against the cuff. "We thought it was Bonnie and Clyde we were shooting, them no-good cop-killing blackhearts."

Sal peeled the shirt away from this shoulder. "You're lucky, it's just the one bullet and it went straight through. Imagine if you were hit say, a hundred and fifty times."

She began wrapping the improvised bandages around his shoulder. "We need to come to an understanding right here, right now. It was Bonnie and Clyde in that car, and not a young couple named Samantha Ebbon and Roy Spinner who were engaged to be married. Because if it wasn't Bonnie and Clyde, and you had advance warning of that fact, I believe you'd be facing the electric chair for your transgressions. Not to mention the scorn of every good person in the country for your reckless behavior."

She paused in her ministrations, waiting for her words to sink in.

He looked up at her, a mixture of fear, respect and revulsion in his eyes. "Let's pretend for a minute it wasn't Bonnie and Clyde," he said. "Why? Why would it be different people in their car?"

"How would I know?" Sal asked. "I work for the government. I trust that the government has my best interests at heart. I follow orders. You didn't."

"I won't be quiet about this unless you can tell me why anyone would try to save them outlaws."

She wound the bandage ends into a knot, securing them in place. "If they were still alive, I would tell you that everyone has a purpose in life, and perhaps they are fulfilling theirs. And I would tell you that you don't use good dogs to guard the junkyard, you use the meanest goddamn dogs you can get a collar around. But since they are not alive, all you need to know is that this is all for the greater good, and you are officially off the case."

He glowered at Sal, cleared his throat and then spit on the wooden floor, trying to get the bad taste out of his mouth.

"Are you aware that Brenda—the one you call Bonnie—saved your life out there?" Sal asked.

"I find that doubtful."

"She could have, indeed perhaps should have, let you die. You're complicating our work here. The dam is under threat and we are trying to protect it. She would have good cause to let you bleed out. I certainly would have. But she has a better nature than that. Does that sound like something Bonnie Parker would do?"

"Bonnie Parker is a whore and a killer."

"Then obviously, that sweet young thing out there so worried about your demise is not Bonnie Parker."

She motioned Carl closer, and he loomed behind her.

"Here's what's going to happen, Mr. Black. My man will drive you to Las Vegas where you will get medical help. Then he's going to put you on a train back to Texas. If so much as one word of this misunderstanding leaks out, your career is over and I'll see you in prison. And not a good prison. Way worse than Eastham. Don't come around Brenda and Clarence Prentiss ever again."

Carl slipped the key through the handcuff and helped Black up.

"You're banking a lot on my silence," Black said.

"Quite the opposite," Sal said. "You are banking on mine. Everyone knows Bonnie and Clyde are dead. You're just a sad old man who can't seem to stay out of trouble, and now you're making up wild stories."

"What am I supposed to tell them about how I got shot?" he asked as Carl guided him toward the door.

"You'll figure out a good lie, I'm sure, with all the experience you have fabricating evidence."

When they were gone, Sal went to the kitchen and found a bottle of gin in the cupboard. She poured a shot into a glass and walked out to the stoop.

"Help yourself to our booze," Clyde said.

"How much did you hear?" Sal asked.

"All of it," Bonnie said.

"So, you know Black had your mom arrested?"

"What?" Bonnie said, leaping up. "When?"

Sal took a sip. "So you heard nothing. Good, it's better that way."

"You are smooth as spring corn silk," Clyde said. "You enjoy our liquor. We're gonna go talk to Jimmy about where he'd stick six crates of dynamite if he really wanted to bring the dam down."

CHAPTER 46

Taking out the trash

Jimmy was propped up in bed, playing cards with Claudette. The room was crowded with families and friends visiting the patients, and nurses coming and going.

"Hey, Jimmy," Clyde said. "You're looking better."

"Hey, Clarence, Brenda," Jimmy said. "Yeah, it's amazing what a little special attention from a volunteer nurse can do for you." Claudette blushed.

"Wonders, apparently," Bonnie said.

"What brings you round?" Jimmy asked.

"Got something we need to discuss," Clyde said. He pulled up a chair and sat down, smiling lightly, but his hand was close to the pistol under his jacket. Bonnie stood behind him.

"We got interrupted last time, but I recall the night nurse saying you've been slipping out when no one was looking," Clyde said quietly. "Like two nights ago, for example. When that bomb was set."

Jimmy sat up straighter. "What are you getting at, Clarence?"

"Nothing in particular," Clyde said. "Just pointing out that someone has been trying to slow Six Companies down. Lots of people think the unions are behind it. And you being here in the hospital seems like a pretty good alibi, especially since you been slipping out. Also, they found one of your little circles of truth drawings at the last bomb blast."

"You're not accusing Jimmy of something, are you?" Claudette asked, dropping her cards onto the pillow.

"Hon, you ought to stay out of this," Bonnie said. "There's more going on here than you know about." She turned her attention to Jimmy. "Like how one of your buddies lost that carbon monoxide lawsuit under questionable circumstances."

"It was a travesty," Jimmy said with a scowl.

"Which means getting revenge against the bosses puts you right at the top of the list of suspects," Bonnie said.

"Are you...are you working for Six Companies?" Jimmy asked.

"Nope," Clyde said. "We work for the government of the United States of America. And I'm tired and sore from breaking my back all day and I want to put an end to all this nonsense so me and Bon...me and Brenda can get back down to sitting on the beach in Mexico drinking tequila and watching the sunset."

"That does sound nice," Bonnie said.

Disappointment flashed across Jimmy's face, and he turned his head away from them. "I knew there was something off about you. I guess that explains the guns."

"Son, we ain't the enemy," Clyde said. "But six crates of dynamite went missing on your watch, and I found a little piece of alarm clock at the last blast site, the same kind of clock we found in a box in Fitzsimmons's office, right next to the form you signed two days ago keeping the dynamite here. I need you to convince me you ain't in on this so we can all go on being friends."

"Our friendship days are over," Jimmy said. He held his broken arm up. "Anyway, does it look like I could sign anything with this?"

"He makes a good point," Bonnie said. "But all the evidence points either to you trying to settle a score, or the union trying to slow things down."

Jimmy looked at her, exasperated, contorting the bruises on his face into a new arrangement. "It's not me. Yeah, the way they treated my friend was shabby, but I wouldn't put good men's lives at risk just to try and settle their wagons. And it ain't the union either. We're not organizing to make more money than we should. We're in a union so we have some muscle when big business tells us we can't take a break, or have clean water, or get medical care when we need it. We're in a union so, when the working man is lined up with each other, we're at least as strong as their money."

"That sounds real inspiring, and for a while I thought you even believed it, but you've still been slipping out at night, and for an injured man right in the middle of all the shenanigans, you can see how that looks bad," Clyde said.

Claudette's face twisted with disgust. "He snuck out so he could be with me," she said. "You got this all wrong."

"Don't perjure yourself, sweetie," Bonnie said. "Some mistakes you can't undo."

"I'm not in the habit of lying," Claudette answered. "Unlike you."

"I swear, the union ain't behind any of this nonsense," Jimmy said. "We can't figure out why in the hell anyone would want to slow things down."

The foursome went quiet, trying to take the measure of each other, and the situation. Claudette collected the playing cards, and began to shuffle them. Clyde looked back at Bonnie's pensive face.

"I can," Bonnie said suddenly, after a few minutes, as the threads of the plot wove themselves together into a clear picture. "They are killing two birds with one stone."

"But who is throwing the rocks?" Clyde asked.

Bonnie noticed that the hospital had become eerily silent. "Darling, where'd all the other people go?"

"Shit," Clyde said, reaching for his gun. The door swung open. Chief Hoskins and two deputies walked in, covering them with a shotgun and a Tommy gun.

"Keep your hands up where I can see them," the chief said. "Jimmy, you're under arrest for sabotage. You're going to jail."

"You're gonna arrest a man in a hospital?" Clyde said.

"He's faking it," Hoskins said. "He's been slipping out at night. That's probably when he stole the dynamite. He signed for it two days ago, and forged Fitzsimmons's name, now it's come up missing."

"That's peculiar he signed for anything, since his writing arm is broke and in a cast," Clyde said. "Hard to sign something when you can't hold a pen."

"Now you believe me," Jimmy muttered.

"You're too smart for your own good, Prentiss," Hoskins said.

"I never really understood that saying," Clyde said. "Seems like you could never be too smart, or too handsome."

The chief pulled out his revolver, cocked the hammer and aimed it Bonnie. "You can be too stupid though, that's for damn sure. Hands behind your back, or the skirt gets it."

"Now you've done it," Clyde said, watching the fire rage in Bonnie's eyes. "Would it do any good to tell you that we're working for the government and this man is our prisoner?"

"Don't you worry, we'll get this all sorted out at the jail," the chief said. "When we saw you nosing around the office last night with Black, we knew something was up. Where is he, by the way?"

"Not far behind us," Bonnie said. "We work together a lot."

"I don't think so," Hoskins said. "I think he's dead and in a ditch somewhere. We found an awful lot of blood in his car."

"You ought not to count on people being dead until you actually see the bodies," Clyde said.

"That's real good," Hoskins said. "They teach you that in fed school? Boys, take their guns and put them in cuffs. For their own safety, of course."

The deputies cuffed them all and extracted the .45s from Clyde's shoulder holsters.

"Get them out of here," Hoskins said. "I'll be along directly. Stick to the plan."

The deputies marched them to the paddy wagon— past a row of nurses excited by the drama—and locked them to the seats in the back as the chief roared away in his own car into the night.

"Wonder where he's off to?" Bonnie asked.

"Official business," one of the deputies said, as he shut the door. He was young and earnest looking, with red hair and ruddy cheeks. His partner, an older white man with a shiny u-shape of carefully pomaded hair, snickered.

Shackled in the paddy wagon, Clyde looked at Bonnie and shook his head. "We've been wrong from the start. It wasn't the anarchists, it wasn't the mob and it wasn't the union," he said.

"Who the hell are you?" Jimmy asked.

"You wouldn't believe it if we told you," Bonnie said. "We aren't going to jail, are we?"

"Doubtful," Clyde said. Right on cue, the truck rumbled past the turn to the jail and rolled out into the desert.

"Where are they taking us?" Claudette asked. She was frightened but held Jimmy close so he could lean on her.

"We're about to find out," Clyde said.

The truck stopped next to a car with its lights off and the engine running. Fitzsimmons and Chief Hoskins stepped out and waved at the driver.

"Howdy, Chief," the young deputy said, rolling down the window of the paddy wagon. "We drove them on out here just like you asked."

"Boys, don't get out of this car," Clyde shouted, stomping his feet. "You do it, you're gonna regret it."

"Shut up, prisoner," the pomaded deputy yelled.

"Come on out here, boys," the chief said. "We need you to drive this car back to town."

"What about the prisoners?" the driver asked, as he turned the key off and opened the door.

"Don't do it," Bonnie yelled. "Please, I'm begging you. Don't get out. Turn around and get back to town. Think of your momma."

"What's she on about, Chief?" the young man asked.

"Don't mind this union-loving rabble," Fitzsimmons said, stepping toward the passenger side. "We'll deal with them." He smiled and gestured for the older deputy to get out, and he obliged.

Fitzsimmons pulled a revolver from his waistband and shot him right between his surprised eyes. The body fell with a thud against the side of the truck and Claudette, who was watching through the slats, began to scream.

"What the hell?" the young driver shouted, finally catching on and reaching for his gun.

The chief pulled his revolver faster and shot the kid twice, right above the belt buckle. He sat down heavily on the sand, the air and blood and life leaking out of him, and looking up at the chief with confused, blinking eyes.

"Looks like that damn Jimmy killed two cops trying to escape," the chief said, swinging the chamber open to replace the spent rounds.

Fitzsimmons opened the back of the truck and pushed in a crate of dynamite between the four captives. "Shame about that," he said. "I guess him and his addle-headed floozy died in the explosion that brought the dam down."

He returned with another box, then another. Bonnie and Clyde stared at them gloomily.

"And what about the two government agents?" Bonnie asked.

"Don't worry, Mrs. Prentiss," he said. "You'll always be remembered as the feds who died trying, and failing, to save Boulder Dam."

CHAPTER 47

Learning to love the bomb

"Are you planning on walking us to death," Bonnie said. "Because I do not have on the right shoes."

She was handcuffed to Clyde, who was handcuffed to Claudette, who was handcuffed to Jimmy, who was weak and struggling to shuffle along as they wound their way deeper into the guts of the generator house at the base of the dam, taking a longer route that would skirt the night work crews.

"I can just shoot you here if you prefer," the chief said. "And then your husband can drag your body to the turbine room."

"We ain't married," Clyde said. "It's just part of our cover."

"We got reports from your neighbors, complaints actually, that would suggest you did a pretty good job faking it then," Fitzsimmons said.

"Oh, that wasn't fake," Bonnie said, hoping her banter would distract Claudette and Jimmy enough to keep them from falling full throttle into panic.

Gerald, his face still bruised and puffy, pushed a cart with the crates of dynamite and leered at Bonnie. "Maybe you and I could go undercover before we're through."

Clyde bristled. "You're gonna regret saying that before the night is over."

"Keep moving," the chief said, jabbing Jimmy in the back with the barrel of his shotgun.

Jimmy staggered, and Claudette caught him under the arms and murmured reassuringly. Clyde, still glaring at Gerald, helped her support Jimmy, who was breathing hard, and rattling phlegm. His face had taken on a sickly gray pallor from the exertion and worry.

"What's this all about anyway?" Clyde asked. "Why are you all so dead set on blowing up your own dam? Ain't there better ways to get at the union? All this water backing up, it's gonna wreak havoc on the folks below the dam in the canyon."

"Guess that's their bad luck," Fitzsimmons said.

"All because of that new carbon monoxide law suit?" Bonnie asked.

Fitzsimmons paused, then picked up the pace. "You're a clever one. But no. The new lawsuit is inconvenient but we'll get through that little bump in the road well enough."

"Are you working for the mob then? Murder, Inc.?"

"Corporate America could buy and sell the mob," Fitzsimmons said.

"The dam's not sound, is it?" Jimmy whispered. "Some of my boys have been paying attention."

"You win a prize," Fitzsimmons said, turning on the lights in the generator house on the east side of the dam, where eight of the seventeen turbines were located. The newly manufactured and installed turbines gleamed like a submarine, with the massive blades whorled up inside each like metallic wreaths.

"Six Companies is in a bit of a bind," Fitzsimmons said. "We signed a contract with the federal government, your employers," he said, nodding toward Bonnie and Clyde. "We were required to meet certain deadlines or else forego bonuses. The deadlines were too aggressive, given the unskilled rabble workforce we had to use."

"You pretty near worked us to death," Jimmy said, his voice stronger now, bolstered by anger. "You should have hired more men."

"And run over budget?" he asked, truly bewildered. "Too expensive, and a black mark on our reputations for contracting and poor forecasting. The government is building more dams and we aim to be their private sector partner of choice."

He gestured at the machine works of the nearest turbine and the chief prodded them along.

"We hoped with the union under the microscope for sabotage, our federal regulators might be a little more lenient," Fitzsimmons said. "But they haven't seen their way to provide the expected slack. And now we're behind, and the rushed construction won't stand up to any kind of engineering scrutiny, so we're going to level it, let the union take the fall, and then after the government breaks up the union once and for all, we expect they'll be inclined to renegotiate the terms of our contract. We'll double our profits, and all we're out is a little dynamite."

"I may not know much about how business gets done in the fancy boardrooms," Clyde said, "but there's no way Hurry Up Byrd would stand for that."

"He doesn't know," Fitzsimmons said. "He's a damn choir boy in a starched white shirt. Hardly anyone knows. A few members from each of the Six Companies, two board members. Only those who truly think big can make the hard choices, the right choices."

"Right choices for who?" Bonnie asked.

"Well, the investors, for one," Fitzsimmons said. "And the executives. And that, in turn, helps everyone, jobs and all, isn't that what's generally said?" He stopped and looked at her curiously, and then laughed. "You don't really think business exists to help the little man, do you? The workers, or the housewives, or the poor?"

"That's kind of what we've been told," Clyde said.

Fitzsimmons prodded them forward again. "That's one of those little lies we all sort of agree on to make sure things keep ticking along, like how we tell our kids Santa Claus is watching, or tell our wives we're not sleeping with other women," he said.

They stopped in front of the turbine. Clyde crashed into the back of Bonnie, and Claudette crashed into Clyde. Jimmy stumbled but caught himself before falling.

The crates of dynamite were arranged around a thick support beam. Two men began twisting detonator cords together and a third wound the alarm clocks—batteries taped around them—and set the timers.

The chief cuffed Bonnie to the railing around the turbine, then looked at Clyde, who smiled evenly—waiting for his chance to jump him—and jabbed the butt of his shotgun into his gut.

Clyde collapsed, dragging Jimmy and Claudette down with him. Bonnie swore and took a swing at the chief, but it only grazed his shoulder and he backhanded her, knocking her off balance and into the side of the giant metal turbine housing. She crouched by the railing that circled its top, eyes burning like a cornered bobcat, dabbing blood away from her split lip with the back of her free hand.

Moving quickly, the chief cuffed Clyde to the rail, then the other two.

"Don't you think four sets of handcuffs will seem a little suspicious?" Bonnie asked.

"Girl, there's enough dynamite here to blast your hands into mush," Hoskins said. "And enough water about to rush through there to wash every shred of evidence way out into the ocean."

Claudette spat at him. "And you call yourself a law man."

"No, I call myself a rich *former* law man," he said.

"Hurry up," Fitzsimmons said, as Gerald and his men set the rest of the timers.

"All done," Gerald said. "We've got an hour before these start ringing and the place goes to hell."

"Some of us have less than that," Fitzsimmons said, casually shooting Gerald in the chest. Gerald, surprised and dying, looked at Clyde.

"You picked the wrong side," Clyde said, with a shrug.

Fitzsimmons turned the gun on the other two men. He shot the first one in the forehead as he fell to his knees and begged for his life. The second turned to run and took a bullet between the shoulder blades, collapsing near the door to the generator house.

The sound of the gunfire echoed loudly, and Bonnie turned her head at the sight of the brutality. She heard Claudette crying.

"You might have saved me the trouble of killing Gerald for disrespecting Brenda," Clyde said, "but I still think you're a mean, backstabbing son of a bitch."

"Just a businessman," Fitzsimmons said. "Who happens to be especially good with handling people."

"Let's go," the chief said. "We need to be back in Boulder City when this thing goes up. Should we shoot them too?"

"Nah," Fitzsimmons said. "If they find any big enough pieces of their corpses, bullet holes in our suspects might look suspicious. Plus, I'll enjoy knowing they spent the last hour of their sorry lives terrified."

He moved closer to Bonnie, but out of reach. "You really were a terrible secretary."

He looked at Claudette. "You actually weren't bad, honey, and you were a treat to look at. But you should have stayed away from the union. You made bad choices."

CHAPTER 48

Time flies

Tick tick tick tick. The sound of more than two dozen clocks echoed maddeningly in the half-lit chamber and Claudette cried softly as Jimmy tried to comfort her.

Clyde tugged on his cuffs, rattling the metal against the railing. "Think they're good and gone?"

Bonnie nodded. "I imagine so."

"Let's get the hell out of here then," he said.

"But we're handcuffed to a bomb," Claudette whispered, distraught.

"Calm down, honey," Bonnie said, pulling a hairpin from above her ear. "This is not the first time we've been handcuffed."

"And likely won't be the last," Clyde said. He pulled his fedora off and slipped a small square of metal out of the hatband and folded it into a V-shape.

"There's three ways out of handcuffs if you don't have a key," he said. "You can pick them, like Brenda's doing. But it's takes time. Or you can use a shim, like I'm using."

"But if you use a shim, you have to tighten them up a notch," Bonnie said, "and it hurts."

Clyde winced as he clicked the cuffs one notch tighter to slide the shim under the teeth. "But it's faster."

"Is it?" Bonnie asked, holding her hand up to show she was already free.

Clyde laughed. "It's always a competition with you," he said, opening his own cuff.

"You said there's a third way?" Claudette asked.

"Cutting your hand off," they said together.

"Obviously though, that's like a last resort kind of deal," Clyde added.

Bonnie fiddled with the other cuff until it clicked open and then dropped the handcuffs in her purse. "I'm saving these special for Fitzsimmons here directly."

"Spring them, would you darling?" Clyde said to Bonnie. "Now that they led us right to the bomb, we can shut down these goddamn clocks before this whole place lights up."

"This was your plan all along?" Claudette asked as Bonnie worried her handcuffs open.

"Once it was clear who was behind the whole thing, it didn't make no sense to shoot it out with them at the hospital until we figured out what they had in mind," Clyde said.

"It might have made sense to us," Claudette said, stamping her foot. "Then we wouldn't be down here in the middle of a bomb."

"I can't believe you pegged the union for all this," Jimmy said as Bonnie used her hairpin to pick the lock on his cuffs.

"It looked pretty bad," Clyde said. "Who would've thunk the company was behind the whole thing?"

"We would've thunk it," Jimmy said. "A company that's willing to cover up poisoning miners, that thinks workers ought not to have clean water, those are not good people."

"Real sorry about that," Clyde said. "But it all worked out in the end. Long as we don't get blowed to hell." He cracked his knuckles and reached for the first alarm clock.

"Hold on," Bonnie said. "Are you sure you know what you're doing?"

"How hard could it be?" Clyde asked.

"Plenty hard," Jimmy said, struggling to stand next to him. "The batteries are wired to the hammer on the clock. If it touches the clapper, the circuit is completed and the detonator blows. And if the detonator blows—"

"We get turned into applesauce," Bonnie said. "Maybe you ought to let Jimmy help you."

"You know an awful lot about bombs," Clyde said, stepping back.

"I'm in the union, not the boys' choir," he said. "Claudette, don't stand so close to me."

He nodded toward one of the dead mean. "Toss me the wire cutters in his belt there," he said to Bonnie.

She pulled out a pipe wrench and he shook his head. "No, the wire cutters. With the yellow handles."

Bonnie tossed them underhanded across the narrow room.

"Soon as I snip the wire, you get rid of the alarm clock," he said to Clyde.

Bonnie pulled her little .25 auto from her purse. "They never think to look for this," she said. "I'll watch the door in case those snakes slither back in."

Working together, Clyde and Jimmy started removing the detonators. As soon as each clock was free, Clyde hurled it against the wall and the ticking gradually subsided until, with the last clock, the room was silent.

They looked at the mound of shattered clocks. "Well, I guess we just saved Boulder Dam," Clyde said.

"For now, anyway," Bonnie said. "We need to get our hands on Fitzsimmons. Specifically, around that scrawny little neck of his."

"And don't forget the crooked law man Hoskins," Clyde said.

"How are we going to catch up to those sons of bitches?" Bonnie asked. "They've got a good head start."

"There's a radio in the office there," Jimmy said, pointing to a windowed room housing the power controls. "We could call back and have them arrested."

"Pretty tall order to have the cops arrested by the cops. We need to take care of this personal like," Clyde said. Bonnie nodded in agreement.

Jimmy pointed toward the back wall. "Use the spillway tunnel. It leads to an access tube designed for future repair work, goes right up to the top of the dam. You get started now and step to it, you might just beat them to the top."

"What about you?" Bonnie asked.

"We'll be all right down here," Jimmy said. "Someone ought to make sure all this dynamite stays safe. But don't forget us. Come on back down after you settle the score."

"And bring a stretcher for Jimmy," Claudette said. She helped him sit down next to the wall and then she picked up a wrench and tested swinging it like a club. "He's not walking all the way back up."

Clyde nodded and grabbed a flashlight from the tool belt of one of the dead men. He and Bonnie walked to the rear of the generator house to the spillway and he shined the light up into the access tube, illuminating a column of darkness stretching up out of sight, with rough iron bars bent into rungs stitched along the seam.

"I'll go first," Bonnie said, slipping her pistol back into her purse.

293

Clyde caught her by the waist, kissed her, and then hoisted her up into the opening. She pulled herself upward, hand over hand. "Stop looking up my skirt, Clarence," she said.

"Then stop being so damn beautiful, Brenda." He jumped up and caught the first rung, then hauled himself up after her.

CHAPTER 49

Gravity

By the time they got to the top of the access tube, Bonnie's hands were raw from the rough iron and the muscles in her arms and back burned. She peeked over the edge. It was a perfect cloudless night with a gaudy splash of stars above.

"Good timing," she whispered, "I hear them."

She pulled herself out of the tube and looked around. They were at the top of the dam near the west bank of the riverbed next to a storage shed, an area that had been completed last year. Clyde followed behind her.

The chief and Fitzsimmons walked toward them completely unawares, moving fast toward the eastern edge under the impression the dam would soon be reduced to rubble.

"We ain't got a prayer against those two without some heaters," Clyde said.

Bonnie pulled out her little automatic. "Remember, we've got this."

He shook his head. "I've said it before, that barely qualifies as a gun, Bon."

"It's all we've got though, and we can't let them get away. You've got your brass knuckles, right?"

He nodded, slipping his hand into his pocket.

"We'll surprise them. I'll cover Fitzsimmons and you knock down the chief. Piece of cake. We'll be on the road to Mexico by midnight," she said.

"You make it sound so easy."

"It will be easy, as long as you knock the chief out cold," she said.

Clyde pretended to polish the brass knuckles against his vest. "I'm gonna hit him so hard it will knock him plumb into next week."

They crouched in the shadows next to a couple of five gallon buckets filled with grout and a long coil of rope. When the two men drew close, Clyde squeezed her wrist and nodded, and they leapt out together.

"Don't move," Bonnie said, the gun leveled at Fitzsimmons.

The two men jumped, startled, and Clyde lunged toward the chief and took a mighty swing. Hoskins backpedaled and stumbled, so the punch barely grazed his jaw. It was enough to knock him backward onto his ass where he landed with a curse, but he was plenty conscious and reaching for his revolver.

Fitzsimmons swore and reached for his gun, and Bonnie fired at him three times. The first bullet missed, the second knicked his sleeve and the third thumped into the flask in his shirt pocket. A dribble of whiskey fountained out.

"Well, dammit," she said, looking disappointedly at the little gun.

Fitzsimmons drew his pistol and cocked the hammer, but Clyde pivoted and punched him in the kidneys, twisting at the waist, putting his full weight into it. Fitzsimmons fell to his knees, clutching at the explosion of pain in his lower back. He dropped his pistol and it skittered toward the edge of the dam. Clyde scrambled after it, but the chief was already up and aiming his revolver.

"Get down," Bonnie screamed and Clyde ducked low as Bonnie shot her last two bullets. One missed, digging into the stone in front of the chief, and the other clipped his thigh. Hoskins stood, touched the gouge on his leg, then pointed the gun at Clyde.

"You so much as blink and I'll perforate you."

Clyde raised his hands, then looked at Bonnie. "I told you that dainty little thing was no good."

"You also told me you were going to knock him plumb into next week."

The chief limped closer, stopped to retrieve Fitzsimmons's revolver and then flung it off the edge of the dam. It clattered against the concrete and was gone. He nudged the barrel of the pistol at Clyde. "Keep your hands up where I can see them, boy," he said. "And turn around."

Clyde turned and laced his fingers together.

"You okay, Fitzie?" the chief asked.

Fitzsimmons groaned. "I think so."

"Gonna be pissing blood for a week though, hoss," Clyde said.

"Shut up, white trash," the chief said, cracking the butt of his gun into the back of Clyde's head.

Clyde slumped down and Bonnie, swearing, lunged at the chief, but the bulky man was ready and backhanded her with a vicious blow that sent her reeling into the shadows where she collapsed next to the shack.

The chief stood over Clyde, triumphant, and rolled him over with the toe of his boot, pistol aimed at his head. "I always knew it would end like this," Hoskins said.

"You with a split lip and a hole in your leg, standing on top of a new dam? You missed a hell of a career as a fortune teller then," Clyde said.

"You're funny, for a dead man," the chief said. "People like you, you think you're special, think you can beat money."

"We already have," Clyde said. "We took apart all your little fire crackers down there. In case you hadn't noticed, the dam's still standing."

"Yeah, but you're not, and there will be plenty of chances to bring the dam down," Hoskins said. "But you? You're all out of chances. I'm gonna blow your head off and roll your body off the dam. And then me and Fitz will have some fun with that cute gal of yours, and when we're all done, I'm gonna send her over the edge after your corpse."

"I was wrong about you," Clyde said with a grimace. "You're not just a two-faced chisel buzzer, you're also a sick fuck."

"And a rich one," the chief said, taking careful aim.

There was a sudden tug at his belt followed by a metallic click and he spun around to look. Bonnie was behind him and danced out of his reach as he struggled to make sense of what he saw. A full bucket of grout was perched on the edge of the dam, a coil of rope beside it— one end was tied through the bucket, the other was tied to the handcuffs she had just snapped through his belt.

He reached for the rope, confused, then for his belt buckle, then looked at the gun in his hand and up at Bonnie.

"Drop the roscoe or this bucket goes over the edge," she said. "It's real heavy. Pretty sure it'll take you with it, and it's a long way to the bottom."

"God dammit," Hoskins said, spinning back around and aiming at Clyde who was crabbing sideways.

Bonnie looked over at Clyde with a question in her eyes, and he looked back at her with the answer. There was no choice. They would have blood on their hands one more time.

She shoved the can over the edge.

The chief shot once, twice, three times at Clyde who was rolling away from him, but then the bucket hit the end of the rope and jerked him backward off his feet like a cork out of a champagne bottle. With a screech, he dropped the gun and tried to grab Bonnie on the way past, then the edge of the parapet, but the force was too great and with a final shriek, he shot over the edge and tumbled down the front of the dam.

He stopped screaming half way down, but it was a quiet night and they could hear the bucket and body clattering for a long time, then heard it hit.

"You gave him a chance," Clyde said, picking up the gun and checking to see how many bullets were left.

"Terrible way to go, though," she said.

"A dam shame, you might say," Clyde said.

"Don't make jokes about folks dying, honey," she said. "It's not proper."

"Man said he was gonna rape and murder you, and I'm not proper," Clyde said.

He pointed the gun at the battered, bleeding Fitzsimmons who was retching in terror at what had transpired. "Come on Fitzie, let's go see how your old pal Jimmy is doing."

"We need to hurry," Bonnie said. "The place will be swarming as soon as they discover the body down there."

"Or what's left of it," Clyde said.

CHAPTER 50

Transmission

Bonnie gave his handcuffs a little tug and Fitzsimmons winced. "Want to say something catty about my secretary skills now?" she asked. "Or maybe stare at my ass again?"

He was chained to the metal ladder leading up to the top of the turbine. "Bitch," he said. "Killer."

"Ain't that a little like the pot calling the kettle scorched?" Clyde said. "You killed so many people tonight, I lost count."

"I had a feeling about this one," Bonnie said. "His tie was always knotted a little too tight. What are we going to do with him now?"

"I guess we take him back to town, let Sal sort it out," Clyde said.

"No one will believe your white trash lies. You ought to just kill me," Fitzsimmons said.

Clyde shook his head. "For such a big shot businessman, you ain't very good at negotiating. You ought to lead with how much your life is worth, and save the murdering for the very last offer."

Bonnie pulled him to the side and whispered in his ear. "He might have a point. It's all just his word against ours now, and it's not like Sal would be itching to march us up in front of a jury, given our unique background and all."

Fitzsimmons watched them whispering. "I'm not scared of you," he said. "You two work for the government, so you can't kill me. With the trail of bodies and missing people, and everyone who saw you four getting hauled off in the paddy wagon, the whole country is going to be looking for the four of you for a date with the electric chair."

Claudette looked up, tired and overwhelmed. Bonnie felt a surge of pity for her friend. "I don't want to go to prison," Claudette said.

"You're all going to prison," Fitzsimmons said. "But don't worry, it won't be for long. You'll be sizzling like sausages before you know it. You murdered three lawmen."

The four drew together into a huddle, leaning their heads in close to talk. "Any ideas?" Clyde asked.

"He's about as dirty as a catfish in a manure pond, but we're not exactly reliable witnesses," Clyde said. "It's going to be hard to prove he was behind all this. He's been setting the union up the whole way."

"No one will ever take our word over his," Jimmy said.

Fitzsimmons began to laugh, then leaned back against the cool metal, his face smug in the certainty that he might actually survive this fiasco with his reputation intact. "Seems like you're between a rock and a hard place. Only five people know the truth, two of them are rabble, two of them are soft, and I'm an expert liar."

Bonnie glared at him. "We need more people to know the truth," she said, then winked at Clyde. "I've got a plan. When does the next shift get here?"

"These interior areas only get one crew scheduled a day, the finishers, and they should be here soon," Jimmy said. "At daybreak."

"Good," Bonnie said. "Jimmy, we're going to need your help. And Clyde, you'll need to knock that asshole unconscious for a while."

"I'm not even sure what it is yet, but I'm already warming to your plan," Clyde said, as Bonnie whispered to Claudette and Jimmy.

He walked over to Fitzsimmons, pulled the brass knuckles from him pocket, slipped them over his hand and made a fist. Fitzsimmons looked up at him defiantly, and laughed again. "Is this where you threaten me?"

"Nope. This is where I turn the lights out." Clyde swung a vicious right hook into the man's jaw that jolted Fitzsimmons's head sideways. With a groan, he slipped into unconsciousness.

"He's out?" Bonnie asked.

Clyde nudged him with his foot. "Colder than a December outhouse."

"Okay, let's get to work. Clyde, string him up so he's above the turbine blades. Jimmy, I need you and Claudette to get up to the main job site and take care of your side of things."

"He can't walk, he can barely stand," Claudette said.

Jimmy struggled up and put his arm around her. "Come on, honey, I can rest up later, now we got to do what Brenda says. Let me lean on you."

An hour later as the sun lifted its rays above the horizon, and a soft dawn light drifted toward the turbine house, the room was still shrouded in shadows.

Fitzsimmons hung from the top of a safety walkway, dangling by his cuffed arms above one of the giant turbines. The rope holding him up was tied off to the base of the ladder on the floor of the turbine room.

From inside the windowed control room, Bonnie nodded and Clyde threw a pail of water at Fitzsimmons as she hit the red switch controlling the turbine. He came to, sputtering and cursing, just as the giant blades roared to life, clanging and whirring through their circular motion.

"What the hell are you doing?" Fitzsimmons screamed, squirming and turning helplessly, his arms stretched far above his head. Clyde climbed down the ladder and started untying the rope, then let some slack into it so that Fitzsimmons lurched down closer to the blades.

"We had a change of heart," Bonnie yelled. "We'd rather live on the run than let you get away with this."

"You kill me and you'll go to prison," Fitzsimmons screamed. "You wouldn't dare."

"You're not leaving us much choice," Bonnie said, calmly. She nodded. Clyde dropped Fitzsimmons closer.

"Wait, wait, wait," he screamed.

Bonnie pressed the button and the turbine shut down. Clyde tied the rope off again as Bonnie yelled out from the office.

"You're a cagey one, Mr. Fitzsimmons," she said. "All this effort trying to sabotage the dam and blame the unions, then when that didn't work, you tried to blow it up for real. And for what?"

"For money, of course," he yelled.

"And you were willing to risk lives and all this work, just for a few lousy greenbacks?"

"No, you idiot. For tens of millions of greenbacks. Let me go, and I'll cut you in on it."

"We don't want your blood money," she said.

"What do you want?" Fitzsimmons yelled. "I'm ready to make a deal."

"The same kind of deal you cut those two deputies you killed, or Gerald and the other workers you killed?"

"No, no," he moaned. "I felt bad about killing those men, but there was no other way. I'll tell everyone the chief did it. He was in on it from the very beginning, what do I care if his name is ruined? And you can have a head start, I swear."

"I don't know how trustworthy you are," Bonnie said. "You tried to blame those bombings on the unions and hang Jimmy up to dry, when in fact they were blameless in all this."

"So, what?" he snapped. "The unions will be the death of American business, who cares what happens to them? It's their goddamn fault we were so far behind. Always yapping about working too hard—"

"Or wanting clean water to drink, or to not breathe in poison gas, or not be worked to death, those kinds of things?" Bonnie yelled.

"It's a goddamn patriotic service to get rid of the unions. Nobody cares what workers want or think."

Bonnie held her hand up to reveal the radio hand set. "It will be interesting to find out if the workers agree with you," she said. "Because we just broadcast your little confession across the whole dam site. Jimmy and Claudette made sure to air it through the siren system."

She dropped the radio.

Workers started filing into the room and staring up at the man hanging like bait above the turbine. Jimmy was in front of the group and tried to stand straight, even though the pain from his injuries was searing. Claudette stood by his side, steadying him.

"We did what you asked," she said. "Ran the radio through the main emergency line. Everybody heard."

By now, the generator house was filled with workers, along with managers.

"You cheating mother fucker," one man said.

"Reckon we ought to kill him for this," said another.

"Ain't gonna be no killing here," Clyde said. "This is for the laws to figure out now."

"Anyone still standing here when I count to three is fired," Fitzsimmons yelled. "These criminals are lying to you. They tricked you and I got men lining up to take your jobs now. One."

Nobody moved. "Fuck you," someone said.

"Anyone who leaves now still has a job," Fitzsimmons said. "Two."

Just then a woman emerged from the shadows of the doorway, followed by a tall man.

"Sal?" Bonnie said.

"Mr. Byrd and I were listening to the most wonderful radio story." Her heels clicked-clacked across the stone floor as she walked over to Bonnie. "About a common criminal who threatened two government agents. But we didn't hear the ending yet."

The men fell to a hush when they saw that the tall man behind Sal was Hurry Up Byrd.

"You say 'three' and I'll drop you into the goddamn turbine myself," Byrd said. "All of you men, get back to work. We've got a lot of ground to make up. No one is getting fired here today except for this greedy little son of a bitch."

The men burst into a cheer.

CHAPTER 51

Amends

"Anything in your car back there you can't do without?" Donnie asked.

They pulled onto the highway past the truck stop. They were in a cramped little AMC Pacer, the radio blaring *We're Not Gonna Take It,* and Royce fiddled with the dial until he could turn it down.

Royce shook his head. "Nothing but a sweated-through baseball cap, some empty Chinese take-out containers and a worn-out Merle Travis cassette. What about your car?"

"A car is just a thing, and mine can sit alongside yours until it rots, for all I care," she said. "Although, some cars are certainly worse than others." She tugged on the seatbelt. "This is like sitting inside a dung beetle made out of glass and plastic."

Royce pulled onto the freeway and the Pacer labored to reach the speed limit. "Yeah, but at least we'll give them the slip for a while." He tilted his head. "Wait a minute, why exactly are we giving them the slip?"

"There's something we need to do," she said. "If this all turns to crap, I want to get something off my chest, and make my amends."

"I'm not following you."

"I want to go visit the Ebbon lady."

"Now? That seems risky," Royce said.

"It's not a might-be-nice kind of a suggestion," she said. "It's a we-need-to-do-it kind of a thing. If those fellows in cowboy hats start shooting at us, I want to go to my maker knowing I made this thing right with her."

"Wait a minute, you think they're going to start shooting at us? I'm not ready to go to my maker. I want to write this story and get accolades and a Pulitzer and have a bunch of groupies trying to get into my pants."

She laughed. "Is there such a thing as journalism groupies?" She patted his arm. "Don't worry, if things get rough, just get behind me."

"I couldn't fit even half of me behind you," Royce said. "I wish we'd taken a piece of pie before we lit out of there. Now my last meal is gonna be a half a plate of chicken fried steak and some truck stop coffee."

"Yeah, but the company was divine," she said. "Where does this gal live?"

"She's widowed. South Lubbock, near Clapp Park."

"That's a nice little park," Bonnie said. "We used to go there occasionally after chemo. Lots of trails appropriate for a wheelchair."

"Yeah, we've still never talked about how he ended up in a wheelchair."

She lowered the visor and checked her hair in the mirror, pushing a few errant curls back into place.

"Do an old woman a favor and let me keep my memory of him intact for a little bit longer. We'll get to that soon enough, and I've kind of enjoyed living in the past these last few weeks, with Clyde whole."

Soon enough, he pulled the car into the driveway of a modest ranch house with a struggling yard and grapevines stretching down the chain length fence between the lots.

"Want me to wait in the car?"

Bonnie shook her head. "Nope, you're part of this now."

He followed her to the porch and waited as she knocked and then, when no one answered, knocked again—harder this time.

A dog barked inside, a high-pitched yapping, followed by shushing sounds—"Tinker, be quiet"—and labored footsteps.

A woman, a decade or so younger than Bonnie, opened the door. She had white hair and leaned heavily on two canes as she peered up at the strangers through thick glasses. Tinker, an asthmatic Boston terrier, growled and wheezed and peeked out from under the bottom of her frayed house coat.

"Yes, may I help you?"

"Miss Ebbon, my name is…Brenda Prentiss, and this here is Royce Jenkins. He's from *The Dispatch*. The newspaper."

"Afternoon," he said.

"What's this about?" she asked. "Did my subscription run out?"

"Oh, no, ma'am," Bonnie said. "It's about your sister."

The woman sucked in a ragged breath, half lifting her right hand toward her throat but then thinking better of it and extending the cane back to the floor.

"Samantha?" she said. "All these years, I knew something would come of it. Come in, come in."

She guided them toward the living room, shushing Tinker every third step. "Did you know Samantha?" she asked, pushing a stack of TV Guides and Reader's Digests off the sofa with her cane to make room for the guests.

"No, Miss Ebbon, I never had the pleasure."

"Ebbon is my maiden name. Just stick with Claire," she said, collapsing back into an overstuffed, well-used easy chair. Tinker hopped up beside her, breathing heavily, stretching his head out on the arm like a canine gargoyle.

Bonnie sat uneasily on the couch, and Royce sat next to her. "Claire, I know you probably held out hope all these years," Bonnie said.

Claire shook her head. "No, I didn't. I knew right away she was gone. I felt it. I felt her die all those years ago. But I always wondered why, that was the part that made no sense to me."

"It's not going to make much sense now, either," Bonnie said. She leaned forward to take a lemon candy— the kind dusted with powdered sugar—from a bowl on the coffee table. Tinker growled.

Claire swatted him on the haunches. "Stop it Tinker. Behave. Please, Brenda is it, go ahead."

Bonnie leaned back. "Actually, I might need something a little stronger than a lemon drop candy. Any chance you have something to drink, something with alcohol in it?"

"There's some sherry in the kitchen," Claire said. She gestured with her cane toward the open door. "Young man, would you? Glasses are above the sink."

Royce nodded and disappeared into the kitchen. Bonnie and Claire smiled awkwardly, silently at one another. Bored, Tinker contorted his body and hoisted one leg and began methodically, wetly, licking his groin. He stopped when Royce returned with a little tray and three cordial glasses filled with sherry, the bottle tucked under his arm.

Bonnie downed hers, then held it up to Royce who tipped the bottle to fill it again.

"Claire, do you remember anything else that was going on about the time your sister disappeared?" Bonnie asked.

She thought about it. "Things were starting to get bad over in Germany."

"I meant more local."

"Bonnie and Clyde were gunned down over in Sailes."

"That's right. Do you have a picture of Samantha from back then?"

"Of course." She pointed at the wall with her cane at a faded picture of a young woman with a klieg light smile and mischievous eyes.

Royce retrieved the photo and set it on the coffee table, scooting the lemon drops to the side. He pulled a photo out of his jacket pocket, the famous one of Clyde holding Bonnie up in his arms.

"Notice anything unusual about these pictures?" Bonnie asked.

Claire squinted at them. "Not really. One is my sister and the other is them outlaws."

"Don't you think they look a little similar?"

"Oh, sweet Jesus, they do," Claire whispered. Bonnie saw a look of confusion pass over Claire's face, and recognized the fog of age. "Samantha was Bonnie Parker? That doesn't make any sense."

Bonnie handed her the cordial glass. "No, no, Claire, nothing like that. But I think you should take a sip of this here to fortify yourself for what comes next."

She took a sip, and Royce topped off her glass. Bonnie leaned forward, risking the wrath of Tinker. "Claire, what I'm about to tell you is a secret almost fifty years old. Telling you is a risk because if word gets out, a lot of plans will be wrecked."

"Like my Pulitzer," Royce mumbled.

"Claire, Bonnie Parker didn't die in that car that day. It was Samantha. She wasn't supposed to die. Bonnie and Clyde had already been arrested, but the law didn't want anyone to know it, so they conned a young couple who sort of looked like them into driving on through Sailes. The couple was Samantha and Roy."

Claire looked confused, then looked at Royce, and he nodded.

"A Texas Ranger had been told to arrest them, and then the people who hired your sister were going to sneak her and Roy out of jail later, but the other rangers didn't know the plan," Bonnie said. "All they knew was a couple of no account cop killers were driving through and so they executed them. Only it wasn't Bonnie and Clyde. It was two innocent kids thinking they were doing something good to help the government. They trusted the wrong people and it cost them their lives."

Tears welled up in Claire's eyes, magnified by her thick glasses. "I don't understand. How do you know all this?"

"Because I'm—"

Royce caught her arm. "You sure about this?"

Bonnie nodded. "Sure as I've ever been. Claire, my real name is Bonnie Parker. I go by Brenda now, but it was me, I'm the one that was supposed to be in that car. I should have died. And I deserved it, me and Clyde, we deserved it. But instead we got to live and Roy and Samantha died and I'm very sorry you had to live not knowing all these years."

Claire, stunned, let the glass drop from her hand and it landed on Tinker, splashing him with sherry. He yelped and jumped down and began wheezing and licking and then sneezing, the full bodied little dog kind of sneezes, at the alcohol.

"How could you live with that all these years?" Claire asked. The knowledge seemed to weigh her down so that she shrank into herself, suddenly smaller and more vulnerable, like a sad owl peering up at two unexpected humans.

"She only recently found out who was in the car, that it was your sister," Royce said. "I've been investigating it for her, and we caught a break." He pulled out the picture of the ring and handed it to Claire.

"Her ring," Claire said. "Those stones were from our grandmother's ring." The tears were really flowing now.

A bolt of anger recentered her back into her body and Claire shot a hard eye at Bonnie, any sign of confusion gone. "Tell me it was worth it. Tell me you made something out of your miserable lives, something that was worth the life of my sister."

"I don't think anything would be worth their lives," Bonnie said. "But we went straight. Well, mostly straight. We worked for the government. We saved the president. Two presidents, actually. Even kept Hoover Dam from blowing up once, but I'm not sure any of it was worth what happened to your sister and her beau."

"I appreciate you stopping to tell me this, I really do," Claire said. "But I want you to leave now. And don't ever come back. Get out. Just get out."

Bonnie nodded and Royce helped her up. Tinker, a sticky, sherry-marinated mess, growled and gasped and followed them toward the door, yipping and barking.

"I can't tell you what to do," Bonnie said. "But if you could see your way clear to keeping this secret for a little longer, I promise you that Royce here will tell the story in a way that gives your Samantha her due."

If Claire heard her, she chose not to answer, and as they left, she was holding the photo of the antique ring close to her heart, and sobbing.

CHAPTER 52

Intents and purposes

A knock at the front door woke them up. "Who the hell could that be at this ungodly hour?" Clyde asked.

It had been two days since Fitzsimmons spilled the beans. Bonnie and Clyde spent the time holed up inside their little company cottage, sleeping late, making love, drinking gin and eating meals sent over from the hotel and paid for with stolen money.

"It's almost ten," Bonnie said. "And after last night, it's probably the neighbors coming by to complain again."

"I'm never getting up before ten o'clock again," Clyde said, fluffing the pillow under his head.

Bonnie pulled a robe on over her nightclothes and padded barefoot to the front door. Carl stood outside. "Come on in," Bonnie said. "I'll put some coffee on."

Carl wore the chauffeur's uniform, and blushed at the sight of her bare legs. "No thank you, Mrs. Prentiss. I'm more of a Postum drinker. The caffeine is heck on my nerves."

Clyde came out of the bedroom in his undershirt and pants, suspenders hanging to the sides and a .45 stuck casually in the waistband. "Hey, Carl."

"Hey, Mr. Prentiss. Sal wanted me to give you the all-clear. Your cover with Six Companies is handled and there's a new car out front. She wants to talk to you. Can you meet her at the hotel lobby in an hour?"

"An hour?" Bonnie said. "We can be packed and ready to go in half that time."

"I'll tell her," Carl said, as he left.

Clyde grabbed Bonnie and swung her around. "Finally, we can get out of this shithole."

Bonnie laughed and when he put her down, she ran outside and flagged down one of the neighbor kids. He came over shyly and she gave him a nickel. "Go tell Claudette down at the main office Brenda needs to see her," she said.

It took them thirty minutes to pack up, and most of that was their guns.

"That's the last of it," Clyde said, slamming the trunk.

Bonnie pulled the door shut behind her and walked down the pathway from the little cottage.

"Room for one more bag?" she asked, throwing the valise stuffed with stolen money into the back seat.

Claudette walked up with Jimmy. He was still pale and drawn, but looking stronger, and leaned against the hood with his unbroken arm around Claudette.

"Y'all sure you can't stay?" Jimmy asked. "There's a lot of work to be done here. Good, honest work."

"Not for all the tea in China, son," Clyde said. "Good honest work definitely ain't my strong suit." He stuck out his hand and Jimmy shook it. "You got a lot of work here to help out these men. Don't get too distracted." He winked at Claudette.

"I don't know how to thank you," Jimmy said.

"Thank us by getting the union going strong," Bonnie said. "And taking care of my friend."

Claudette hugged Bonnie. "I'm gonna miss you. I can't believe my best friend was a spy."

"You keep that to yourself now, hear?" Bonnie said. "Word gets out, we might just get caught up in something bad next time."

"We're itching to get on the road," Clyde said, ushering Bonnie into the car. "We'll see you two on down the line."

Jimmy leaned on Claudette as Bonnie and Clyde drove down the street. "We'll never see them again, will we?" Claudette asked.

"Nope," Jimmy said. "Not a chance."

At the hotel, the sight of Sal waiting for them at a table in the lobby quickly dampened their moods.

She sat in a chair reading the company newspaper, and Bonnie and Clyde sat down across from her.

"Now don't go ladling all the sweet words on us for saving the dam," Clyde said. "It was our pleasure."

"It was a barely missed catastrophe," Sal said.

"You have a hard time passing along praise, don't you?" Bonnie asked.

"If you ever do anything well, I'll be the first to note it in your report." She handed an envelope to Bonnie. "This should cover your expenses for a while."

"How about covering our expenses forever? Seems like we've done enough," Bonnie said. "We saved FDR, and now we kept Boulder Dam from getting blown up."

"Both good things, poorly done, but all in a day's work for rehabilitated criminals," Sal said. "It will be a long time before we put paid to the debt you owe."

"What happens now?" Clyde asked. "Here, at the dam, I mean."

"First reports suggest that some elements of the Six Companies consortium did shoddy work. Parts of the dam itself, near the base, are leaking," Sal said.

"Why didn't they just fix it, why go to all this trouble to cover it up?" Clyde asked.

"As Fitzsimmons confessed, a substantial bonus from the federal government would have been forfeited if the dam was not been completed on time," Sal said.

"I'm guessing everyone's going to get away with it," Bonnie said.

Clyde shook his head in disbelief. "You gonna let all those people downriver live in danger."

"Of course not," Sal said. "The dam will be opened as planned, the country will celebrate the achievement, but its operations will be quietly curtailed. Repairs will go on behind the scenes until it's fixed."

"You're lying to the American people," Bonnie said.

"What's better for the country? Thinking a few bad apples could rig the project for their own profit or seeing that Americans can work together to build an engineering marvel as magnificent as the pyramids?"

"People aren't as dumb as you think," Bonnie said.

Sal looked at them both stone-eyed. "If this dam goes down, if public opinion turns, how much congressional support do you think there will be for more government investment in infrastructure? It's that investment that will put people back to work. That's what's important now. If it means a few companies get away with their reputations intact, so be it."

"They always get away with it," Bonnie said, lighting a cigarette.

"There will be arrests of those we can directly link to the plot. Business leaders must be held accountable for illegal activities just like the common criminals they are."

"What about the union?" Clyde asked.

"As you know, FDR is supportive," Sal said.

"He could start by giving every working man here a share of that completion bonus," Clyde said.

"Fat chance," Bonnie said.

"Think big, you two, I know you have it in you. If they can get the union going, imagine the future it will bring," Sal said.

"Maybe workers would have enough influence to really change things," Clyde said.

"Exactly. Imagine a world twenty or thirty years from now, when wages are a thing of the past and workers are offered part ownership of a business," Sal said. "Or in a project like this, they do get to share in those bonuses. Maybe unions can get the working class—everyone, not just the ones with the jobs—health insurance, good housing and education. Find ways to spread profits around to build a better society."

Bonnie exhaled a thin stream of smoke. "That's just what Jimmy has been saying."

"Jimmy's right, and strong unions are a way to level the playing field, so that the working class and capitalists have equal say in how profit is used," Sal said. "That level playing field is going to make this country the greatest in the world."

"If they can pull it off," Clyde said. "And that's a big 'if.' Money has its ways."

"There's a chance," Sal said. "The legal framework is in place. It's up to the unions now. Change always happens from the ground up. If union leaders can avoid the pull of money and power, I think things will go well."

"We're doomed then," Bonnie said.

"Always so negative," Sal said, standing. "I'll be in touch with your next assignment soon."

Bonnie stood too, leaning in close and blocking Sal's exit path around the low coffee table. "What about Hank Black? How did you get him off our trail?" Bonnie asked.

"That's need to know," Sal said. "And you don't."

Bonnie leaned in even closer. "You didn't plan on those two people getting killed, did you?"

"Again, need to know."

"I've been thinking hard on this, and the only way you could get Black to back down without a fight is if he knew he killed the wrong people," Bonnie said quietly. "And the only way he'd believe you is if you warned him that day. But men with guns get crazy when they get their blood all worked up. Your mistake was that things got out of hand on that road in Sailes. Is that what happened?"

"You have an active imagination," Sal said. "Maybe you should write a poem about this little theory of yours."

"If I'm right, that makes you a murderer," Bonnie whispered.

"There are many variables to consider in battle," Sal said. "The secret to a clean conscience is always staying on the right side of things."

Sal pulled a thin sweater over her shoulders and pretended to stifle a shiver. "It can get chilly in the shadows." She pushed past Bonnie, and then stopped. "I'll be in touch. Don't go far, or else your families will find themselves on the field of battle."

Leaving Bonnie and Clyde inside, Sal walked outside, dabbed at the corners of her eyes, then nodded at Carl who let her into the backseat of the waiting car.

"I'm sorry about them two kids," Carl said to Sal. "I know it eats at you. It wasn't your fault."

Sal straightened and pulled on a pair of sunglasses. "Let's go. I need to be back in Washington before the Six

319

Companies lawyers start weaseling their way out of responsibility."

Thirty minutes later as they drove toward Las Vegas, Bonnie and Clyde roared by Sal and Carl, honking and waving and almost careening into an approaching car before disappearing down the highway, leaving them in a trail of dust.

Clyde watched them in the rearview until they disappeared from sight.

"Where to now?" Bonnie asked.

"Mind if we make a stop in Hillsdale?" he said.

"Texas? That will be sight for sore eyes," she said, leaning in to fiddle with the radio. Fred Astaire came through the speakers singing *Pick Yourself Up*. "Pretty good tune for us now."

After a few hours driving, the sun—at the peak of its arc in the cloudless blue sky—poured through the windows. The red landscape shimmered with the glaring heat and a turkey vulture circled above. Warm air flowed through the open windows. Bonnie's head dropped down and then she jerked it back up. She bobbed a few more times. Clyde stifled a laugh. Finally, she leaned her head back against the car seat.

"I'm so glad to be back on the road," she murmured.

"Me too, Bon, it's where we're meant to be."

"That nine to five routine really took it out of me," she said.

"Go on, take a little nap," Clyde said. "I got the radio and the road to keep me company. And I like to watch you sleep."

Within minutes, she was sound asleep. Clyde smiled, and then sped up, wanting to make good time getting to Texas.

CHAPTER 53

Benevolence

The next day, they drove slowly through Hillsdale, Texas, down Waco Street, past a row of low-rise brick buildings—half of them boarded over and empty—and then turned at the Gulf gas station where a few cars idled while the gas jockey filled their tanks. At the end of the main road, they passed the gleaming white sandstone courthouse.

"Let's not tarry long in this vicinity," Bonnie said, smiling. She pulled on her oversized sunglasses. "Some folks might still recognize us."

Clyde tromped on the gas pedal and they sped through the rest of the tiny town. As the buildings gave way to farmland, they pulled onto the county road and fifteen minutes later drove by a general store.

The screen door swung crookedly in the wind, the upper hinge barely hanging on. A woman in a plain white dress rocked back and forth on a chair on the porch. Bonnie waved, and the woman nodded. Tumbleweeds blew across the driveway.

Around a bend in the road, Clyde pulled the car over onto the shoulder beneath a sprawling pecan tree. Late afternoon clouds, bruised and billowing, gathered across the Texas skyline, threatening to unload a storm.

"Was that the widow?" Bonnie asked.

"Couldn't be sure from this distance, but likely."

"Seems like she's sitting just about where you said her husband bled out," Bonnie said.

Clyde looked out at the dusty, windswept fields and abandoned farm buildings. A gray horse wandered up to the sagging barbed wire fence lining the road, nickered, and looked at Clyde.

Clyde had been in a dark mood the past few hours, and Bonnie was worried. It pained her to see him sad. "Socks?"

"Yeah, wasn't that a crazy thing to say we wanted to buy in the middle of the night?" he asked. He whistled at the horse.

"Shall we get to doing what we came here for?" she asked.

"Bon, I don't think I can go in there," he said.

"But you were in the car, she didn't ever see you that night," she said.

"Don't matter," Clyde said. "That woman was the momma of some kid I knew. I met her before."

"You were friends with her son?" she asked.

"I wouldn't call us friends," he said. "But there's a strong possibility she would recognize me, even with this fancy haircut."

A dark cloud cast a shadow over the parked car. Fat, lazy raindrops splattered against the windshield. Bonnie took the envelope from the glove box, tucked it beneath her jacket, and stepped out of the car. "I got this one, baby. You sit tight." She held her purse over her head and ran lightly back toward the store.

The old woman was surprised to see a fine-dressed young lady appear on foot from the road. She remained seated, but stopped rocking as Bonnie walked up the gravel drive. Bonnie climbed the four steps to the porch, sheltered by a wooden overhang and a drooping tree. She shook off the water droplets from her purse. A chained-up dog barked behind the store.

"Howdy, ma'am," Bonnie said.

"Afternoon," the woman said. "Quiet down, Chester," she yelled at the dog.

Bonnie glanced down at the porch and saw a faint brown stain, about as large as a kitchen sink, to the side of the rocking chair. Blood. Odd that she never replaced the wood, Bonnie thought.

"You got car trouble?" the woman asked.

"Nope, I came for an orange soda if you have one."

The woman stood and Bonnie followed her inside. The shelves were sparsely stocked. The woman rummaged behind the counter, found a dusty bottle of soda and held it up.

"Don't got no electricity here, and the ice man stopped coming on account of, well, he just stopped coming, so you're gonna have to drink it warm."

"I prefer it warm," Bonnie said. "Otherwise, I get a cold headache."

The woman flipped off the bottle cap with a metal opener and offered the soda to Bonnie.

The woman still wore her gold wedding band.

Bonnie took a swig. "Are you Mrs. Butler?"

"Do I know you?" Mrs. Butler asked. Her hair was gathered into a loose bun behind her neck. She didn't look much more than forty, Bonnie thought, not too much older than her own momma, but life had been hard on her as well. And Bonnie knew she and Clyde were mostly to blame.

Bonnie pulled a handkerchief from her pocket and dabbed her eyes. Green eye shadow rubbed onto the white cloth. With a trembling hand, she took another sip of the orange soda and swallowed, trying to calm herself.

"When I was passing through town, I got stopped by some man, a good-looking fellow, a stranger to me, and he said to give this to Mrs. Butler at the grocery store," Bonnie said, handing the woman the envelope. "He said to tell you it's money from the Parker Barrow Benevolence Fund."

"The what now?" the woman said, looking curiously at Bonnie's face.

"Did those awful people, Bonnie and Clyde, do some harm to you or something?" Bonnie asked, trying to keep up the pretense.

"You could say that. Their gang killed my husband. Right out there on the porch," she said. "It wasn't neither of them personally, but it was the Barrow gang all right. He was in the getaway car."

"You know for sure Clyde Barrow didn't do this to your husband?" Bonnie said.

"Not sure how much difference it makes, but he didn't pull the trigger. What I don't know is why a stranger is in my store drinking warm pop and dredging up the past."

"I'm just following directions from that fella I met in town, who said to give you that envelope. I got the feeling he was trying to make amends somehow for what those two did."

"That sounds like a bunch of stuff and nonsense to me," Mrs. Butler said.

"I don't know anything about that, I just know he said to tell Mrs. Butler that nothing can bring her husband back, but he hoped this would help make her life a bit easier."

Mrs. Butler opened the envelope and gasped at the thick sheaf of bills.

"Maybe you can get that ice man to start up his deliveries again," Bonnie said. "Now I have to be going. What do I owe you for this soda?"

"Don't you worry about that," the woman said, fingering the money, seeming to forget Bonnie all together.

The screen door squeaked as Bonnie ran out of the store before the woman could say anything else. She walked quickly back down the road—the squall had already passed over and the air was filled with a clean, crisp smell. When she got to the car, Clyde wasn't in it. She crossed the road and looked over at the far end of the field. He was on the back of the gray horse, riding bareback. He trotted up toward her, holding on to the horse's mane to steady himself. He pulled up short by the fence, and smiled down at her. His hair was plastered against his head, slicked back from the rain.

"Come on, get on."

"Get on? Clyde Barrow, do you even know how to ride that thing?"

"Who in Texas doesn't know how to ride a horse?"

"Me, for one," she said, shaking her head, and ducking under the fence.

"Come on, now," he said. "Your gonna hurt her feelings."

Bonnie grabbed his outstretched hand and he swung her up behind him. Bonnie wrapped her arms around Clyde's waist. He clucked, gently nudged the flanks of the horse with his heels, and the mare lunged forward, enjoying the chance to show off.

Clyde trotted them around the field once and then coaxed the mare into a good-natured gallop and for the briefest of moments, the two riders felt truly free.

CHAPTER 54

Old habits

Bonnie sat in stony silence after they left Claire's house, watching the tidy little neighborhood give way to strip malls, then to a less tidy neighborhood, then to the Interstate, rimmed by fallow fields and gas plants.

Royce matched her silence and aimed the little Pacer in the direction of his apartment.

The sight of an oil pumpjack, stark and recursive, brought her back to the moment. "Where are we going?"

"Given the current state of things, I don't think it's safe for you to stay alone," he said. "I'm going to swing by my place and pack a bag, stay with you for a couple of days."

"You do remember who I am, right?" she asked, looking at the city lights as twilight settled over Lubbock. "The one and only Bonnie Parker." Her voice was clipped and edged by bitterness.

"Fine, maybe you can look after me then," Royce said.

He nudged the turn signal and pulled off the Interstate, looping back into the sprawl of fading apartment complexes and body shops making up his neighborhood.

"What do you suppose is going on up there?" Bonnie asked. The end of the street was choked with fire trucks and ambulances, their emergency lights flashing strobes of red and blue.

Royce slowed, rolling the car borrowed from the waitress closer to the swirl of activity, the trucks and steam and smoke and people milling back and forth. "That's my apartment building," he said. Thick, oily black smoke billowed from a corner unit with the windows blown out. "And that's my goddamned apartment."

Firefighters directed streams of water through the shattered frames with steady precision.

"Oh shit, my cat. Mephisto."

"You named your cat Mephisto?"

"It fits him."

"Is he kind of a big yellow looking cat with a sour disposition?" Bonnie asked.

"How did you know that?"

She pointed at a woman in a bright purple housecoat, her hair in curlers, standing on the corner holding the cat.

"Bless you, Mrs. Tanner," he whispered.

"Keep your eyes on the road and don't speed up yet," Bonnie said. "It's them fellows from the restaurant."

He froze but kept driving slowly, trying hard to seem nonchalant. Out of the corner of his eyes, he saw the two men in dark suits and cowboy hats watching the crowd.

"Things are heating up," she said, slipping her .25 automatic out of her purse. "Pun intended."

He looked at the gun in her hand. "Wasn't it you who told me not twenty-four hours ago that gun was too small to do any damage?"

"Ammo got a lot better these past fifty years," she said. "I wouldn't bet against me now." She looked back at the fire in the side view mirror "Do you think the fire destroyed all your work on the story?" He heard the worry and fear in her voice.

Royce turned onto a side street and sped off at the upper limit of the borrowed car. "I likely lost some photos and files from the Historical Society, but I mailed copies of everything important to Terrence, our intern, when I started getting nervous. The work is safe."

"Good," she said. "Nervous makes you smart. So, nothing lost."

"Only all my stuff, my clothes, my pictures, my cassettes, my—" he said. "There was a really expensive bottle of Irish whiskey. I was going to crack it open when the first story ran."

"All of that stuff is replaceable," she said.

"That's easy for you to say, it's not your stuff, and it's not your whiskey."

She waved him off with dismissive gesture. "I can't tell you how many times we lost everything. You're young. Well, you're not old, and you've got plenty of time to build your life up again once this story breaks."

"If it breaks," he said, then slammed his hand on the wheel. "Shit. I have to call Larry."

"Put a little more distance between us and them first," she said.

He followed the Interstate that cut through town until they were miles away from the arson, then pulled into a gas station. There was a pay phone booth next to a field with two bedraggled donkeys and a goat, patiently chewing its cud.

Royce parked next to the phone booth, left the car door open and the engine running, dropped in two dimes and dialed Larry at home. Larry picked up on the third ring and just before he spoke, there was a metallic click on the line.

"Larry, it's Royce."

"Don't say another word," Larry said, his tone light, but conveying something deathly serious. "Yes, I got your note, you can take your vacation. No questions asked. I'm sorry I've been pushing you so hard. And also, I think that story might be a nonstarter."

"The uh, the one story?"

"Yes, that one," Larry said. "I want you to forget about it. I want you to just go and enjoy yourself. And don't even tell me where because I'd be tempted to send you more work. Take as much time as you need to, you know, relax and refocus."

"Understood," Royce said. "And thanks."

"Take care of yourself," Larry said.

Royce hung up and pushed open the door to the phone booth and got back in the car.

Bonnie was still holding her little pistol and watching the parking lot nervously. "Everything ok?"

"No. He knows we're in trouble and he's warning us off. I think someone was listening in." He rubbed his eyes tiredly. "Now what should we do? Hunker down at your place?"

"That's where they'd make a run at us first off."

"What about all your stuff? The money, the paintings?"

"The safe is fire- and blast-proof, and a neighbor comes by now and again to keep an eye on things. Any strangers come slipping around and I'm not home, they'll call the cops."

"What do we now? I've got like twenty bucks on me and banks are closed."

She handed him a business card for LokTite Rentals. "Go here."

Fifteen minutes later, they pulled into the storage facility and she directed him to a unit near the back.

Bonnie slipped a key from her purse and turned the lock and Royce raised the overhead door, revealing the outlines of a car in the shadows. She clicked on the light and a fully restored dark red 1934 Ford Sedan gleamed under a single bulb hanging down on a cord.

"Damn, it's beautiful," Royce said, whistling under his breath.

"Glad you like it," Bonnie said. "We're ditching that little dung beetle."

He ran his hand over the sleek paint. "You're not suggesting we drive this, are you?"

"Did you really think anyone in 1984 would look for Bonnie Parker in an actual Bonnie and Clyde car? There's no better place to hide than in plain sight."

She opened the back trunk and pointed at two suitcases. "One of those is filled with cash, and the other with clothes. You're a little bigger than Clyde, but might be something that fits."

Royce flipped back a blanket and underneath he saw the wooden gleam of a pump shotgun. "And this?"

"We ain't going to a picnic, son," she said, channeling Clyde. "We're going on the run."

"Don't take this the wrong way, but you sound a little bit excited."

"You can't begrudge an old woman for wanting one last thrill," she said. "Go on, give it a try. The keys are in the ignition."

Royce slid into the driver's seat and it felt like he was traveling back in time. The car turned over on the second try.

She smiled happily and climbed in the passenger side, sighing as she settled into the stiff seat. "Let's go, Clyde," she said, her eyes wide with distant memories.

He didn't correct her, just stepped on the gas and the old car rattled and bounced out into the Lubbock night. Top speed was never more than forty-five miles an hour, so it took almost twenty minutes before they got past the city limits, and passed into rural farmland. Lulled by the motion of the car, Bonnie soon fell asleep, her head against the window and a secret, serene smile on her face.

The End

AFTERWORD

President Franklin Delano Roosevelt dedicated Boulder Dam on September 30, 1935. (In 1947, it was renamed Hoover Dam, the name it retains to this day.) The dam was one of several taxpayer-funded infrastructure projects undertaken during the Great Depression, helping create thousands of jobs. The dam also provided electricity, irrigation and recreation opportunities, further stimulating the regional economy.

Hoover Dam—visible from space—is an engineering marvel. However, as alluded to in *Dam Nation*, the project was plagued by construction irregularities. After the 1935 dedication, behind-the-scenes repairs to shore up the integrity of the dam and associated elements continued for more than a decade.

In response to the New Deal push to support unions—as a potential counterbalance against the drive to maximize profits inherent in capitalism—their membership began to grow in the U.S., peaking in the 1960s, at about one-third of all employees nationwide. The growth of union membership correlated with the midcentury expansion of the middle class and its broad-based prosperity—as collective bargaining delivered wages, benefits and more to workers, with spillover effects to non-union employees.

Similarly, the decline of unions in the second part of the twentieth century is linked to the increasing difficulties of working class America.

Real wages and benefits are down, job security has largely evaporated, and profit is routinely redistributed upward to shareholders and those who own or control capital at the expense of the workers creating that profit. With the decline of the workers' voice in capitalism, the concentration of wealth at this top echelon of society has unleashed a new gilded age of modern Robber Barons.

Many factors underlie declining union membership. As the midcentury gains for the middle class became normalized, it was easy to forget that these outcomes were due to efforts to organize workers, demonstrations and collective bargaining. In short, workers began to forget their own history.

Before long, some workers began to buy into the demonization of unions led by corporations and other well-funded entities who saw an opportunity, due in part to globalization and advanced technology, to exploit growing economic insecurity with coordinated and Orwellian messaging campaigns focused on the "right to work," painting unions as hindering competition.

Union leadership itself played a role in their declining influence for a number of reasons. For example, the movement became delinked from a collective working class-wide purpose, retreating to narrower profession- or trade-based goals. The union "brand" was damaged because in some cases, early in their history, membership was restricted to white males. Further, during their midcentury apex, to some degree, unions paradoxically mirrored the same hierarchal power structures of capitalism they were designed to check, exposing themselves to the corrupting influence of greed. Last, the inability of unions to fundamentally align with the civil rights, feminist, environmental and other grassroots movements of the 1960s to leverage this collective passion and push capitalism into a new worker-centric era was a tragically-missed opportunity.

But, of course, the story of unions is not yet done. The need for and potential impact of a reinvigorated vision for the 21st century any beyond has never been greater as the working class continues to fight for a fair and just economy for all people.

```
┌─────────────────────────────────────┐
│  TELL THE WORLD THIS BOOK WAS        │
│                                      │
│   GOOD    │   BAD    │   SO-SO       │
│           │          │               │
│           │          │               │
│           │          │               │
│           │          │               │
│           │          │               │
│           │          │               │
└─────────────────────────────────────┘
```

Bonnie and Clyde: Dam Nation

ABOUT THE AUTHORS

Clark Hays, a native of Texas, was raised on a Montana ranch and spent his formative years branding cows, riding horses and writing. His work has appeared in many journals, magazines and newspapers. He was nominated for a Pushcart Prize for a short story appearing in Opium Magazine.

Kathleen McFall was born and raised in Washington, D.C. During more than a decade working in journalism, she published hundreds of articles about natural resources, environmental issues, energy and science. Previously, she was director of communications and senior advisor at a major research university. Kathleen was awarded a fellowship for fiction writing from Oregon Literary Arts.

In addition to the *Bonnie and Clyde* books, Clark and Kathleen are the authors of the award-winning, best-selling *The Cowboy and the Vampire Collection*, which was named to Kirkus Reviews best books of 2014 list, included in IndieReader's best books of 2016, and was awarded a 2017 IPPY Silver Medal in horror.

Connect with the authors:

www.pumpjackpress.com
www.facebook.com/cowboyandvampire
@cowboyvamp (Twitter)
@cowboyvampire (Instagram)